THE LOVELY LADIES

NICOLAS FREELING

THE LOVELY LADIES

VINTAGE BOOKS
A Division of Random House
New York

First Vintage Books Edition, March 1981
Copyright © 1971 by Nicolas Freeling
All rights reserved under International and Pan-
American Copyright Conventions. Published in
the United States by Random House, Inc., New
York. Originally published by Harper & Row,
Publishers, Inc., New York, in 1971.

Library of Congress Cataloging in Publication Data
Freeling, Nicolas.
The lovely ladies.
Reprint of the 1971 ed. published by Harper &
Row, New York.
I. Title.
[PR6056.R4L6 1981] 823′.914 80-6129
ISBN 0-394-74694-5

Manufactured in the United States of America

THE LOVELY LADIES

PART ONE

THE THREE LOVELY LADIES
OF BELGRAVE SQUARE

As a child his favorite happening was to be taken to the market. An experience loved by all children: ecstatic smells, thrilling hubbubs, loud delightful arguments. His first—and never forgotten—impression of the police: remote majestic figures in splendid boots, walking heavily about, thumbs hitched into their belts, pretending Olympian detachment but apt, excitingly, to intervene and create melodrama. The English police, he thought irrelevantly, walk the same way but have no belts. . . . They hitch their thumbs into breast pockets, giving an unfortunate impression of a bra whose shoulder straps have given way.

Ah, the markets! Holy places of an Amsterdam childhood in the early thirties. This, thought Van der Valk sadly, is very different: hard to say what fun a child could get out of this. Saturday afternoon in the shopping center of a provincial Dutch town and he was being trampled under foot; they were all in such a hurry—was all this collective insecurity desperate to get back to the reassurance of cars (penis symbol), television sets (womb symbol), or horrid suburban houses (prestige symbol, but wasn't he getting them a bit muddled?)?

If he had been an adult during the Depression, his souvenirs would be different. But a nostalgia for childhood is permissible, he decided: not gravely reactionary; not sinfully Fascist. Everyone had been poor, and there was pleasurable suspense in one's mamma's lengthy feeling (lips pursed suspiciously) of printed cotton, in the trying on of stiff and smelly serge trousers—pleasure lessened there by the protesting child being déculotté in public, painfully aware of its underpants. But as a reward afterward, there was the sniffing of oranges, the rejecting of some as unripe, the ceremonious purchase of one orange.

Just look at them now, scurrying along with their anxious frightened faces; couldn't wait to get rid of their money. Small children being dragged along in nasty new shoes from which they got no pleasure, not even from pestering everyone with the balloon (spoilt by the beastly shoeshop's beastly address displayed on its squeaky smelly flank). . . . Children odious in little terylene suits, self-conscious copies of their parents. Older children with imitation-leather briefcases, pretentious files and loose-leaf notebooks, pencil sharpeners like plastic sputniks and erasers like giraffes—the new school year began on Monday morning. Vive la rentrée; roll on Mother's Day; vive all such rackets.

Mums were lugging plastic nets of obviously unripe

4

(yet somehow dried-out) oranges, a kilo at a time. No longer possible to buy one orange. As for smelling them, that helped nobody: they smelt, like everything else, of plastic. But this is the Grote Markt, the Big Market. Sursum corda, thought Van der Valk; get up off the floor.

In the street, he had his legs banged by heavy things with sharp corners. A mum pushed her pram over his foot and glared as though he had deliberately joggled her fat immovably sleeping plastic jellybaby. A travel agency, all large posters of happy skiers gazing at ice-cream Alps as though about to eat them, was already imploring him to leave instantly for the winter sports: to set a cap on exasperation, it was a brilliant, hot, sunny day. He wanted a nice cup of tea and to sit; he'd been to the winter sports.

He was supposed to be working—well, he was working—though there was no real need for him to run about like this. Shoplifting was getting out of hand: when one caught them, they were never ashamed, never sorry, had pockets full of money, and generally said "So what?" He had to write a report, and was making a survey. He had, too, to talk to some terrible people, committee members of the Shopkeepers Association; a powerful municipal lobby that must be cosseted if it was not to make his life needlessly tiresome.

The crowd was always thickest outside Vroom & Dreesman, and of course the street bottlenecked just there, the pavements were medievally narrow, and accidents frequent. He could not stop traffic passing this absurdly tiny street; he had tried, and the shopkeepers complained he was taking the bread out of their mouths: they would never be able to afford the closed-circuit television spies they lusted after.

Hmm, the crowd was unusually thick; a bus was waiting patiently to get past, and a human bee swarm (hooked no doubt to one another's abdomens) had spilt onto the roadway. He caught a glimpse of a policeman—thumb out of your belt, stupid; why aren't you breaking them up? The uniform disappeared as though devoured by bacchantes: smelling drama, Van der Valk used his stick as a tin opener.

"Run over, poor soul."

"Heart attack—anyone can have one—anytime, I tell you, anyone."

"I tell you I saw the bus hit him."

"How could it when it was standing still?"

"Standing still—he was walking, amn't I telling you?"

"Will you all please move further back."

Half in the road and half on the pavement lay an elderly gentleman in a gray suit. The policeman was grateful to Van der Valk.

"Move—Officer, clear the roadway."

"Here, I've got a first-aid diploma." The barrier of chewing gum gave a little, stickily, as a man shouldered to the front with the same unconscious authority, eyes indifferent, so that he was allowed to pass.

"Ich bin Arzt—deutscher Arzt." He felt the pulse and frowned.

"Umdrehen," he commanded briefly: Van der Valk and the fat housewife showed off their first-aid diplomas together, she a bit mutinously: had been taught *not* to turn people over, and what good were German doctors anyhow?

"*Kein* Herzanfall," a little unecessarily. The handle

of an antique dagger emerged from the center of the man's old-fashioned waistcoat.

A reproduction, said Van der Valk's mind automatically as he stared at the weapon.

"We'll get him into that shop—you can't do anything on the pavement."

"Who are you?" asked the doctor.

"Polizeikommissar."

"Ach, so." Thus surrounded by experts, the man was brought into a shoeshop and put on a settee.

"Phone," mimed Van der Valk at the manager.

"Already have," an egg-shaped mouth mimed back.

The pharmacist across the street arrived with an armful of stuff he thought might be useful: the German doctor picked at it dubiously, pronouncing unfamiliar languages on labels.

"Neinei—spielt hier keine Rolle."

"Notfall . . . schwere . . . Herzstimulant," laboriously.

"Ja, ja, ich weiss," impatiently.

Outside, an ambulance sounded its siren furiously, unable to get past the still-immobile bus.

"Shall I come?" offered the doctor conscientiously, as the men were getting the limp body onto their stretcher.

"Neinei," said Van der Valk. "If you'll just write down the address where you're staying." He had collected a couple more policemen by now, all busily writing things down on their slates exactly like the jury in *Alice in Wonderland*. A dozen Saturday shoppers, half scared and half self-important, had been herded in: he addressed them.

"This is a death by violence; you may have witnessed an assassination. Directly you have given your names to the officers, you may go home. Please be at home tonight; an officer will call to interview you. Try meanwhile to concentrate, and don't"—politely—"imagine things that didn't happen."

In the ambulance was a great deal of equipment and precious little room for him; he wrinkled his nose at a smell of ether. Under the oxygen mouthpiece, the man mumbled something: Van der Valk stopped himself snatching it off, bent forward to listen, collided with an attendant's hair oil.

"The girls . . ." said the man.

"Who attacked you?"

"The girls . . ." It was not an answer. But he had to be content with it, for the man had died. Van der Valk took the gaudy dagger—it was, as he had thought, a paper knife—looked for a handkerchief, had to be content with a sticky bit of cotton wool. On arrival, all he could do was tell an excited intern to keep the man and his clothes untouched.

"I'll call the professor." But the man was beyond resuscitation even by a professor. Zealous busybodies fiddled at him. . . . Van der Valk had small hope of the witnesses, either, having recognized the man who had seen with-his-own-two-eyes the poor fellow hit by the bus. . . . He went back to the Grote Markt and found one of his inspectors making chalk marks.

"Didn't choose the handiest spot." It was littered with ice-lolly wrappers and used bus tickets. "Rope it off, Chief?"

"Just photograph it and measure everything, or else,"—dryly—"we'll get complaints about spoiling business." He shrugged. Even if the man's clothes had all been bought in Riga, and there was nothing in the pockets but a hand grenade and a Gideon Bible, it would still tell more than this trampled strip.

As it happened, identifying the man was no work. He had cards in his pocket in a little case: hmm, engraved, said the police fingertip testing the creamy surface.

F.-X. Martínez

An address off the Rivieren-Laan, in Amsterdam South. A telephone number; he rang it. A woman's voice answered, young and fresh.

"Martínez."

"Who is that, please?"

"You tell me," said the woman tartly.

"Who is on the line, please?" Official drone.

"This is Madame Martínez, and who are you, if I may ask?"

"Good afternoon, Madame, this-is-the-police." Ritual.

"If it's that car again," irritably, "I repeat; I know nothing about it."

"This is the Commissaire."

"Oh. . . . Er—is there something wrong?"

"A man has had an accident. We have to ask you to come and see whether you can identify him."

"You mean my husband's had an accident?" The usual tone of disbelief, that it happens to others but not to me. The usual note of shock, of alarm, almost of anger—but there was an unsurprised sound. Come, one couldn't tell—especially over telephones.

"I'm afraid so, Madame, if the cards we find are to be believed. A tall man, with gray hair."

9

"Oh, God—of course—I'll come—at once. Where must I go?"

A tall man with gray hair: he knew nothing else himself, but now was the time to look. Mr. Martínez did not lack individuality, even in the little curtained-off cubicle next to what hospitals call the Reanimation Center: it is where they put the failures.

The face was long and bony, Dutch—or Nordic, at least, whatever his name was. Gray eyes, high forehead made higher still by thinning receding hair. An intellectual face; the wide thin mouth had been decided and vigorous, the long shaved jaw authoritative. Ears large, flat, well shaped; the nose slightly acquiline; the skin fine-grained and healthy, and it had been tanned not so long ago. Both the face and the slim active body belonged to a man of sixty: when he learned that Mr. Martínez had in fact been seventy-six, he was surprised, but by then there had been several more surprises.

About both man and clothes there were exterior signs of wealth. Or should one more properly say breeding? A meticulous, fastidious quality, of taste as well as money always possessed and easily carried. A linen handkerchief smelt of Roger & Gallet; the gold teeth had been made by a good craftsman and so had the spectacles in the worn morocco case, which matched the card case, and the wallet, and came from an expensive shop. There was a broad wedding ring and a heavy signet ring, a Sulka tie—the shirt and the socks were silk. Both, admitted, were old, much worn, and finely darned, but it still came as a shock to find cheap cotton underclothes. The shoes came from London—or had, rather, before the war, at a guess: they had lived all their lives on trees and been polished every day. The gold stamping was obliterated, but he guessed it was one of those curtly named haughty shops—Block, Brock? Shoes, umbrellas, bowler hats . . . But the suit was very mass-production, very nearly cheap. The label had been cut, and he suspected out of snobbery. It seemed a queer mixture.

The wallet—so often a disappointment—proved so again. A little money, some stamps, the scraps of paper one always keeps religiously long after their purpose has been forgotten. A few more cards—printed this time: "F.-X. Martínez. Import and Export. Harbor Building, Amsterdam." There was a tiny pocket diary with appointments, names, and numbers, but that could wait. Van der Valk rang the Harbor Building.

"Martínez, please."

"Who?"

"Martínez—import and export."

"Never heard of it. Not here. Some mistake."

"Elderly man, tall, well dressed. Distinguished."

"It's possible—this is the switchboard; I only know their voices."

"Give me the concierge, would you?"

But was that not curious? If—it did not seem to fit in with what observation could tell him about Mr. Martínez—if one had cards printed with a spurious commercial address, one did not, he would have thought, do it so incompetently: one telephone call . . . And the Harbor Building, a vulgar commercial block near the Central Station; it did not seem to fit. Import-export, by all means, but this man? He was curious to meet Madame.

Devil take the woman; what was keeping her? He had leisure to discover that his own police department knew nothing about Martínez, which meant nothing,

11

and that the Criminal Record office knew nothing either, which meant precious little.

She arrived. A woman like her voice. Trim, pretty, and young—thirtyish. A fur coat despite the warm weather. The Dutch fair hair, the large teeth, the high complexion. Small; shopgirls would call her petite. Quiet and composed.

"I'm sorry to have been so slow—trams; trains . . ."

"Not at all," said Van der Valk politely. "I had supposed, without really any reason, you would take a car."

"I haven't one," abruptly.

"Your husband had it—What was he doing here, do you know—some business appointment?"

"I presume so; I'm afraid I've no idea."

"Well, we'd better look: I'm sorry to inflict it on you."

"I'm ready."

"It seems unnecessarily painful, but we do, as you realize, have to have a formal identification."

She looked at him steadily with clear pale eyes, prominent but pretty.

"I am calm, Commissaire, because I have known this day would come, and in a way I've practiced for it."

"You've expected an accident?"

"There are so many accidents." He bowed and said nothing. She showed little emotion in the mortuary: her cheekbones showed, she went white around the curve of the nostril; her hands clenched on her leather gloves.

"Poor Vader," she said softly. Note of affection, of respect . . .

"Vader?"

12

"He was old enough to be my father," composedly. "Did he have a heart attack?"

"He had a weak heart?"

"Not especially—that I know of. But he was no longer young, he worked too hard . . . His blood pressure was rather high; that I do know."

"It isn't quite that simple." She seemed puzzled.

"He doesn't seem injured; was it a car?"

"We'll go back to my office, perhaps. A few formalities, and some explanations—may I offer you a lift?—a few questions, no doubt very futile, to put to you."

She went on being composed, though in the car her nostril kept whitening and twitching, and once tears came quickly down before she could regain control, staring determinedly in front of her.

At police headquarters, busy little plastic plates were screwed helpfully to doors. His said, "Commissaris: Criminal Brigade." He never noticed it, but when it caught her eye she stopped and stared at him.

"Criminal Brigade?"

"Please do sit down, Madame. I have to explain."

"But what does this mean? What has happened?" Shock, astonishment, but not fear.

"We have the habit of talking about accidents because it sounds less upsetting—a professional cliché, in a way. But I'm afraid I have to tell you that your husband was stabbed with a kind of dagger. A paper knife. This one."

She shuddered violently and bit into her glove.

"But that's—is it?—does that mean—?"

"I rather think it does. Do you recognize this? Have you seen it before? It's a paper knife."

"No—no—how, stabbed?—where?"

"Here in the town, in the street, in the Grote Markt to be precise, around four this afternoon." Blank astonishment, and shock.

"Would you like a cup of coffee?"

"Yes—no—some water—if you don't mind."

"No trouble."

"God . . ."

"Take your time."

"I am so sorry. I will not be stupid. I promise you."

"Are you in a hurry? Somebody waiting for you—at home? Children?"

"I have no children. Nobody is waiting." Bleakly.

"You won't mind, then, if we do a bit of paper work? Very good. The usual, then, to begin with—full names, date and place of birth, yes, your husband and yourself, nationality, both Dutch?—very good—address . . . the Harbor Building is a business address, I take it?" She went on writing without looking up.

"I'm afraid I know practically nothing at all about my husband's business affairs, Commissaire," she murmured.

"Shall we begin, then, with the personal angle? A cigarette, Madame?" He lit it for her, staring at her peaceably, as cowlike as he could get, which was quite cowlike.

"To get it clear from the start . . . a death by violence, which is incontestable. And, yes, I'm afraid, murder, as self-evident. Leaving aside any inherent possibilities of suicide—forgive my bluntness—people do not stab themselves in the middle of the crowd at four of a Saturday afternoon in a busy shopping street. Nor do they trip and fall on a paper knife."

14

She let out a short yap of hysterical laughter and cut it off at once.

"Quite so," he said calmly. "There's no need to apologize—it is ludicrous. So we are faced with a criminal investigation and that is my job, my affair, and explains the notice on my door. Eventually, too, a judicial instruction or process. When we find the assassin," he explained bluntly. "So that at this point, Madame, you have a kind of choice. I am the investigating officer, and will have questions for you. We will be as discreet as possible, but these questions might be personal, embarrassing, even painful. I would go fingering through your house."

She gazed helplessly, not seeming quite to understand; but plainly she was in shock.

"What I'm trying to explain to you is that you may feel you want advice, professional help, a kind of protection. No, no, that doesn't make you in any sense suspect or imply the slightest guilt. It's a sort of prudence. You might feel I was in some way taking advantage of you—do you follow?"

"You mean a lawyer?"

"I mean a friend, who could advise you. You're in no sense obliged to have a lawyer. You might, shall I say, decide against it?"

"What difference could it make?" with a sort of vague helplessness.

"It would reduce my role, you might put it, to fact-finding and verifying. And it does make things more complicated, lengthier, more laborious. I would notify the Officer of Justice, because then the whole affair gets in the hands of the examining magistrate, who asks you to come and see him and—why, then he takes whatever steps he sees fit. Which can be all

15

very wearisome. I would work in a simpler, less official, perhaps less oppressive manner. If"—he spread his hands out—"you allow me to." Quite the little civil servant: a model of prudence.

She smiled very slightly, thought it over, taking her time.

"I think I prefer to leave things to you, Commissaire. I don't think I need a lawyer; as for friends . . ." She thought a little more, and sighed as though tired. "I realize that being much younger than my husband I must look an attractive prospect—a kind of candidate, is it, for this criminal you will look for . . . Lawyers—magistrates—all these formalities . . ." She sighed again. "I'm afraid it's all going to be quite complicated enough as it is."

He thought about her, driving her back, wordlessly, to Amsterdam. Reasonable woman, balanced, not going to make his life a perfect misery. Detachment—yes, in the voice, too. That phrase "preparing myself for the day"—resignation, even a certain humor. She spoke of Martínez with undoubted affection and respect. "Vader"—begun perhaps as a joke, and turned into genuine feeling. It did not sound the slick, simplified gloss of someone pretending. Still . . . "Women criminals are consummate actresses"—quite so. The saying, however classic, is nonetheless itself a little slick. He had a solid Dutch distrust of aphorisms: they tended to appeal to immature minds.

He had not asked her any of the obvious questions yet. Not even why she wore a fur coat on a hot day.

The Rivieren-Laan is not one of Amsterdam's old quarters. Built after the war, but not so long after that one of the streets missed being called Stalin-Laan, an enthusiasm that later caused the municipality embarrassment. A wit had suggested "Stalinweg"—"weg" means a roadway in Dutch, but it also means "gone." He was not thought funny. It was renamed "Liberty-Laan," which does betray a certain laborious lack of imagination. But there, municipalities are like that and the whole quarter is anyway drearily unimaginative, too. Behind these heavy blocks live many rich people; there is the thick silence which more than anything means wealth in an apartment block. Picasso lithographs, and a little safe built into the wall behind. Gilt-edged, but lots of lead within. Behind the lumping boulevards named for lumping great heroes are narrow noisy streets full of poor people, who go to work of a morning along the busy tramlines of the Van Woustraat and the Ferdinand Bol. Van der Valk, during twenty years in the city, had mined the seams often but still never knew which of the little streets were which.

"Left . . . second to the right . . . you can stop here." There was resignation in her voice. A big row of letter boxes showed that the flats were small and crowded. The stairway was cramped: no lift. Junior officials and undermanagers, not distinguished old men with morocco card cases. She walked in front of him to the third floor, slipped her key in the lock, gestured him in, and slipped off the fur coat. Under it was a cotton frock, which his Arlette-trained eye could see was homemade, not very well homemade. He knew these flats all right: minute, with a little hallway, doors to broom cupboard and bathroom, both the same size; doors to kitchen and living room. He knew the kitchen would have a little balcony where one hung out the wash, that behind the living room were two bedrooms, the one a scrap less cramped than the other. He needed no telling that the Martínez household was not rich.

The living room was furnished in the solid mahogany of the thirties now despised in Holland and sent to junkshops. He was asked to sit down, in a fat little armchair with a chintz cover hiding the worn plush upholstery. Madame Martínez had determined upon uncompromising honesty.

"I can't offer you a drink, because there isn't one. In fact, it's a miracle the phone hasn't been cut off. Still, he would have paid that if he possibly could—was there any money in his pocket?"

"Not a great deal."

"How I'm to pay for the funeral . . . Well, there it is. We hadn't a penny and you may as well know it."

"Was it always like that?"

"Oh, no—no, often we were—how to say, we ate in expensive restaurants, the place here was full of champagne—ah, there is at least a cigar I can offer you—everything riding high, but suddenly, without any transition, one would be wondering how to pay the phone bill." And Van der Valk felt a little spurt of interest and admiration. In a boy of twenty-five, yes, it was commonplace, but at seventy-six! However improvident, or irresponsible, or whatnot—what vitality the old boy must have had! She read his mind from the pursed lip, the twitch of amusement, and the tiny whistle.

"He wasn't all stiff and chalky and incapable of movement," warmly. "He had mettle."

"You loved him." It wasn't really a question needing answering.

"Yes, I suppose we lived squalidly—but whatever he was he wasn't squalid."

"You didn't work yourself?"

"He was also very proud. He'd been a more than adequate breadwinner for fifty years, and wasn't a man to live on women's earnings."

"You didn't get bored, with nothing to do?"

"Never," with conviction.

Van der Valk smoked his cigar, which was good.

"He had mistresses?" in a peaceful, tranquil tone.

"Certainly not," indignantly, and then suddenly saw through his little deception and said, "And I didn't have any lovers," even more indignantly.

"I did warn you that I would ask this kind of embarrassing, rude question."

"That's quite true. I beg your pardon." Tensing herself to a lot of desperate honesty.

"Perhaps you might have been his mistress before he married you?" She did not frown but thought it over carefully.

"Well—I was his secretary—how am I to explain this? He didn't have mistresses; that would be a most immoral thing to do." Suddenly a little click of intuition gave it to him.

"He married them instead?" To the surprise of both, they found themselves laughing a little, but in a sort of admiration of Martínez.

"Well, yes, I'm bound to admit he did. And—and —well, you'd find out easily enough—I'm bound to admit I'm his fifth wife. Such cows, really—so often exploiting him—making so little effort—did they ever really even try to understand?"

"How long have you been married?"

"Seven years," with an innocent enough kind of pride. Quite an achievement.

Van der Valk was becoming quite attached to Martínez, who had been an engaging old rogue. Did they get killed, then, the engaging old rogues?

"Was he dishonest?"

She made her mind up quickly.

"Well—he's dead, poor Vader—I suppose I can forget about—oh, loyalties, and the whatd'youcall'em, the necessary deceptions—it wouldn't be a lot of use now. But one can't really answer that simply: I suppose, yes, you'd call him dishonest, but you'd have to call him honest in the same breath."

"Moral and immoral."

"He had high principles, which he would die rather than infringe." Her warmth was a scrap edged, as though stung by his indulgent tone.

"Like, for instance, always marrying his mistresses?"

As a match will sometimes sputter as it is struck, before flaming, she gave again a tiny flicker of laughter before regaining her gravity.

"There's a great deal more to it than that," severely, so that he, too, had to laugh a little in his turn, because yes, certainly, he bet there was!

"Who are the girls?" he asked suddenly.

"Why do you ask that?" astonished.

"I was with him in the ambulance. He was still alive, for a few minutes. He spoke—that is to say, he uttered, 'The girls'—twice, nothing more."

"A last effort to keep his grip." She was crying now, but not noisily, a steady trickle of tears that did not disrupt her calm; left her calmer, in fact, because less strung up. "He was very attached to life: I've never known anyone so—difficult to kill." She looked dismally into the distance at the back of Van der Valk's head. "He was often ill—he used to get bronchitis every winter, and very often pneumonia, but he had colossal recuperation. He was tremendous fun, you know . . . The girls; they live in Belgrave Square."

"Isn't that in London?"

"I suppose so, but not that one. This one's in Dublin. I used to live there myself once," with a moment of nostalgia. Another of Martínez's little surprises.

"What does it mean, then, the girls?"

"His daughters—there are three of them."

"And they all live there—a sort of Martínez colony?"

The idea, and his tone of voice as though he could not take all this altogether seriously, seemed to strike her rather as though she had never thought of it that way before.

"Well, there's a sort of family bond—a strong sense of attachment—I mean they're all married women, around my age; we were more like sisters, in a way. . . ." She broke off in some confusion, whether because it was embarrassing or too complicated to explain he could not tell.

"Madame, there is one question which you haven't put to me, which surprises me a little, so I will put it to you."

"Which is?" seeming puzzled.

"Who it was that killed him."

This flustered her: she reddened and lost countenance, as though the main point had been forgotten, like doing an hour's shopping in a store, and then discovering one has forgotten one's purse.

"I've simply no idea," in a great hurry to get the

words out. "No notion; I simply can't understand it."
Self-possession had vanished; she was floundering.

"I can't suggest any reason at all," she gabbled on.
"I mean he might have enemies in the sense of people
who disliked him, or envied him—but I can't see—
I mean one doesn't kill people. I'm expressing myself
very badly: he could be sarcastic, snubbing, very fierce
sometimes, even rather cruel—but that's all I meant.
Mortal enemies, that's the word I wanted, not mortal
enemies."

"And of course you didn't kill him yourself." A police remark made in a police voice, as if making in a
joke a nasty suggestion that yes she had and somehow he knew all about it.

She recovered her dignity, and smiled politely. "I
don't think you can be serious, Commissaire, or if you
are I don't quite know what you mean. If you mean
actually kill him like that, with a dagger—well, I don't
know exactly when he was killed, you did say around
four o'clock, I was here all afternoon. I can't prove it
because I was alone. I ironed some shirts. I pressed a
suit—no, I did go out a moment to buy some eggs, and
tomatoes, you can ask the shop. No—I can prove it—
I was here when you rang up; I answered the phone.
I suppose in a story I might have had time to do it
and get back very quick, in a helicopter or something."

"That kind of story is for laughing at," politely.

"Then you mean you don't believe I killed him but
perhaps I wanted to kill him, did I have a reason for
killing him, something like that?"

"Partly," in the agreeable, almost joky voice. But
she was now very much on her dignity.

"Then apart from the idea being revolting, disgusting—you wouldn't care about that"—her tone said

that he was no longer intelligent—"no, the answer is no." Proudly, bitterly, the pale, slightly protuberant eyes no longer so pretty but glaring with anger and pain at the infliction of a gratuitous wound. He had to break this tension.

"I'm not so unimaginative as to think you a splendid suspect just because I've nobody else. You were closest to him, you knew him best; it's in him I'm really interested. I want two things, essentially. I will ask you to come to my office tomorrow to help one of my men piece together all you can recall of his doings and movements this last fortnight, shall we say? His telephone calls, letters, meetings, conversations."

"But I don't know the half—I couldn't remember, anyway. I'd get it all wrong."

"Very likely you will, as anybody would: we're used to that. A patient man used to such work will help you. Memory plays one tricks—just a matter of disentangling it."

"I'll do what I can. I don't see that it's likely to be much use. I've told you nothing of his business, because I know nothing—I didn't listen when he talked on the phone, say—I had no curiosity about it, so it left no print on my mind."

"The second thing," disregarding all these explanations and justifications, which were common form, "is that I want your authorization to go through all his papers, and perhaps take some away, here and his place of business."

"I don't think he had one, really. He was just one man. He always worked alone."

"He had cards printed with an address in the Harbor Building. It's true—though only on the strength of one phone call—that they don't seem to know him there." She was again a scrap confused, but not disconcerted.

"I told you—there were all sorts of little shifts and pretenses, and some you might think a bit dishonest, whereas really they were only pathetic."

"This particular little shift seems so very easily penetrated."

"No, you don't understand, I think. There was actually—is actually—a friend of his who works there, who took messages and things—I really don't know his name. Oh, do try and understand. He never talked about business. When it went well, it was unimportant—contemptible, somehow—and when it went badly it was humiliating. I know a couple of names. The papers—well, even if I said you couldn't have them you'd only go and get a mandate or a warrant or whatever you call it."

"Of perquisition, yes, probably I would."

"Then take what you like. They're in the bureau there. It's locked, but he carried the keys."

"We found them." It was the solidest piece in the room, and too large for it: a large old-fashioned "ministry" bureau.

"It wasn't that he didn't trust me," she went on pathetically, "but he was terribly orderly, and meticulous, and couldn't bear things being touched."

"I have everything here." Van der Valk opened his briefcase, and handed back the sad, luxurious contents of Mr. Martínez's pockets: the plaited straw cigar case—empty—and the sterling cigar cutter. A gold clip—Mexican twenty-dollar—holding so slim a fold of ten-gulden notes; a leather key holder. Door key, street door, yes, bureau. Ignition key, with a Mercedes plaque, the three-pointed star a flashy gold on silver.

"I've a man looking through the town for this car, which must be parked somewhere."

Her smile was acid. "Just for show, Commissaire. He used to play with it ostentatiously, or pretend to forget it on people's desks—he hadn't a car at all."

"I see." Yes, he felt sympathy, and again admiration. A man of seventy-six!

"The tram stops ten meters from the door. I need hardly tell you the trains are frequent and efficient."

"Have you a suitcase, Madame, for these papers? You'll get them back in a week or two. Any that may appear relevant to our inquiry will be photostated, but no originals will be taken or indeed any paper used without your knowledge. I'll give you an official receipt."

"Very well," in the resigned, half-dazed tone in which most people acknowledge this bureaucratic claptrap.

"Are you going to stay here by yourself? You could go to friends, you know."

Her desolate look held courage. "I do have friends —but I prefer not to trouble them. I am an adult woman; I prefer to sleep in my own room and my own bed; I shan't be frightened."

The bureau was in apple-pie order; paper classifiers, neatly labeled. One drawer, marked "girls," held four bulging folders labeled "Lotte," "Agnes," "Agatha," "Anastasia."

"These are the ladies of Belgrave Square?"

"Three—Lotte is older, she lives in Venezuela. I hardly know her, met her once on a trip to Europe with her husband—he has some vaguely diplomatic post: they're rich. The others I know, of course."

"You'll come to my office, then, around nine if that suits you?"

"What about my husband?"

"There are a few administrative details, but don't worry that's all quickly cleared up. We'll discuss it tomorrow."

Van der Valk went jauntily down with his suitcase, nobody seeing him, apparently, or at least showing any interest. People did not seek much intimacy with the neighbors hereabouts, and doubtless Mr. Martínez had not been one of those men who are pally with the whole block.

He climbed into the car and drove round the corner to the local bureau.

"Commissaire in?"

"Yes, sir. Can you state your business?"

"I have a criminal brigade of my own, son, out in the sticks."

"Sorry, sir."

"Is it still Mr. Keur?"

"Yes," soberly. Bit of a tartar with his staff, Harry Keur.

"See if he's free." The young man picked his phone up.

"Sir . . . Mr. van der Valk . . . Yes, sir . . . Right, sir . . . He says will you please go on up."

It was not a man Van der Valk knew well—younger than himself. But in bygone days their paths had crosssed often enough for an understanding to exist.

"Hallo, Harry, how goes?" He was not only older but in hierarchy superior. But for some years he had been regarded as a half failure, as a somewhat bizarre and eccentric fellow, and for a while now as "a provincial." Once, in foreign fields, a woman he had been running after had shot him with a rifle, and the resulting disability had disbarred him on medical grounds for further service in Amsterdam. The reaction of his colleagues had been, roughly speaking, "That *would* happen to a fellow like that," and there were a couple who inclined to be patronizing. Was this, now, a bit like the "friend" in the Harbor Building, who let Martínez use his address sometimes?

"Hi, there," quite warmly. "Good to see you— what's your news?"

"Oh, only a customer, here in your territory." He explained: Keur smiled and rang his bell, and within a few minutes a folder was brought in: Van der Valk whistled politely at this smartness. Any civil servant beams at praise of his administration; Mr. Keur was pleased.

"He'd no criminal record—nothing in central archives, at least."

"No, this is just the usual—requests for information like credit rating—hmm, pretty untouchable, the credit rating, I see. Mmm, a heap of doings more or less legal—note here from finance squad; fellow knew his law, skated on the brink a couple of times— but here 'generous,' see for yourself."

Van der Valk reflected that it is difficult to have much private life nowadays. Ask for a bank loan, an insurance policy, a license for some commercial activity—and information is requested. And a whole dossier is collected of tiny off-white peccadilloes, anything from paying your rent irregularly to giving noisy parties. Any criminal proceedings, of course, be it only a

27

misdemeanor like shooting a red light, are there, too. Good administrators like Mr. Keur have all this stuff on file, but Van der Valk also knew that really interesting things are rarely found in these files.

"Thanks, Harry, and if over and above you cared to do me a favor I'd like an eye kept on her for a day or so. Not a filature of course, just her movements, any visitors, stuff like that—could that be possible? And, by the way, when I rang her up saying police, she started by complaining that if it was that car again she knew nothing about it—does that ring any bells with your boys?"

"We'll soon find out. . . . Karstens, did somebody ring up a Mevrouw Martínez about a car. . . . Bakker—well, look on his desk. . . . No, just read it out. . . . Yes, I see; thanks, no, no need. . . . No, nothing, just a car that was irregularly parked a few days running in the same place, and since it was outside her flat—We can always get the patrolman's report if you want."

"Don't bother—if it seems relevant, I can always ring up to find the number. Kind of you, Harry."

"Remember me to your wife," said Keur politely.

"What an awful lot of stuff," said Arlette, eying the suitcase. "Is that all work?"

"I do hope not—orderly as it is, it would take a week. Give me a drink, would you?"

There was no real correlation between working and drinking. But when things were slack he had leisure, or so Arlette said, to be hypochondriacal, fussy about alcohol and mashed potatoes. Whereas work, meaning anything passing a certain level of concentration and perseverance, meant eating and drinking a lot more with no apparent ill effects. Improved metabolism, said Arlette, with a French fondness for abstract nouns.

He got into a Victorian armchair with a high back and wings: not an object of beauty but good for working or sleeping in. Once in, it was notorious that one could no longer get out. Arlette brought a drink and promised supper on a tray.

"What is supper?"

"Minestrone."

"Not terribly exciting," unfairly.

"What else do I have to do?" snappish.

"Take your clothes off."

"Coarse!" One of her snubbing words, meant to floor him. Well, he was coarse. Though he preferred to say he was robust.

He arranged a little table for the suitcase, a little table for supper, a notebook, a ballpoint that didn't work, another ballpoint, and was nicely settled when he found he'd forgotten an ashtray. He attacked the business files first.

After a little while, he began to discover a pattern.

The Machine Tools Kantoor
Westeringschans 612
Amsterdam

My dear Xavier,

Well—water under bridges—we don't get any younger, you and I. It was exceedingly pleasant to relive a more youthful decade in your company, and I got back to the office feeling the better for that slightly self-indulgent lunch!

I looked up the correspondence as promised, but I don't think there is an awful lot to be done, since they

29

were infiltrated, for the levers of decisions are now in other hands. I can of course put you in touch with Masterson, but frankly he is become a figurehead, and I fear that the gentleman from Akron would not be disposed to give much continuance to your notion. But I will of course think around your problem in more general terms. Do please remember me to your charming Aglaia.

> Yours youthfully,
> Alfred

Plainly a frost. Businessmen's smoke, masking a diplomatic refusal to help, despite the personal approach from an old pal.

Lyon, le 20 mars, 19—

> Siège Social
> Rue Taitbout
> Paris IXe

Cher Monsieur,

We acknowledge the receipt of your study concerning the proposal outlined in your verbal communication to Monsieur Martin in Rotterdam, and we have studied the modalities thereof with an interest wholly sympathetic.

You will forgive our laboring the point (already in all probability well known to you) that the credits available for payments of American-owned patents are parsimoniously distributed by the Ministry. Copyright in a license of this nature would in our opinion be unduly onerous, and in the Ministry's eye tending to outweigh the indubitable technical advantage attractive to ourselves and rightly emphasized in your interesting presentation. It is therefore with the utmost regret that we decline.

We beg you, cher monsieur, to have the goodness to believe in our most distinguished and sincere sentiments,

> Matthieux, for the Company

Antwerpen, 24 maart   Vereenigde Vlaamse Chimie NV
                                        Oliebollenkade 97

Esteemed sir,

It is with considerable sorrow that I am compelled to point out an error which has inadvertently crept into your calculation, based to the best of my knowledge upon the figures supplied by our Textiles Division in Kortrijk. Due to an unfortunate lapse by a clerical junior in, it must be said, a hasty telephonic communication, these figures are not altogether as advantageous as you were then led to believe, since they fail unluckily to take account of the recent tendency toward a universal upgrading in raw materials.

> Begging to undersign with
> highest and most faithful esteem,
> Moers

Poor old Martínez.

There were successes, too, to be sure, and even coups, glad confident mornings of wouldn't-you-like-a-few-oysters-to-begin-with, but in a world growing ever more bland and slippery, too few. The carbon flimsies of Martínez's own letters, carefully typed at home, sparkled with wit, ingenuity, imaginative enterprise, and grasp of detail, but the cautious deadness of professional commerce choked too many young plants.

None of the letters showed trace of anything construably illegal. To be sure, Martínez might have been engaged in contraband, industrial espionage, bribery, tax evasion, and tra-la-la, and had simply been too prudent to put things on paper; but one had no right to assume any such thing. No apparent motive for murder. Van der Valk hoped the personal files would be a less barren field.

Caracas, December 9th

Dearest Father,

We were overjoyed, naturally, to hear from you for the St. Nicholas. The little parcel—sweet breath of Holland far away—arrived on the exact date and gave much pleasure. I had to stop Joaquin being greedy!

I am infinitely sorry to hear that your health gives anxiety, and Paquita, I must tell you, is making a special Advent Novena. She was entranced with the little Bavarian figures, which are quite unobtainable here and gave me an especially happy memory of that summer in Tyrol long ago.

I quite see that your conscience must often pain you; none of us, alas, is a stranger nowadays to this unhappy type of moral compromise and our prayers go with you.

Felipe is as usual dreadfully overworked. His department is deeply involved in the efforts toward peaceful settlement of the endless troubles arising out of the sordid greed of You-Know-Who. Anxieties and uncertainties beset us. I fear I see no prospect of Europe this year. We have sympathy for your present straits, for our position is by no means rosy! This nasty expropriation talk has made the market more than nervous and some of my own shares as good as valueless. I need only mention that I had to cut down on Paquita's pony.

Both the children send warmest affection to Opa. Rest assured that during the Nativity Season that is so dear to us all we will ask for an especial blessing upon all that is dear to you. My warm love to Anna.

> Your ever-loving daughter,
> Charlotte

Nothing there. Poor old boy had hinted at a bit of help and got the rather odious mixture of piety and the Bourse which so often characterizes bourgeois women. Still, she was one of "the girls": his hand stole out toward his notebook. He shrugged: what could he write? Convent-bred; flowery in style, handwriting, and doubtless appearance. Heavy, hairy blond women taking such pains to be neither, unable to prevent the attention of their overshaved and overpowdered husbands straying toward supple youthful flesh, flashing shiny brown thighs. . . . Come, come, he was being literary. He couldn't help imagining Charlotte, decidedly overperfumed, drinking coffee over the financial columns that were her substitute for sex, but he didn't think she had anything to do with the death of her father.

Belgrave Square, January 8th
Dear Papa you are sometimes really—with all respect—insufferable. Your Christmas letter was intolerably full of moral unction. Do try and realize that letters are seen by Jim, and vu his morbid jealousy I have a great deal of trouble pacifying him ensuite. What you call "regularizing my position" is impossible unless we suddenly get a new bishop more flexible in his views, and even then. . . . Well, to happier topics! Snow in Holland—and pea soup, no doubt—I can smell it! Dublin is muggy and moist as usual and we all have colds, Jim a nasty bronchial cough. That ghastly raw wind is so trying and you know how damp this flat is. I am thinking of rounding out our income by giving German lessons—Jim doesn't like the idea but at least it's at home! There are firms enough here doing business with Germany and Holland, and I could earn a worthwhile salary in a secretarial post but the bee in Jim's bonnet about married women working stops each and every effort (and please spare me sar-

casms; render to Caesar what is C's). Jim was not very impressed, either, by your strictures on Dublin business practice. In this climate one just doesn't get up early and anyway this just isn't Holland but why I tell you this I can't imagine since you know it perfectly well. What you don't grasp is that attitudes have changed a great deal—we are not so isolationist and antiquated as you appear to believe—but I have scolded enough. Knowing you as I do, your irritability is just nervous tension: I sympathize—you didn't really need to tell me what the doctor said because he says it to me! We wish you all possible New Year blessings and especially peace and health with very much love from Agnes.

Van der Valk, who had been biting his ballpoint, clicked it: this was better. The overneat, overregular writing was as uninteresting as Charlotte's rococo twirls, and they seemed to have gone to the same convent. But there was more conflict; a sharper lecturing tone, more self-pity. A husband who wasn't a husband and was "morbidly jealous," apparently no children. Not much money and plenty of frustration; the bossy querulous tone was unattractive. However . . .

Our Lady of Lourdes Hospital, June 4th
    Dear old silly Father—
    I'm on night duty this month and have time for letters, though not that much I warn you since next week I have an important exam, indispens. for SRN. Your letter gave me pleas.—your being sunny and serene means I worry less about you and worries heav. knows I have enough. Poor Mal has such rot. luck—he went for a radio we were all cert. wld be neg. and that accurs Tierney said there was still a shad. rnd the apex—really hvng tb.

34

nowadays is too absurd & its only T's dnd incomp. that he didn't shake it off long ago.

Sorry many interrup. I have a whole squad of priv rms as well as the ward & must study too. Yr sugges studying at home isn't v. clever you know—one no lgr gets the maids & gvrness & all that folk we had when we were little! The new kindgrt—thk heav. Francis goes to school in Spt.—is v. handy, but Lil is nowhere nr old enough to be given rsponsblty at home and cnot "take them off my hands" as you so blandly put it! Mal does his best I mst say but he's often away in winter & when at work at home is blind & deaf to all but his wrtng & he too is chldsh enough heav. knows blast I have to fly—

Later I hv been so much delayed that I will send this as it is. More news soon yr Loving Agatha

The last file was different from the others. For a start, it was twice the size, and the writing was more interesting. Van der Valk was no expert, and he despised graphology anyway—something much believed in by earnest German businessmen!—but this struck him as elegant, incisive, intelligent. The first two had been rather stupid. Agatha's large slightly backward-sloping "lecture notes" had more character, perhaps—but this one—Anastasia . . . the youngest? All three were saints mentioned in the Mass in those lists one always skipped. She had the same convent upbringing, the same fluent pietistic jargon, but there was, he felt at once, more to her.

The writing was rapid and hurried, strongly sloped, but legible and well formed. There was a powerful will, an aesthetic sense, a feeling for form. The words had wide even intervals that made reading agreeable and, he did not quite know why, attractive.

Belgrave Square, April 11th

Dearest Papa,

I have not, I know, written for some time; writing has been difficult and painful. Poetry as you know has been impossible to me for some years, and yet this winter I was moved to begin again. But on the paper nothing would come; the old familiar gap. This time it took a new form, for my whole arm was paralyzed, as it were, frozen. A pen brings me no peace.

Winter was shadowed. E. is drinking less, but he knows that unless he maintains—at best it is intermittent, at worst the schrecklich existence that needs—bears—no description—then he will not hold his job. I wonder if he sees—really sees—how close he is to the kind of dégringolade that ends in the Salvation Army Hostel. I myself see little chance; he is characteristically sanguine and optimistic at all times. The lendemain he is abject with apologies and resolutions and seems genuinely to believe that each time is the last. I envy him his illusions. The physiological cross that I have to carry complicates existence . . . To finish with the woes, yes, my health is irregular, but nothing to cause concern: rassurez-vous.

I have not yet read the book (I prefer to put it off than to read it badly). I have a disinclination to effort which annoys me, which I combat, not always well. Lack of conviction . . . Speaking of books, I have one on which I should value your opinion, which I send you. The translation is stiff, and reads awkwardly, but the thought I found compelling and very lucid. It has influenced my recent thinking.

Of the little train-train there is not much to say. Children, thank God, well, garden beginning again to give me pleasure (the crocuses were remarkable this year) and the feeling of again living out of doors, walking, finding "countryside" still not too far away (Killiney is still just Killiney)—all this does me good, makes me happy for once to eat and breathe and be alive. You know how my disgust with the world has given me a somber outlook.

How I sympathize with present trials. How I wish I could help! E. is well meaning, but his own position is too shaky . . . anything but the solid planks you need for a venture. Jim or M. would *not* strike the right note. Oddly a student acquaintance is the son of an "influential personage"—but said i.p. sounds a pompous ass. It is a pity—Anna's old flat is empty again too just now, not for long of course.

Do let us hear from you soon. There are one or two paragraphs in your letter that I have disregarded, as you see, but I imagine you will prefer it so. Your finishing "stroke" could only cause a bitterness likely to be more lasting than we could wish—or endure. There—my love to Anna. How I should enjoy coming to spend a few days with you: spring in A'dam—I think of it with longing. E. would have a fit!

Your always faithful loving
Stasie

More talkative, more fluent, more literary. Brighter; closer to Pa.

Closest resemblance/affinity to Pa? What is all the mumbo-jumbo?

What is "physiological cross"?

What was the "finishing stroke"? Neurotic-sounding woman.

Whatever it was, it had just finished him, with a smart tap between the eyes. He yawned enormously: Arlette looked across at him.

"Little man, you've had a busy day."

37

"What I need is something as silly, frivolous, and utterly superficial as one can get."

"In that case, turn the television on."

"No cowboy pictures this time of night," said Van der Valk sadly.

It was such a beautiful day that he was vastly disinclined to sit in the lousy office. But he had to: when a homicide came one's way, it occupied the whole of one and everything else could go hang. He had often noticed that they chose to arrive when the weather was unusually nice or—more frequently—unusually nasty. The September sunshine was delicious, not too hot: he opened all the windows as wide as they would go and turned to be mellow—he felt mellow—with Madame Martínez, who had abandoned her fur coat, and taken pains with her appearance.

"How do you feel?"

"Numb. Not believing it yet, quite. But calm. Reasonable."

"Thinking of the future?"

"I have to, I suppose."

"A job?"

"That's no problem. I'm a trained secretary. I must work because I have not a penny. And it will be good for me. I can't sit heaving sighs in white linen. Poor Vader's dead. But I knew the day would come." Her voice went momentarily off-key. "I must react, you know."

"He was murdered, you know."

"I'm trying—been trying—what do you say?—to rationalize. Oh, it sounds awful. All night . . . but what can I do? It's the same, to him. Better, maybe. He couldn't have endured something lingering . . .

impotence. He'd have fretted himself into dying: perhaps he'd have suffered more. Do I sound abominable? Callous?"

"No."

"The hospital said he didn't feel pain. I suppose they tell everyone that. But it can't have lasted long."

"It's true. It's even possible he never realized he'd been stabbed. Stabbed," he repeated, "I don't care for the word. Too melodramatic. That is my job, in a way —to deflate melodrama. You are talking sensibly— but neither you nor I can talk away the fact, can we? He was stabbed. Knifed. Pricked. And you've no idea how?"

"How could *I* have any idea? Everything seems so unlikely."

"I treat you as a detached person, Madame, since you give me proofs of detachment. He had several wives. He married you when he was already old but you were a young woman. He had exceptional charm —and shall I say sap? I don't wish to cause you pain."

"I'm ahead of you."

"Very well; had he a new girl friend?"

"No," unhesitating. "It's not that he couldn't. No, you don't give me pain. I thought of it. At one time I feared it. I'm not a fool. But I would have known."

"I don't wish to force you to go into details of your married life."

"I won't, either, unless you do force me to. Can I put it—I'm young, as you say, yes, but in these years . . . I have learned a good deal. Can I leave it at that?"

She had dignity, sitting there. Excellent legs, neatly crossed, skirt carefully arranged. Pretty woman.

Nose a bit too long, features a bit heavy, real blond hair a little too stiff—fault of a cheap hairdresser, that. Nice figure. Firm, sensible woman.

"I don't know him," Van der Valk said. "I have to get to know him. Was he a jealous man?"

"I see that I have to explain. Jealous—the word is so crude. He was proud, touchy, sensitive. He observed me carefully. He took great pains that I should be interested, occupied. To settle the point once and for all, I had—have—no lover. He was punctilious, generous—and passionate, if you must know. And very fair. You've seen how poor we are just now. Well, I'll tell you that I have a few items of jewelry given me in better times—nothing very wonderful but a good ring, a clip, some earrings. I offered to sell them to help tide us over. He would have none of it."

"It suggests pride."

"Of course it does; it also suggests that he earned my fidelity and loyalty." It was said warmly; it was also, thought Van der Valk, not badly answered.

"You'll sell them now?"

"I've no choice if I'm going to pay for the funeral."

"Have you notified his daughters?"

"I sent telegrams, but I don't expect them to come."

"I've only read some of their letters, superficially at that. They seem very attached to him."

"It's not for me to judge, Commissaire. They all have husbands, two have small children. They wouldn't find it easy to get away."

Van der Valk, who had the strong Dutch "family feeling" and approved of the Martínez family having the same, was a scrap shocked; he would have thought that one or more could well get away. A father who dies like that! Especially the young one, Stasie, who had a deeper bond with him than the others, perhaps. They all lived on the same street—one of the others could look after her children for a couple of days. Oh, well, it was irrelevant to the job in hand.

"So to conclude, Madame, you see nobody who could gain by this death."

"I most certainly do not," very warmly.

"You refuse the idea of an entanglement with a woman. I take your word for this, but we will have to check it, as you will understand."

"Check away."

"And you discount any quarrel over a business deal."

"Sounds as though he was smuggling drugs or something," sarcastically.

"No. But if in straits—and he was—he might have laid his hand to something he would not ordinarily have done—something outside the law?"

She flushed, disquieted, angry. "You don't understand him. He was a gentleman. That sounds old-fashioned. But there were things he would not do, would not accept."

"I don't like having squalid ideas, either," said Van der Valk calmly. "I've got to remember, though, that he was murdered—we keep coming to that. Most people are decent, have standards of ethics, values, scruples. But nearly all murders are as well committed by decent honest people. I wouldn't suggest that Mr. Martínez pinched a tin of peas in a supermarket."

"Or that he caught somebody else who did," she said bitterly, "and was killed in a scuffle. I wish you'd understand. I don't try to stop you doing your job, but leave me a few rags of peace and self-respect. He has a right to some private life—to be left in peace."

"I won't pester you any further, Madame." The phone rang as he got up to let her out. "Hold the line," he said irritably; he was not quite happy with her and he was not quite happy with himself. "Goodbye, Madame."

"I'm sorry—I was a bit sharp."

"That was quite understandable. Good morning, Madame. . . . Yes, who is that?"

"Rivieren-Laan bureau," said a young cheerful voice. "You wanted to know something about a car."

"So I did. Well?"

"Well, nothing, really. I mean a patrolman saw it two days running parked on the wrong side, and he was asking in the houses around. So we checked the number back here. Rented car—you know—so we let it go."

"You mean Hertz or something—rented to a foreigner."

"Right—these tourists, you know, leave a car anywhere and say they hadn't understood the notices—what can one do? Just thought you'd like to know."

"All right. Give me the number and the date, in case I need to check it."

Cheeky boy. Not very ruffled—it had no importance—Van der Valk picked up his hat to go and have a stroll around the Harbor Building in Amsterdam.

Martínez was not altogether unknown, meaning the police photograph Van der Valk had in his pocket wasn't. He had often "popped in and out." After a couple of false starts, inquiry led Van der Valk quite easily to an office called Lindbergh Import Export Agentschap, where, in an air-conditioned room, comfortable and prosperous, he found Mr. Frits Niemeyer.

Youngish middle-aged, thickset, athletic, dark wavy hair, handsome bluff teeth and eyes, easy smiling manner. Very frank and forthcoming.

"Delighted to see you, Commissaire—cigarette? —coffee?—I was meaning to come and see you, didn't quite know who or where, or how to go about it. I was going to get my secretary on the job and you turn up just like that—detective, what?—ha-ha. Yes, I saw it in the morning paper—poor old Vader."

"Vader?—no thanks, not just now."

Niemeyer, very relaxed, snapped a lighter, lit a very long American filter tip, looking just like a color spread in *Life* ("one of Amsterdam's dynamic young businessmen"), and swung his chair from side to side.

"We had a family relationship—sort of halfway ex-son-in-law, that's me. Briefly, his former wife married again and I was the result."

"Divorce?"

"Lord, no, Vader didn't divorce. Very Catholic. Annulled, my dear Commissaire, Vatican Court, Rota, or whatnot—I'm a bit vague, except that it costs more than divorcing, takes longer, and is a lot more trouble. But has a lot of prestige. Sort of thing Italian aristocracy does—typical Vader," laughing, remembering suddenly about the death and straightening his face in a hurry. Van der Valk reassured him by grinning—yes, it did sound the Martínez style, the grand manner.

"Won't say there wasn't ill feeling to begin with," went on Niemeyer lightly, "but when I grew up that was all forgotten. I met the old boy in the way of business somehow a few years back, knew who he was, of course. Bound to say I took to him—never saw anyone with such a marvelous way with headwaiters." He chuckled appreciatively. "Well, how can I be of service to you, Commissaire?"

"You had a little arrangement."

"Well, not formally. Didn't amount to much. If I came across something not really in our own line of country, I'd let him know. And to—well, help him out occasionally, I have fronted for him—a telephone call. And I'm bound to say he helped me. He knew people all over the place, was very skillful in certain areas, knew his law very well. Mustn't think of me offering a charity—he had great experience. Had a factory here once, and another later on, before the war—that'd be in Ireland, I do believe. I couldn't employ him, you understand? False position, so much older than me and so on. He wouldn't have stood for it anyway. Prized his independence. No nine-to-five for Vader; not his style at all!"

"What do you know of his transactions?"

"Nothing at all. Friendly agreement, as I said. Outside that—my business is mine, his was his; that's obvious, surely. We didn't 'compete.' He interested himself in things that can advantageously be done by one man, without office apparatus. Go-between call it. Doesn't sound grand, or very creditable. But it can be useful, profitable, valuable, and necessary. And not in the least dishonorable," he added as an afterthought.

"Have you—accidentally, incidentally—any knowledge of what he was doing over the last fortnight or so?"

"None whatever," cheerfully. "Come. Commissaire, you're almost beginning to hint that he might have been doing something questionable and I might be aware— no, no. Unethical. I've no guilty knowledge. If I had, you'd never get me to admit it. Make me an accessory or something. But I'll say this—you're backing the wrong horse there. I understand he was stabbed in the street even, and that does sound like a gangster serial—you know, O'Brien knows too much, have the Syndicate rub him out. No, Commissaire, he wasn't the man for any dirty games, however thin a patch he might be going through."

"Just what his wife said, but I'd be interested to hear your reasons. You know her, by the way?" (very by-the-way).

"Know her, no—know she exists. Didn't ask to know her—wouldn't have been maybe very tactful— remember I'd be a sort of bastard stepson," laughing. "But Vader—well—he was too experienced, too level-headed. And too genuinely honorable—a straight dealer. Agents—we somtimes dodge regulations, cut through red tape. Doesn't make us shady, Commissaire."

"Don't sound defensive," said Van der Valk. "I'm not the financial squad."

"I only mean to say," hastily, "why, there's an office on this floor, specializes in tax advice—use it myself. What is it? Consultant telling you legal ways to dodge tax, avoid quarrel with the Excise Branch, and so on. Doesn't make him illegal or even a twister; as respectable a man that walks the pavements of this town. Fair enough?"

"You needn't get warm," smiling. "I have to verify everything, however absurd."

"That's all right, we understand each other. Anything else I can help you on? Believe me, I've nothing to conceal."

"You've never met the wife?"

"Oh, yes, I've seen him with her—restaurants or what not. Young, pretty woman—great eye, Vader. Althea?—no, it isn't Althea, get her mixed up. Whole heap of ex-half sisters on the other side of the blanket. I can't tell them apart, their names all begin with 'A.' "

"Never come across any of them?"

"No, they all lived abroad—mostly in Ireland, yes, wasn't it? Like I said, Vader had a factory there. I've seen photos. After a couple of drinks, Vader would often talk of his beloved daughters—amused me, as I say, sort of my sisters. He was an eccentric old boy, tremendous card. Like old Kennedy, sort of patriarch —less rich, that's all, but more aristocratic; nothing Boston-Irish about old Martínez. I'm awfully sorry, Commissaire, my girl's waiting with a heap of files. If you need me, I'm at your disposition, not tonight, though. I'm going out. I give you my card—that's my home telephone number."

Van der Valk had two or three more interviews of this kind. He took some pains over finding out whether Mr. Martínez had been seeing any girls—he hadn't. He also took pains to know whether any of these businessmen had been seeing anything of Mrs. Martínez —they hadn't. Nor was there anything fishy about her account of her movements. She seemed to spend most of her time at home. A quiet, shy woman by all accounts, and genuinely devoted to her husband in a touching, youthful way. Almost as though she had been his daughter. The name "Vader" was not altogether a joke. Some people had even thought she was his daughter. She had a lot in common—age, looks—with the three lovely ladies of Belgrave Square. One kept coming back, somehow, to these ladies, the three lovely ladies. . . . It "made a phrase" such as he liked; it had an agreeable rhythm.

He had studied their photographs with some interest. A family resemblance that was strange and came no doubt from their mother—the same fair hair and strong, slightly raw-boned features with something faintly Slav in the conformation, especially in Agnes, the eldest. Agatha was heavier, rounder in the face, with a lot of bosom and a fine pair of eyes. Anastasia the youngest, was the prettiest, but the photo was somewhat out of date, he thought; she didn't look more than twenty-three or four, with finer, more delicate features. The photographer had given her a misty, romanticized expression that was probably misleading into the bargain.

His last visit was to Alfred, in the machine-tools firm on the Weteringschans, one of the older generation who had known Martínez for years, had been to the university with him, had belonged to the same club before the war. Jovial, high-living, smooth-tongued old boy. No family connection. Had "been able to do dear old Xavier a good turn from time to time," he said. Hmm. He said, thought Van der Valk, remembering his letter. But it filled more gaps.

"Have a cigar, Commissaire—no, no, I insist. Now, how shall I say this without seeming scornful? Why, he was cleverer than me." Quite something that, in Alfred's estimation. "A bit—a bit unstable, if you follow me. Had a trick of finding trade a bit unworthy. Old-fashioned paternalistic view of commerce. Bizarre—given to sudden impulses. Overimaginative

47

—now, perhaps I go too far. Level-headed enough, no really harebrained schemes, but didn't always show sufficient—what?—prudence, long-sightedness—call it what you will. Or was it patience, perseverance? Perhaps. He could be notably impatient and above all with fools.

"Very talented. Marvelous palate—great judge of a drink or a cigar. Man of the world—urbane, cultivated, knew a lot about art, that kind of thing." It did rather sound, thought Van der Valk, as though Alfred considered knowing all about art the biggest handicap a businessman could possibly acquire.

"Made two or three fortunes in his life and lost 'em again—no, I don't know how. Didn't speculate, no. We've all made a few duff investments in our time. Yes, I knew his wife—that's right, I recall those girls when they were little. Three little charmers with long blond hair, tied up in big bows, white satin ribbon. Had a big house then out in the country along the Vecht, packs of servants, cars, horses—on his way to his first million and suddenly smashed it all up. No, I don't know why, never did. Threw the wife over—never understood that either—ran off abroad somewhere—just before the war, didn't see him again for years. Heard he did well—something else bizarre happened. No, I've no idea, just as though he suddenly got tired of riches and success. And women all the time, great collector of women. Something irresponsible—no, no, not what you're thinking; he married them, always married them, invariably; some odd quixotry; great mistake to marry them, Commissaire, great mistake."

The old gentleman took the cigar out of his mouth to laugh, which made him belch noisily.

"Too much dindin," he said, unconcerned.

"And since he came back?"

"Ah. Bit sad, really. Hadn't gone soft, but lost his touch—lost his luck, perhaps, or pushed it too far, maybe. Not modern. Always on the scratch for a big killin' and never quite getting there because he didn't really understand the postwar world. He got older, girls got younger, what . . ."

"You've met the present wife?"

"Sure, little Anna, when was it, now—we had dinner together—a year ago? I've no idea any more. Quiet little girl, no harm in her. Very devoted. Old boy very deferential to her in public, holdin' her chair, that sort of thing, very courtly. Bit of a tyrant at home, I believe. Notable coxswain right up to his last years. Poor old boy, whatever could have happened to him? Got assassinated by one of these maniacs we have about the place now—what is it they do?—inject themselves with peanut butter or something. Go mataglap. Old boy pushed young ruffian off the pavement and gets knifed for his pains. Big crowd, ruffian runs away—never catch 'em. Police no good—no disrespect to you intended, my dear feller."

"Might there have been a new little girl?"

"I doubt it, doubt it very much. Didn't have hole-'n'-corner affairs, not his style. If he had a girl, he had to show her off, display her in public, and above all create a whole system to prove the old one was all wrong. No hypocrisy—understand me—made me laugh, in the past. Convince himself it had been a big disaster, that he was making her suffer, it should never have happened, and the only thing was to pretend it had never taken place—and all this in affection and respect, etcetera."

A lot of moist chuckling, another massive belch. He swallowed a bit of smoke and had to cough, which made his eyes water. He rolled about and slapped his massive stomach.

"My girlie days are over," he said regretfully. "Eatin's what I enjoy most, nowadays. No, no, I would have known. Capable of it—wonderful man for undiminished virility an' all that. But he would have shown her off. We saw one another frequently enough, in restaurants and so on—we're creatures of habit at our age, y'know, go where the waiter knows you. Not at all, Commissaire, not at all. Only sorry can't be more help. Something illegal? Good heavens, man, you don't know what you're saying. The type to pay a bill twice rather than be thought close-fisted—his downfall, in one way. Always was overfree. Breedin' perhaps—old Dutch family, distinguished, none left now. Never had a son, kept trying. This girl never gave him a child, I do believe—can't have been his fault, that. Can you find your own way out?"

Van der Valk went back to his office to meditate.

He didn't believe in the long-haired mayonnaise addict! He didn't believe in Anna having a lover. He didn't know what he did believe in. Casting about for any conceivable loose end he had forgotten or hadn't noticed, he saw the note he had made upside down on his blotting paper that morning. What was that? Couldn't read his own writing now. . . . Oh, yes, Anna had been here; it was Amsterdam ringing up about a hired car; something totally irrelevant—why did one's time always get wasted with rubbish? . . . Oh, well . . . pooh . . . yes, pooh . . . Oh, well, why not? Yes, yes, he knew all about maxims written in manuals. Stuff thought up by imbeciles to be learned by more imbeciles. Never neglect the most insignificant detail, which may turn out. . . . Samuel Smiles wrote that one. Oh, well, why not, when all was said and done?

"I want some information—no, I don't want your charming hostess. I don't want to hire a car at all, I've got one. This is the police. . . . No, I said this is the police. Van der Valk, Commissaire, Criminal Brigade. . . . Yes, that's right, yes, good morning, good evening. Now I want details of who, in the course of last week, hired a car. . . . Yes, of course I'll give you the number. I want to know if it is still out and, if not, where it was left. I want to know what mileage it did and—Don't be so damned silly, man, I'm not asking the color of his eyes. You don't just hand out cars like toffees. You make out a form. You make a driving-license check. I want the number of that license. And when it's a foreigner, don't you make a passport check? . . . Left at Schiphol on what date? . . . Yes, I'm still here: Denis James Lynch, spell that. . . . American? . . . Yes. Yes. No. No. Nothing for you to worry about. . . . Nonsense. You tell your area manager from me, Commissaire van der Valk, if he doesn't like it he can tell me so."

The car that had been parked for two days on the far side of the street from the Martínez apartment was booked in the name of a young Irishman called Denis Lynch. Which was something of a coincidence, interesting Van der Valk, no great believer in the long arm, enough to want to know more. Alas, before he knew enough he was bidden to attend the Officer of Justice. Evil-minded personage.

"This," said the Officer of Justice, "is not at all satisfactory. I can't issue a warrant on the basis of a hired car someone left in the street. She denies all knowledge of this car, you tell me. The man may have had business, or relations, or an acquaintance, anywhere in the district."

"The local commissariat has done a door-to-door. Nobody knows Mr. Lynch from Ireland."

Officers of Justice do not say "So what?" but they think it. "He was just taking a stroll. Visiting an antique shop or whatnot."

"All day? Two days running?"

"Proves nothing. Now, if you could place this car in your area around the time Martínez was attacked—I might be willing to listen then."

"Who notices a rented car? Nothing distinguishes it."

"Why should anything distinguish it? It was parked on the wrong side, a thing all foreigners do. Otherwise it would have attracted no notice."

"Nevertheless," said Van der Valk obstinately, "KLM tells me that Mr. Lynch flew out of the Amsterdam airport on the evening of Martínez's death after changing his booking at short notice."

"Yes, yes," impatiently. "It could be most significant and no doubt you imagine it is. But I must have a peg to hang it on. I can't see myself," sarcastically, "asking for an extradition order on account of a parking offense. Did you find out where he stayed while in Holland?"

"Nine days in all, in a little hotel in the Paul Potterstraat. Slip correctly filled in. Occupation given as student: reason for visit tourism."

"Quite. And what criminal activities were noticed in the Paul Potterstraat?" Fortunately, Van der Valk was used to the heavy humor of magistrates exercised at the expense of the police. It is common form.

"He went out every day after breakfast, and slept in his bed at night."

"You appear, Commissaire, to entertain a hypothesis that a tourist came expressly to Amsterdam to murder this Martínez, but took nine days to make his mind up. You are wasting my time."

"It's all we've got." Which did, yes, sound excessively feeble.

"The paper knife?"

"Made in Holland," drearily. "Tourist souvenir with the town coat of arms."

"This town?"

"Yes. But they're still made by the hundred and sold everywhere."

"What was that tiresome Martínez doing here, anyway?" muttered the magistrate crossly. He felt he was being played with, too. But he could show irritation; Van der Valk couldn't.

Self-respecting people did not get stabbed on a Saturday afternoon outside Vroom & Dreesman.

It was still such marvelous weather; everyone exclaimed over it. The great thing, they agreed earnestly, was that, being autumn, it wasn't too hot. Didn't they call it an Indian summer? That couldn't be, surely; why, everyone knew that summer in India was insufferable. Or. St. Martin?—what had he to do with it? There was no lack of rambling talk, much sententious opinionating about atom bombs and jumbo jets. Meteorological law—lore?—got laid down in every café. Everybody enjoying themselves but me, thought Van der Valk self-pityingly. It had become plain that he was condemned to the kind of police investigation never mentioned in crime stories, because it is far too dull.

He even failed to see humor in making an Identi-Kit photo, generally good for a laugh. People—the hotel porter, the car-hire "hostess," the airline-booking girl—produced regulation clichés from women's magazines. What was a sensitive mouth, a firm jaw, a fresh complexion? They came to the laboratory and did their best: as usual, the compromise arrived at satisfied nobody. A camel is a horse designed by a committee, thought Van der Valk, not for the first time, cursing all eyewitnesses—not for the last time—from the bottom, or dregs, of his heart.

With this wooden object, and a ten-year-old photo of Martínez, who had, like a wise man, disliked being photographed, the inquiry hobbled upon flat feet in circles.

Two antiquated plainclothesmen from Central Recherche, characters who had learned nothing in thirty years but professional insensitivity (indifference to disturbing anyone on absurd and futile grounds, refusal to be snubbed, veneer of unconvincing and threadbare politeness upon utter lack of consideration, whether for people, mealtimes, television programs, or just comfort in general—comfort means not being involved, that terror of all populations)—these two dreary old bores were beating up Amsterdam. Not all of it, naturally; that would have taken a year. The tourist quarter. Since Lynch was a tourist, said Van der Valk with hate in his voice, he had gone to the Rembrandt House, or Anne Frank's garret, or gone for a ride on the water bus. He just might have been seen there with Martínez.

54

Two more old bores were shuffling round his own town, which was at least smaller, so that concentric circles could begin with the pavement outside Vroom. They came one day with the information that Martí-nez had been seen in the municipal art gallery, pos-sibly on the day in question. He had been with a man, but the attendant didn't think it was anyone like that, staring in disbelief at the Lynch reconstruction. Man in glasses. Van der Valk could not feel convinced that this item really advanced the inquiry very much.

Meanwhile he had read more letters. The three lovely ladies had private lives seeming both confuséd and bizarre, and so, as the magistrate might say, what? He thought that any fluent and prolific letter writer —Arlette, for instance—would give the same impres-sion.

There was nothing to be had out of Anna. She said she had never laid eyes on the mysterious car, had known about it only through the police inquiries, had never heard of Mr. Lynch. Yes, the ladies of Belgrave Square had sent long emotional telegrams and Inter-flora wreaths, but had not come: they couldn't get away. They were under the impression that Vader had had a heart attack; she hardly knew how to tell them he had been stabbed. What good would it do, anyway? She supposed she would have to tell them sooner or later. No, none of them read the Dutch pa-pers.

"You wouldn't think of going back to Ireland your-self?" fishing vaguely.

"It would be attractive in a way, I suppose," as though she had never thought of the idea. "It would be pleasant to be near them all again, and I enjoyed

55

Ireland. But earning a living would be harder: that's what I've got to think of."

"None of—more natural to call them your sisters, isn't it?—their husbands couldn't help you to a job?"

"Oh, them," not sounding much impressed by the stepsons-in-law. "I don't think any of them could help much." Quite.

And at the end of it all it was Van der Valk himself who found out something, by accident arising from his own stupidity. The fact was that while in Amsterdam—to be exact, while drinking black-currant juice in a dismal café near the post office—he left his glasses behind. He had only been wearing them for a year, and then just for reading. Wasn't really even middle-aged; must be all those years of filling in forms. No disgrace, anyway; half Holland wears glasses; but he had not taken to them with any great enthusiasm. Still, he must have been very preoccupied: how had he come to leave them on a café table in full view? It was two hours afterward when he discovered his loss and rang them up. Ah—they'd found them . . . but with a zeal utterly infuriating, instead of hanging on to them, the silly bastards had sent them to the Lost Property Office. As in all major cities, the Lost Property Office is a joke. Incredulously, he thought back but could not remember having ever been there: where was it, anyway?

When he found it, and described the glasses, the clerk nodded sadly, went away, and came back with a large cardboard box full to the brim.

"Good grief," said Van der Valk as two or three hundred pairs were tipped out.

"Your bad luck," with faintly spiteful satisfaction.

56

"Got piled up. People thinks we keeps them a year. Couldn't; too many. Once in a while we has a clear-out."

"Don't people claim these things?" asked Van der Valk, whose experience told him never to be surprised at any vagary or oddity, but a bit taken aback at seeing tape recorders, guitars by the hundred, cameras, typewriter cases, and bags of every description, many expensive.

"Reckon on them being stolen, people say. I reckons it's just too much trouble to come and claim them. Can't think why we bother. People got too much money."

"Here are mine, anyway. Want to check them?"

"You think we ties labels on all these? We only does that with articles of value."

"They are articles of value." He had been strictly brought up.

"Nobody seems to care. Easier to go buy another. Sign here. Seven hundred umbrellas, we got."

Fascinated, Van der Valk was staring at the heap of unclaimed spectacles, wondering what was interesting about it. He did a double take, caught it, and read the gold print on the handsome green leather slipcase a second time: "Murray," fresh and new. "Optician. Duke Street. Dublin."

"You don't tie a label. But you do have a register. You enter a description."

"Well?"

"Can you identify these?"

"What's it to you?"

"Police."

"Oh, well . . . suppose I might. What you want to know?"

"Where they were found, what date—no name on them, I suppose?" The old-fashioned metal cases that shut with a snap, he recalled, had a paper sticker inside for a name and address. People could no longer be bothered.

The old man shuffled back. "Horn rim, brownish black, no metal—hundreds of 'em. Greenish case, leather, stamped Dublin—that's Ireland, isn't it?"

"Yes."

"Uh, uh, uh," turning pages, "goes back a bit. Here we are. Table in waiting room, Schiphol Airport."

"Date," with a sudden excitement.

"Ninth of inst.—here, you can't take those without you gives me an official receipt."

Van der Valk, pleased with himself, as though losing his glasses had been a clever thing to have done, bore the prize away.

Doubtless there were dozens of Irish people leaving Schiphol any day. But how many—that day—sufficiently worried, distracted, preoccupied to leave their glasses on the table, like himself.

"Superimpose them on the photo."

"But nobody said anything about glasses."

"I only wear mine for looking at things. Reading, or the cinema. Not in the street. Or looking at a picture—an art-gallery attendant remembers Martínez with a man wearing glasses. Profile and three-quarter; I'm taking nothing for granted this trip."

"Sure I remember. I look at the pictures because I know them and I'm fond of them. I look at people, too; like they were in a picture. How the light strikes them, and such. Why? You ask why and I tell you—

58

because I've nothing else to do, that's why. Before you asked me, I said no, because of the glasses. Now you ask me, I say yes, still because of the glasses."

It was a typical provincial art gallery, a historic town house with faded elegance, chipped stucco needing regilding; the kind of place that would be very beautiful if intelligently restored but which no provincial municipality will ever consent to spend money on.

"Not so many people come here. They go for the better-known ones, like the Mauritshuis, or the Frans Hals in Haarlem. And here they go for Gallery Nine 'cuz that's the Van Dam Bequest. But there's good stuff here."

"Really," said Van der Valk, staring anaesthetized at a huge boring seascape by Abraham van der Velde (the Elder). Even to himself his voice sounded glassy; the old man was stung.

" 'Course, if you know nothing about pictures."

"No," humbly.

"That one, now, that's a good one, but not obvious, that one isn't. Carel Fabritius that one is, the girl with the parrot. That's what they were looking at and talking about. Knew something about it, the elder gentleman did."

"And the younger?"

"Well, your photo's not much good. But with the glasses, I'd say yes; I'd say yes, and I'd be pretty positive, not maybe to swear but to be pretty positive."

Conscientiously, he went to look at the girl with the parrot—putting his glasses on. . . . Prickles went suddenly from the back of his neck clear down to his behind. He hadn't expected that!

Down off the faded crimson wallpaper out of a baroque gilt frame, Stasie's face was looking at him. Far more living than in her photos; calm and delicious, between youth and age, between innocence and experience, fondling the parrot, mocking, gay, mischievous, extremely sexy.

"Well, Van der Valk, something new? Come a bit nearer toward convincing me this time."

"Martínez was seen in the town, by a good witness, an hour before his death, with a young man in glasses. These glasses. They were found in Schiphol on a table that evening. Young man booked on a flight to Dublin via London. They were looking together at a picture that has an interesting resemblance—here, see for yourself: this is a photo from Martínez's flat. About five years old, his wife says."

"I see the resemblance. What is the significance—it's his wife?"

"Daughter. Who lives," with relish, "in Dublin, Ireland. And this time I've got something. Two elements. Neither strong, but taken together . . . The time factor—afternoon of the death—and the space factor; this same young man, who hired a car seen outside Martínez's flat, lives in Dublin. Where Martínez once lived, where three of his daughters still do. Madame Martínez disclaims all knowledge of the man or his car, but she may be in perfect good faith, because by all accounts Martínez did not tell her about his business affairs, especially when they weren't going too well. Now we know what he was doing in our town— showing this picture. And why does he go seventy kilometers outside Amsterdam to show this young man a picture so strangely like his daughter? And why is he killed within an hour? Case there surely for an international mandate. Is Ireland in the Interpol net? Must be, surely."

The Officer of Justice fell into a profound trance, apparently disagreeable.

"Well," he said at last, "there's ground for questioning, certainly. But even a mandate for interrogation, to a witness in another country, is still a serious step. You're a pest, you know that."

"Oh, I quite agree. But I thought you'd be pleased."

"Pleased! You have this infernal knack of turning things up in other countries."

"Haven't turned anything up there yet. I thought we could get the Irish police to look into it."

"Remember that mess in France—woman got machine-gunned. You always get yourself into these irregular positions."

"I don't want to go to Ireland," defensively. "Haven't the least interest in going there. Position's entirely different." He spoke with sincerity, but realized at once that he was not telling the truth: he would be interested, very, in meeting the lady of the portrait!

"They can surely ask the fellow questions on your mandate."

"I'm none too sure," muttered the magistrate irritably. "It's all very circumstantial."

"Just my sentiment," said Mr. Kevin Nolan, Counsellor at the Irish Embassy. He was like a teddy bear that had a bald forehead, with tiny round eyes, a curly little mouth, a round padded pleasant face that needed shaving often, a benevolent milky voice. "Tenuous, y'know. A pair of glasses, a picture in a museum, a hired car, a changed plane ticket; nothing there that can't bear a construction of complete innocence. Can't expect us to believe—can you, now— that this young man comes over for a bit of sightseeing, since nothing shows otherwise, kills this Mr. Martínez, and calmly takes the next plane back. Maybe he does know Martínez and these daughters of his. Comes over here and looks him up—reasonable. Art gallery together—normal. Chap shows him a picture like his daughter—amusing coincidence. And then he forgot his glasses—so do I, often. So did Mr. van der Valk, on his own showing: not exactly an indication of guilt—is it, now?"

"If I may say," said Van der Valk softly while the magistrate fidgeted and a lawyer from the Ministry of Justice smoked a cigar, "none of my friends or yours got knifed in the street."

"It's a point, to be sure," said the Irishman, "a point—no more."

"But perhaps the essential point," said the lawyer. "The manner of this death. Hardly a premeditated act. The very suddenness of it suggests a violent upheaval. Evidence on Martínez's state of mind would be relevant, and this young man's own state of mind. The car parked outside, the meeting in the art gallery, the resemblance to a person in Ireland—the tie is undeniable. This young man, Mr. Nolan, is thus a witness to Martínez's movements, words, possibly mind, on the last day of his life. We suggest no more than that there is a case for hearing his account. Time enough afterward to consider any—uh, whatever might appear a subsequent suitable step."

"Oh, I'm not trying to obstruct the course of justice," with good-humored milkiness.

"Very well, then, suppose we ask your people to interview him."

Van der Valk said nothing more: too cozy altogether, all these bland functionaries. But once out in the street he realized that this was the way to do things, that he was only cross at things being taken out of his hands. His witness, found by him—and squabbling over legal niceties. But there, his Officer of Justice, dubious, had asked advice of the Procureur Général, and it had been that gentleman who suggested a tactful scheme with, if possible, the cooperation of the Irish.

"We haven't even a case. Even if we did, launched an international mandate, they would sit thinking up excuses for not letting us have him. Remember the fellow who helped the English spy break prison, the one who got that absurd prison sentence—Irish chap, that, too. English wanted him, tried to extradite him; fine fools they looked, never did get him. Irish said blandly he was a political refugee. We don't want any touchy nationalist sentiments: extradition is always a tricky business." A faint volcanic noise rose from the Procureur's lungs, suppressed out of consideration for United Europe.

No, no, thought Van der Valk, better this way; they're quite right—but he did dearly wish there was some way of getting in touch with his opposite number in Ireland for a little heart-to-heart.

Some days later, the Officer of Justice handed him a thick envelope of papers clipped together, the top

63

two or three covering notes, but—"Read it for yourself," with a long face. It was like peeling an onion.

Republic of Ireland, Ministry of Justice, Attorney-General—a few skins in came "Criminal Investigation Department. Dublin Castle. Confidential," which was more up his street.

"In furtherance of instructions received"—he could skip the phraseology, which he could read easily enough, English bureaucracy being much the same as Dutch, and the jargon no different (mercifully it wasn't all in Irish!).

Facts at last. Lynch was a common name; since there was no clue to identity, they had begun with a passport check: this was the subject of a confidential memo to the Irish Embassy in The Hague—yet another skin further in. Inquiry from airlines had produced information that the young man in question had not come on a connecting plane from London to Dublin, nor did his name appear on subsequent lists, which did not exclude possibility of travel by boat ("Or flying saucer," muttered Van der Valk, exasperated). Further discreet inquiry elicited information that the young man was not at home: he had stayed in England, or, of course, gone elsewhere. His home had apparently received no recent news, but he "was always a bad letter writer." Detective Inspector Flynn (plainly jubilant at finding the fellow outside his jurisdiction) felt there was little purpose in pursuing the matter until receipt of further instructions; bloop, bloop, bloop.

What was this memo lark? The Officer of Justice rang the Ministry of Justice. Yes, there was a memo; it had been received, was the subject of study, would doubtless be forwarded on from External Affairs when the time should be ripe.

"What did I tell you?" said the magistrate, almost with satisfaction in his voice. "I knew there would be trouble."

Van der Valk decided by himself that there was a way of getting at the facts, and went quietly to see Mr. Kevin Nolan.

"A confidential memo?" said Mr. Nolan, sounding a little amused. "That will mean it went to the Ambassador and hasn't come my way. I'm curious myself," disarmingly. "I'll pop in for a word with him; he's free, as it happens. Won't keep you more than a minute." And, true to his word, reappeared in a quarter of an hour.

"The Ambassador feels it's a little ticklish: however, he authorizes me to handle the matter. I'm only anticipating, of course, since this will come trickling down through official channels—hmm?—but since you are here and took this trouble, I will give you the gist . . . verbally . . . in confidence, of course . . . oh dear, oh dear."

"Sounds English, that," said Van der Valk comfortably, liking Mr. Nolan, who was certainly doing him a good turn by being human. "Civil servant in receipt of embarrassing instruction."

The teddy bear beamed, pleased by this perspicacity. "It does rather, doesn't it. In Ireland, we would probably say 'Oh, Jaysus. Mmm. I mustn't be frivolous." He gathered threads, coughed, got his fingertips arranged.

"Perhaps I can best explain by putting a hypothesis. Let us assume that we in Ireland have a criminal inquiry, and Inspector Moriarty—in charge of the investigation—forwards a request to the Netherlands government with a view to interviewing a witness of Dutch nationality—a young man of unknown identity. Now, upon checking this identity, Commissaire van der Valk discovers a fact that could, conceivably, embarrass the Dutch government. To wit, the young man in question is the only son of a well-known, highly respected, massively influential member of the Second Chamber. On hearing this, the Dutch government is—undeniably—embarrassed. It communicates a sense of misgiving to the Netherlands Embassy in Dublin, where at this moment the Counsellor, Mr. van der Linden, is trying to explain to Inspector Moriarty, in whom he has every confidence, that his witness, to put it mildly, is red hot."

"I understand perfectly. Can I know the identity of the respected etcetera member of the Chamber—let's see, you don't have a House of Lords, do you?"

"No," said Mr. Nolon sorrowfully. "We are like you—or, rather, since we are a republic, like France. We have senators. You wish to interview the son of the President of the Senate. Imagine what the French police would say to you."

"They'd say 'Oh, Jaysus.' "

Mr. Nolan beamed at him. "Since—oh, Jaysus—you possess the name Lynch, there's no point in hiding under any alias. We are about to be faced with Senator Terence Lynch uprisen in his majesty. Oh, Holy Mother."

"Some cry on the Virgin," agreed Van der Valk. "Mutti, Hilfe!"

"If we had something direct, now." The Officer of

Justice was far from happy. "You must understand, Van der Valk, that I'm under instructions from The Hague. If we had an overriding fact, a strong motive, or an eyewitness. Something we could go into court with. An incontrovertible fact. We haven't, you know. I have received a confidential memo."

Van der Valk groaned, and cried silently upon the Virgin.

"Senator Terence Lynch is a prominent—a most prominent figure. He is a newspaper proprietor, sits upon several international commissions, in his own country chairman of a most important committee on the Euromarket. A man of unquestioned integrity."

"But as liable to bring his son up badly as anyone else."

"Get it in your head: we're *not* getting this boy. Not without more evidence."

Van der Valk went home and brooded, causing Arlette to say many rude things about the opinion she, as a French woman, had of senators. He then put in a request to see Mr. Anthoni Sailer, the Procureur Général for the Province of North Holland. Van der Valk had not seen him for seven years, and found him as alarming a figure as he had then.

"Van der Valk," said Mr. Sailer with the severely upright voice Van der Valk had recalled vividly, "I have sympathy for you. It is undoubtedly a case of conscience. I recall that once before you had a dilemma of a similar nature, and acquitted yourself with credit. I am myself far from satisfied with the apparent cloak of diplomatic immunity presented to me to invite my acquiescence. If you have a suggestion, I will consider it with sympathy."

"I have a certainty."

"Really?"

"An interior certainty—of a tie, a connection."

"Explain yourself."

"Sir—if a Dutch woman marries an Irishman, does she acquire Irish nationality?"

"I will inform myself. The frame of reference?"

Van der Valk explained about the three lovely ladies of Belgrave Square. "And, with what is melodramatically known as his dying breath, he spoke of 'the girls.'"

Mr. Sailer did not draw on his blotter or play with his paper knife; it wasn't his style. He sat immobile.

"Very well, Van der Valk," he said simply. "Leave this to me."

So that when another summons came three days later from the Officer of Justice Van der Valk was unsurprised.

"A compromise—diplomatically speaking—has apparently been reached. I am instructed that if, in pursuance of this inquiry, it is thought useful to interview Mr. Martínez's daughters, who are Dutch subjects by birth, there will be no obstacle placed in our path by the Irish government, irrespective of their present legal status or domicile, all this of course without prejudice to any subsequent steps they may see fit to—uh—"

"Etcetera. Quite. So the Irish police—?"

"Er—no. The Irish police, it is felt, have no role to play beyond a certain informal cooperation: not, put vulgarly, their pigeon. No, it is proposed that we send a Dutch officer."

"Oh, no," wailed Van der Valk. "Oh, no."

"Why not?" startled. "You liked the idea."

"And every conjectured, supposed, or alleged criminal on whom I ever look like laying hands always manages to commit suicide practically within the whatnot, precincts of the court, and I get my head washed from here to Kingdom Come. Anyway, I've never been to Ireland. I know nothing about the place, I talk no Irish. And if I discover naughty things about Senator Thingummy, what then?"—soprano—"then it'll be don't make a fuss, there's a good chap, simply climb into this box we have here, the wet concrete's all ready and the tide won't serve all night."

"Stop talking such nonsense, will you?" said the magistrate irritably. "Even if I were disposed to listen, I can't do anything about it; I have formal instructions, I tell you. You are to proceed to Dublin. The Hague says so. You will contact Inspector Flynn at Dublin Castle—equivalent, I gather, of our Prinsengracht. You speak English, I suppose?"

"I can just barely make myself understood."

"That's all that's needed—if you're going to interview these women, you speak Dutch to them. That's the whole point; they are Dutch. Otherwise, if I may be permitted the expression, we wouldn't get our toe in the door. Vulgar expression, that."

What was there to say? With nothing, on the whole, but a soggy feeling round the socks—that would be the wet concrete, no doubt—he said nothing.

"You will report confidentially to—let's see—Mr. Slavenburg at the Netherlands Embassy, who will be responsible for any diplomatic liaison that may prove necessary. Written reports to me which will go, hmm, to The Hague, and—let's see—oh, yes, the comptroller at the Embassy will see to your expenses. Really, Van

69

der Valk, you've nothing to complain of. What worries me is we've no guarantee whatever of your turning anything up. How can we expect that these women will know anything material about the circumstances of their father's death? I have taken, by the way, a formal deposition from Mevrouw Martínez—nothing to go on there, nothing at all."

Back at home, Arlette was unexpectedly sympathetic to the idea. "Be most interesting and rewarding, I should think. I've always wanted to go to Ireland, sounds fascinating. They drink stout; I don't quite know what that is, sounds horrid. I've a street map of Dublin, which I got to try and help follow the journeyings of Ulysses. It doesn't seem to have changed all that much."

"I don't want to go at all. I'm afraid of the Irish—all much too allusive and oblique for a fool like me—Is allusive the word I want or is it elusive?"

"Oh, stop talking nonsense," said Arlette, sounding like the magistrate. "You'll enjoy yourself. Now, let's see—weather—rains all the time like here, but not so cold. Loden coat, your rawhide shoes, umbrella."

"I refuse to carry an umbrella."

"Very foolish and snobbish."

He was to realize the truth of this.

Schiphol to Heathrow—nasty as ever. Toy plastic airplane, the famous thirty-eight inches between economy-class neighbors, a very Dutch smell, and an ooze of cheap piped Muzak. A chill competence, a politeness as false and oily as the Muzak. Heathrow a sweaty scrum; smell of soft-boiled bread and synthetic lemonade in a plastic thing the English called a "goblet"—unspeakable. . . . But he was beginning to enjoy himself, coming round to the idea of Ireland. And Anastasia—hmm, conceivably as fascinating as her namesake. A little air of mystery that lent seduction: ha.

The Irish airplane was almost pleasant. True, the stewardess stood there ladling out charm over the passengers' spareribs as though it were barbecue sauce, and her uniform was a singularly hideous shade of green, and he had already noticed that Irish women had absurdly short legs. But there was the delightfully haphazard feeling that is so different from Holland; that things are no longer cut and dried; that one does not know quite what will happen next and neither do the Irish, but they will improvise and the improvisation will be brilliant; the sensation one has in France which is so agreeable, of a clown's nimble sloppiness. . . . He would like Ireland.

At the Dublin Airport, a man asked him earnestly whether he had been in contact with cows, and another man stamped his passport and said, "Ah, Mr. van der Valk, hold on a second, now, I've a message for you." It was an envelope, large and thick; coat of arms and "Je Maintiendrai." Fifty pounds in currency, a street map with the Embassy meticulously marked in black ballpoint, a little note saying "Expect you tomorrow 10 A.M., Slavenburg," and a hotel reservation.

"Sheridan," said the official, reading unashamedly over his shoulder. "Doing you well. Nice, that—right in the center, Stephen's Green, best bar in Europe; cheerio, now, enjoy yourself." No different from other countries—every town he had ever been in had the best bar in Europe—but a nice change for the poor policeman to be given an expensive hotel. Not the Embassy's doing, he'd bet. He climbed to the top of a double-decker bus, sat right at the front, discovered his knee space to be a lot less than thirty-eight inches (plainly all the Irish had such tiny legs), and turned happily back into a schoolboy.

PART TWO

THE SENTIMENTAL
SEDUCATION

HE HAD WONDERED whether he would be conspicuous, like the man at Val-d'Isère who went to ski with
his bowler hat on, and was relieved to find he blended
into the landscape. Plenty of local people given to his
kind of checked shirt; as for the loden coat, it was as
correct as in Kitzbühel. There was a fine drizzle, and
no sun—but there, he hadn't expected everyone to be
out picking grapes. It was still warm for September,
with milky, heavy clouds. "Very close, today," said the
reception desk.

Enchanting, Dublin: tatty, deliciously disgraceful;
all the buses looking like much-played-with Dinky toys
—all the corners bent and practically no paint left.
Wasn't like England at all; was like nowhere else he
knew—it must be like Ireland! Traffic went—if that was
the word—on the left, money promised to pay the
bearer quick punt (whatever—aha, pounds?) on demand in London, and the pubs had uncivilized hours,

but the difference was much bigger than the resemblance. He headed instantly for the best bar in Europe.

"Evening, sir."

"Good evening."

"Grand evening, now."

"Is it?" startled. "I thought it was close."

"It is that," unperturbed, "but agh, a bit of rain—make the girls prettier. What would you be liking?"

"Stout," courageously. Where had he seen before those enormous numbers of broken-looking Mercedes taxis? That oatmeal-colored foam looked very attractive. Yes, of course; in Lisbon. Black—odd but nice—where had he heard about black velvet? A bold swig—it wasn't very nice; in fact, it was rather horrid. The barman watched with amusement.

"You need to be getting used to it. Wouldn't it be the same, now, if I went to your country and got the snails? Oysters, now—there's people just can't get their mouth to open in front of an oyster."

"I love them."

"You'll want to try the Guiness, now, with oysters, but I'll take that away. A nice lager now?"

"Some whisky, please."

"A grand drop of Jimmyson. Right away. Where would you be from, now?"

"Holland."

"Is that so? Lot of Dutch people here. Real colony, you might say. Very nice people indeed," hastily, in case of misunderstanding.

Nobody in Ireland wants to hurt one's feelings. Why do they say "now" all the time? Same reason the Dutch say "hoor." And the English say "actually." Delicious whisky; he had some more and went off in search of oysters. In a new town there were always oysters, and one had to learn how to open them: finding out how things worked, what people thought; it was a journalist's knack. He had already fallen into the trap of thinking that because this was the edge of Europe and had a grubby look it would be backward— or cheap. Not a bit of it.

Full of churches—all ugly. Pubs were ugly, too, and shops. Women loved loud colors: emerald, puce, and electric blue in all directions. A people without taste, but with lots of vitality despite the climate—they looked a sight more alive and gayer than in Lisbon. Plenty of prosperity; the shabbiness was deceptive and perhaps only a pleasant carelessness about clearing the rubbish up. Lot of good-humored yelling and general indiscipline—he was going to like it here. . . .

The food was a blow. Pretentious but poor; one just never knew, recalling how badly he had eaten, too, in Marseille: he put himself outside a strapping big meal for all that, nice and slow, studying his street map the while, had Irish coffee—he was going to do all the right things—and went happily to bed having learned several useful things already, like "Avoid soup," "The cake is too sweet," and similar slogans in favor of tea, whisky, and of course oysters. He took a pile of paperback shockers to bed—let this holiday mood last as long as it could—and had great difficulty getting out of bed next morning, but was cheered to find that everyone else in Ireland did, too. The thought of the Netherlands Embassy dispelled the holiday mood, and cast a slight chill across breakfast.

It was only five minutes away; he could observe the Georgian houses which Arlette had lectured about. Very beautiful indeed, or would have been had they not been disastrously turned into offices. The Netherlands Embassy was as bad as any, a fact that did not surprise him in the slightest. Mr. Slavenburg had the cheek to keep him waiting, and when he did get in there was a distant manner, a strong flavor of his being likely to create Incidents. He got a chilly white handshake, a plastic chair, and a cup of weak tea. The flag was being kept flying all over the shop with Leerdam glass and Philip Electrics, not to speak of the tea.

Mr. Slavenburg was pear-shaped, closely shaved, and smelling of Cardin-for-Men. Van der Valk was not surprised at the hostility: all functionaries have a holy horror of interference from another department. Being Dutch, this one was not likely to speak openly of the Procureur Général as "that silly little man back there," but you could see that he thought it, and moreover that he wanted you to notice that.

"Well—er—Commissaris. I understand you'll be here for a little time. Your—er—investigation seems to touch people living here. Now, Senator Lynch—I do hope you have understood that he's not the person to ask bluntly where he was on Tuesday evening." This was so crude—and so obviously only dented amour-propre—that Van der Valk held his tongue. "Well," sighing, "you give me your reports, and I'll have them typed."

"I'm afraid I have instructions that my reports are to be confidential. A copy goes to the Ambassador, of course. Verbally, though, I understand that I have to keep you in touch, and of course this Mr. Flynn. I would, though, be grateful for the loan of a typewriter and carbons: I can do the reports in the hotel room and take pains to bother nobody."

"As for these Dutch people . . ."

"I'm not going to cause you any trouble," firmly. "I can't guarantee that they won't come storming round here complaining of being harassed, but you'll have to take my word it won't be true."

The diplomat was tapping his teeth with a paper knife, seeing if they were sound enough to bite policemen. "That's all very well, but what guarantee have we that you won't—quite possibly with no blame attaching you, but you aren't familiar with the ways of thought here—that you won't get into a false position?" Had he been briefed to the effect that Van der Valk headed at false positions like bears at a beehive?

"I take it that this is the reason I will be giving the Ambassador a copy of my reports. Avoiding false positions—isn't that what this place is for?"

A level look and a level voice. "No need to get hostile."

"I thought I had felt a certain hostility." Van der Valk moved the teacup.

"Well, that may be so—and if it is so, then I'm sorry."

"Well, I was rude—and so am I sorry. The truth is that I'm oversensitive about this because, of course, I'm not happy about it myself. I'm here to try and find a shred of proof for a hypothesis that sounds strong enough, but—and that's a false position by definition."

Slavenburg softened and put his elbows on the table, displaying hairy wrists and a lot of gold cuff link, but it did make him more human. "I don't want to force unwelcome advice upon you," with more sympathy. "I did wonder, and I'm speaking quite informally, whether you knew the role—just for instance—that religion, say, plays in this country. Are you, by the way, Catholic? Good, that's a point acquired. You might know, for example, that divorce doesn't exist here, but you might underestimate the role played by the hierarchy, diminished but still very puissant, in public as well as private—hmm, proceedings. You need to realize that this is a small town in many ways, rather provincial—and extremely touchy. Now, take this boy Lynch: he went to an exclusive boarding school on the English model. All the parents know each other. I'm only, shall I say, opening a perspective. The slightest things are known here, seized on—as tea-party conversations and a chat under the dryer—commented on, and criticized. Beware of that criticism. Beware of a national pastime which is coat-trailing; beware, above all, of comparisons with the way we do things in Holland."

"Which is in general deplorable," and regretted it because the fellow was pinked.

"I must remind you that you are a public servant and that people will judge your country by your behavior. You have—it is said—something of a reputation for indiscretion."

It was undoubtedly a test, to see how he reacted to coat-trailing. "That is quite true, and I suppose quite often deserved. But I didn't come here because I wanted to. I came because I was sent, and I wasn't sent on account of a reputation for indiscretion. However, don't think I have an inflated notion of my importance. In this job, it's important to remember one's nothing but a tool. So are you, if you'll forgive my saying so."

Mr. Slavenburg had a self-controlled expression, as of someone stung by a bee just as he is being presented to royalty, but he managed a nod.

"You're no relation to the bridge player?" asked Van der Valk politely, getting up.

"No. I do play, but only socially."

"Ah. I only play marbles. In the gutter; that's where I was born, in Amsterdam. Learned to cheat at an early age. That's the difference between us; if you cheated, you'd be expelled from school, whereas at marbles one has to cheat; it's expected. We are different kinds of tools, called for as wanted. Good luck, now, as they say in Ireland."

From the Netherlands Embassy in Merrion Square to Dublin Castle in Dame Street is not very far, not much over ten minutes for an active man, or not much over fifteen for Van der Valk, who had an old bullet wound in the hip. But it is another world.

He was not at all disconcerted—on the contrary, he was reassured—to find that it isn't a castle at all, but a courtyard surrounded by blocks of exceedingly dingy offices: to him this was a good deal cozier than the pretty, well-painted, much-window-boxed house in Merrion Square (Georgian, mannered—a town place for Sir Walter Elliot). The smell was dearly familiar—stone, dust, guggly old central heating, cardboard, damp umbrellas, and not very clean lavatories. He was perfectly at home immediately.

Detective Inspector Flynn was tall, thin, and countrified, with the bucolic look that is so useful. (In hardly any other profession is looking intelligent such a disadvantage.) He had a soft voice and a gentle manner, large hands and large feet, shabby clothes, a tweed cap (new, checked, shocking), and all the time in the world. He might have been about fifty and Van der Valk trusted him instantly.

"So there we are. Will you find these cigarettes nice, I wonder? And we've got to have a talk, umm. And about Senator Terence Lynch, so help us. And him."

"He needs it, too?"

"Sure he needs it as much as us if all I hear about him be true, or even the quarter of it."

"You are a man in my heart."

"After my heart, it would be. Why after, now, I wonder."

"My English is, I'm afraid, very bad."

"Your English will do fine, then. Amn't I now just out the bog, and don't speak any languages at all? Now, you'll be speaking the French and German, too, I make no doubt."

This was coat-trailing.

"Yes, that will do me no end of good, being able to speak German to Senator Lynch."

"Sure he's a greatly traveled man, and maybe he speaks the German, too; I wouldn't know. D'you want very much to talk with him?"

"I rather talk with you, or listen better, not quack-quack what I nothing know from. Here to have your advice, not give mine."

"There, now, you'll get on famously with him. He's a businessman. Broad-minded. Goes all over Europe. Represents us in a heap of these international discussions, don't you know, disarmament and all that. Now, what"—Flynn meditated—"does Ireland be wanting with disarmament? Sure we've six tanks and maybe two old fighting planes we got cheap from the English in 1953."

"You don't take Senator Lynch very seriously?"

"Ho, yes, I do then, because he's like me, he looks a damn fool but isn't. But about his son, now—maybe he is. A nice boy, I'm told; I don't know him. Some say he's no good—I wouldn't know that neither. Senator Lynch is, no doubt of it, a proud man, and he wouldn't like to hear people say his boy wasn't any good. Which the boy is as good as any other, do you follow me, but he may be in a bit of a jumble, don't you know. I'm told there's some as says he's no use. Isn't it a lamentable human failing, now, to go about saying things are no good, and isn't it just an excuse now for us, being ourselves too lazy and too uncharitable to take a bit of trouble and inform ourselves properly instead of repeating a slipshod load o' guff?"

Van der Valk was relieved to find that he understood English very well indeed.

"The Senator—I talk too much but just put a stop to me any time—he's accustomed to making a success of things. Good businessman, like I said. 'Course we none of us like to admit failure. He's maybe an unusually sensitive and intelligent man, like yourself. If he doesn't see things, it's not maybe that he hasn't noticed them. Maybe he doesn't want to see them, being human and imperfect like the rest of us.

"As for this boy Denis, now—been to an expensive school, been to the Trinity College, and he's been sent now on a kind of tour, to complete his education, like. The Senator Lynch is a man who has a lot of friends, and all anxious to oblige. If the boy likes to travel round Europe, and he wants to study awhile at the Sore Bone or anywhere you like, he can stay as long as he takes a fancy and the Ambassador will esteem it a pleasure and a privilege, as the saying goes. He doesn't have to find any student's lodgings sous les toits. And maybe he likes that and maybe he doesn't. Being a young man that likes to feel free. When you're a little boy, isn't it so, feeling free is more or less always just having ten bob to clink in the pocket, and small worry who put it there. When you're a bit older, having the money always there put there by your dad, all of a sudden you don't feel free any more. About that I wouldn't know.

"I'm told, too—the hearsay we call it—that the Senator Lynch is not too happy. Why is that? Well, invest your money in the oil or the gold, you can always get it out again. You might have dropped a little, but on the stock exchange even the Pope's not infallible, though I seem to have heard"—he was meditating again—"there's a few cardinals in training, like, to be infallible. But when you invest in a boy you can't just sell out while the quotation's still high. This is a problem maybe our Terence hasn't got quite worked out yet, but don't get me wrong, now, I don't know him. Haven't spoken to him, nor don't yet intend to.

"Me, now, I have this disadvantage coming from Cahirciveen, and Terence Lynch coming out of that backward kind of place himself, and never once looked back neither; he don't like to be reminded of his native woodnotes wild, as the saying is, and with people like me he gets kind of impatient.

"You, now, speaking the German, you'd be very welcome. Mrs. Lynch, now—very nice lady. I could talk to her, sure, but I thought I'd just as soon leave that to you. I'd only be in your way.

"Live out in Ailesbury Road, they do. You know where that is? A bit outside—not far. Enough for some gardens and nice trees and a bit of quiet. Old-fashioned it looks. Where the crust lives and always has since I was a tiny boy in Clanbrassil Street and the Castle here was where the Lord Lieutenant lived;

in the English time, that was. Lot of changes since, as you'll notice. Lot of embassies out there, the Ailesbury Road way," he added, with meditative malice, squinting at Van der Valk.

"Would that be anywhere near Monkstown?" asked Van der Valk with false innocence.

"Ah. Monkstown. That would be just a step further out along the road there. From Ailesbury Road, a quarter of an hour on the bus. Very respectable kind of a little district, all suburbs of Dublin now—built up, it is, all the way along the coast, not like when the tram used to go out to Dalkey; cost you fivepence, it did, an' now it's half a crown. Mmm, these women of yours, I don't know them neither. Reckoned you wouldn't be wanting me to know them. Got no call to know them, myself," with an innocence quite as false as Van der Valk's.

"And does Senator Lynch know them?"

"They wouldn't be his sort of people. You're staying in the Sheridan Hotel, now, and there in the bar you'll find a lot of money just back from the races, and that's where you'll find his friends: call themselves his friends, anyhow, which ought to be good enough for the likes of me. In the right place, you are."

"Come out and have a drink," said Van der Valk, moved irresistibly by powerful springs.

"Why, bless my soul," said Inspector Flynn. "Half eleven already. Maybe I will, at that. Just be getting me coat."

"In Holland, we put the clock back instead of forward—I've no idea why—and say half twelve."

"That's a very interesting place, Holland, and I hope you'll be finding a moment to instruct me a bit about it. Now, here we are"—he did not have to put his cap on, because he had had it on throughout the conversation—"but if you'll excuse my touching your elbow, we won't go to any Sheridan—be full of a lot of rich women around this time; no fun at all. We'll go to the place over there—you see where the big clock is—Mooney's, it's called."

"O.K. by me," said Van der Valk happily, making great strides in talking English, too.

Van der Valk sat in a bus exploring Dublin. He had quickly learned to feel affection for Dublin buses. They looked like English buses; the usual double-decker Leyland with a spiral staircase of nasty slippy metal treads; but they were without the primness and respectability of English buses. They were not bourgeois, but ruffianly, defiantly working-class. Nor, it was plain, did anybody give a damn about what sort of image they projected: they were encrusted with filth, and the shrill stink of unwashed poverty—it was like traveling inside a dustbin—only added to the pleasure. They did not even have the portly movement of an English bus: they were alley cats, with an indecent speed and agility; limber rather than lumber.

He wasn't going to call on Senator Lynch in a bus; might be the wrong approach. It might, though, be the right approach to the lovely ladies of Belgrave Square. The names in Martínez's neat address book—Mrs. James Collins, Mrs. Malachi MacManus, Mrs. Edward Flanagan—had been given a little flesh by Inspector Flynn but still lacked blood.

The bus was pleasantly empty: mmm, two in the afternoon and buses going into town were all packed, so that he felt clever. He sat on top in the front seat, shaken about in this crow's-nest by high winds, and loving it. One couldn't even begin writing in the good tiny notebook, but that would be ridiculous anyhow. One would do that tonight, if one lived that long, over smoked salmon (he had had oysters for lunch)—stop daydreaming. Lansdowne Road. It meant nothing to Van der Valk, though he was something of a rugby fan, but that concrete crown of thorns flying the American flag was plainly the United States Embassy; the large houses had a new dignity, there were broad pavements with trees. He crossed a tiny river by what his map told him was Ballsbridge; a dear little factory made bread and was called Johnson, Mooney & O'Brien, which had surely inspired James Joyce to flights of fantasy.

Respectable neighborhood, full of money. Tall terraced houses gave way to semidetached villas in bulls'-blood colored brick; these villas got steadily bigger, uglier, and wealthier, with Gothic turrets, greener lawns, and leafier trees, and suddenly the name "Ailesbury Road" flashed at him and past him and he felt contentment. These villas were just like Aerdenhout or Bloemendaal in Holland, where people like Senator Lynch lived in houses looking much the same: it wasn't a foreign country after all. The bus fled on.

Yes, he saw; that was the edge, technically, of the town. Thereafter was new suburb—concreting, gnomes, and crazy pavement—which had been countryside not so long ago, and the high iron gates and stone walls of one or two large country houses were still there to prove it. He thought he understood; these houses with rambling basements and acres of field and paddock were impossible without servants. One or two became schools—there—or convents—there—but most were carved up by the speculating builders: gold in those fields.

On the left, suddenly, was flat gray wrinkled sea: he was on a wide dreary boulevard moving fast: the houses thinned out, clustered again thickly round an obliterated village that was now a suburban shopping center with such a High Street look one was surprised not to see Boots the Cash Chemist. "Bray," said a road sign; "Temple Hill," said a piece of painted metal on a wall; "Belgrave Square next stop," said the friendly, dirty bus conductor, who had a blue chin, thick spectacles, and that confidential way the Irish had of talking to one, entrusting you with all their secrets. Van der Valk got off the bus and was knocked sidewise by all the fresh air.

Belgrave Square was a lot less impressive than it had sounded and he had expected, without quite knowing why. The London model, he supposed—he had always thought of something tall and Georgian. This was a squat Victorian terrace with stunted tiny gardens, starveling box hedges, genteel little pear trees too well brought up to bear any fruit. Behind worn strips of bare turf and daverdy gravel, the houses needed paintwork, were weedy round the doors, rusty round the iron gates. Grim little basements had bars over blind windows, flyspecked net curtains needed a wash, and dark poky halls full of prams could do with airing as well as polishing.

Not all were like this. Some houses had repaired their rotting sashes, put on a coat of that violent pink or lilac paint beloved of the French and the Irish, clipped around their tiny rose or rhododendron bushes. But his main impression was of flats with absentee landlords, bohemian tastes, and more children than money. The air was soft, moist, seasidy; there were a few ragged palm trees. But somehow it was very Irish as well as Bexhill backwoods; and subtly mixed with the flavor of curates and daffodils was a raffish scent, as of Mooney's pub, Boland's bread, McCabe the Licensed Victualler, and Ryan's Funeral Parlours. He was delighted to find a symbol crystallizing it all: a letter box of florid cast iron, set in a stone wall; a magic casement opening on the foam. It was painted, to be sure, bright green, but had a crown. He had studied English pillar boxes, columns that stoutly support the monarchy, and knew that "V.R." meant Victoria Regina. He was cheered by this, and no longer so downcast about missing Admiral Nelson, who had presided so long over Dublin, until—belatedly—removed by fervent nationalists with dynamite: Inspector Flynn had explained Irish politics over a glass of stout.

"A great mistake. Sure the good people up in Belfast will come roaring down to blow up Daniel O'Connell, but I don't mind that at all. Nelson, now, was a great help to the police; he held up his hand, so he did, and all the trams stopped right in front of him. Civic-spirited, so he was, and gave the street an air: sure without him it's just a slum."

Mrs. Edward Flanagan lived behind some ratty privet; a child's bicycle and a door knocker the worse for sea air. The door had been amateurishly done up with royal-blue paint that had not been thinned properly. She opened the door herself and he knew her at once.

"Mrs. Flanagan?"

"Yes, what do you want?" How long has she lived in Ireland?—her accent is still strong.

"Commissaire van der Valk: Netherlands Police," he said in Dutch, and watched it hit her.

She showed no fear, but a great deal of surprise. "What on earth are you doing here?" She spoke Dutch, too, automatically, probably without realizing.

"I will be glad to explain."

"Yes. Sorry—you'd better come in. Such a surprise. As though you told me I'd won the sweep or something. Netherlands Police," incredulously, and this time there was a note of fear. But it doesn't mean anything, he thought. Police is a dread word in the ears of anybody Dutch, be they of the most irreproachable virtue. They shift uneasily inside their clothes, wondering what regulation they can have broken. He followed a brown corduroy behind and a solid Dutch upper half in a sage-green pullover needing a darn at one elbow. This is Stasie.

"I hope you'll excuse me. I wasn't expecting anyone. Everything is very untidy."

He had heard that, too, often enough in Holland. In a tone of groveling but reproachful apology, and meaning there is a thread from the sewing box on a cushion, and a flowerpot out of mathematical alignment with the corners of the window sill. But here it was different. The words were said carelessly, not in the least as though she meant them. And the room was untidy; very untidy indeed. But he did not have time to look at it, because he was concentrating upon the woman and she took all the concentration he had. Beautiful?—oh, come. Very, very pretty?—he supposed so; he'd no idea, really. Like the picture?—yes, and unlike.

He couldn't be bothered with any of this, because

of the gust of seduction. Great wafts of sex. Massive gushing cascade of luscious femininity. He sat down gingerly in a small fat armchair with upholstery worn threadbare on the arms, crossed his legs with care, and put his glasses on from self-defense. If he had brought a briefcase, he would have been rummaging in it in next to no time. One saw the shabby sweater and the sloppy trousers—and one simply saw her naked. Remarkable.

"I am the Commissaire of the district in which your father, Mevrouw, was found dead. This has turned out a delicate, even disturbing affair. It was thought best to come and talk with you and your sisters, informally." But he was not listening to these idiotic words; his mind was racing to collect impressions that crowded one upon another. Housewives at the butcher's sausage counter on a Saturday afternoon, dozens and dozens, and he wanted to remember them all. Every movement—she cleared knitting off her chair, looked for a cigarette, found a packet on the chimney piece, found it empty, saw another on a table, searched for matches and found them, too, eventually in the chink between the back and seat of her chair (a bigger chair, covered in worn brown leather)— showed a different woman. She caught the light in facets.

Not a Renoir, whose skin took the light well. This was the moist softness of the Irish air. Her skin was sallow, with a greenish color. Not even pretty—coarse. But the nose was straight, delicate, and the modeling of the forehead fine. Fair eyebrows, full of angles. Small, seemingly uninteresting bluish eyes. Large mouth, mobile, sensuous. Strong Dutch jaw, and

square, not quite heavy chin. Very fine throat, and untidy blond hair that half hid well-shaped ears. Was it
the mixture of crudity and delicacy, of animal force
and spiritual sensitivity, that was so striking? Not a
Renoir. A drawing by Matisse.

She was wearing an amber necklace and tortoise-
shell earrings, knowing that lumpy barbaric jewelry
suited her. The mouth was only slightly painted, as
though penciled along the outline: she had no other
make-up. The eyes were small, their blue a little
muddy, but they were an interesting shape and unusually vivid. There was a strong smell of woman, mixed
up with an ancient classic Lanvin—Arpège?—no. The
voice was warm, heavy for its size, like a peach off the
orchard wall, low pitched, with a characteristically
Dutch metallic timbre. In fact, the whole woman was
metallic. Greenish-bronze armor reflecting red waver-
ing torchlight.

Van der Valk felt that someone had unfairly kicked
him in a sadly un-jockstrapped tenderloin. The
woman had a violent, instant, painful effect. Stasie
Martínez. Mrs. Edward Flanagan. Licensed Victualler
& Grocer. Wines & Spirits. John Power & Son Gold
Label Whiskey. Not a drop is sold till it's seven years
old. Boompsadaisy: get up, you clown.

"There are puzzling details," his voice said. The
hearth rug was off-white and slightly smelly, as though
of cat.

"Would you like a cup of tea?" asked Mrs. Flana-
an.

Suddenly he understood something important. This
woman was a natural, a high-powered piece of rawhide, and the splendid teeth were those of a man-
eater. This would take some watching.

"That would be very nice," he said gently.

Van der Valk was a good policeman in some ways: that is to say, he possessed some essential qualifications: quick intelligence, determination not to be blunted by a discouraging job, a vile wearisome job, and ability to learn from experience. This he thought of as the need to keep both sides of his head separate. He was brutish, lazy, and egoistic, but he had them both, and kept them fresh. One side belonged to the public, and the other to bureaucracy. There was a continual conflict, and reconciling this was a labor of Sisyphus, and at nearly fifty he had not made much progress since the age of twenty, a green trainee sub-inspector fresh out of the army, thinking he knew it all after seeing something of pain and fear, cold and hunger, having learned to lie still under fire and having experienced the pleasure of being bombed by one's own aircraft.

What had he learned in the days since Constitutional Law at the police training college? (He could still hear the whiny voice saying, "Lax law enforcement is more of a menace to the liberty of the citizen than strict enforcement; will you comment on that, Mr. Sluys?"—he had at least got it quicker than most of the class.) Well, he had learned that the public itself stayed absolutely insufferable whatever the law enforcement: feeling tolerant and sympathetic wore off awfully quick. So that one learned techniques for dealing with one's feelings. A bit of zoology, for instance: his relationship with a criminal, say, was much the same as that of Dr. Konrad Lorenz with a goose, bursting out laughing at the observation that "Well, after all, geese are only human." Or visits with his children, when smaller, to zoos or circuses (both heartily detested on his side), which taught one a good deal about prisons, so that he noticed—coinciding again more or less with Dr. Lorenz—that chimpanzees, dissolute and depraved at the best of times, became much more so when shut up in cages. Very like criminals.

Alas, one was never left in peace to pursue these pastoral observations—the great bureaucratic octopus got in the way. Dr. Lorenz, studying his geese, giving them pleasant names like Kopfschlitz (Van der Valk knew several criminals called Kopfschlitz), was a great man, no denying it. But he could get on with his work unimpeded by reams of idiot regulation. The same thing happened all over the world; policemen being told how to do their job by gaga Lord Chief Justices. Damn it, nobody made Dr. Lorenz work in a world where all his rules, methods, working patterns had been designed by the geese: worse still, where his scientific papers, lecture notes, the proofs of his books —even his conversations with colleagues—were submitted to the critical stare of geese having the right of comment, criticism, and final decision.

He could just see Kopfschlitz (a gander with a most interesting homosexual relationship with another called Max) leaning over Dr. Lorenz's shoulder, saying, "Cross that bit out, Konrad: I'm not having it."

The bureaucratic octopus spent plenty of time telling him off, drawing magic circles outside which he might not step, and devising new sets of rules. He broke these, of course—all policemen had to if they were ever to get any work done at all—and wasted a good deal of time in not getting caught: already a terrible indictment of his efficiency, that, when he considered the further immense amounts of time consumed in writing reports. So little of what one did made any sense. One lived in a Kafka world; he supposed it helped him a little to look at the castles and the trials, to realize why the examining magistrate behaved in that neurotic way (so like a goose deprived of its partner in the triumph ceremony), but Kafka was not a writer he cared for.

Pleasant, vanity-tickling notions such as that of the policeman as zoologist would not do, alas. Was he not the centurion in the gospel? A man giving orders; a man under orders.

Human beings are not geese.

The octopus did try hard. Van der Valk had recently been on a "recyclage" training course at the police college in Fontainebleau, and had been amused at recent instructions given to traffic cops.

"Do not lean your hand on a man's car."

Better still:—"If a driver is accompanied by his family, and you have occasion to address him a reproach, ask him to step out of the car. You must beware of injuring his dignity as a man, and his authority as a parent."

What a terrifying gap there was between "We, the people . . . in order to insure a more perfect . . ."—how did it go?—"the blessings of liberty to our posterity . . ." and the sidewalks of Chicago—or Paris—or Amsterdam.

He had, of course, a high degree of detachment. Learned on simple, physiological lines on dreary nights of street duty upon Amsterdam cobblestones. Look at the silly bugger, you with the pain in the shoulder blades, feeling the feet, moist down the neck: stop yawning. It had continued in every report he had ever written, with the other Van der Valk, the goose one, leaning over his shoulder helping.

He had lucidity, simplicity, humility. Poor things, and permeable. He was a shaky fellow, and Mrs. Flanagan not the easiest of exercises. Not when one half of his head was telling him that she was a bit of a chimpanzee, no?, while the other was wallowing upon billows of sex and thinking it lush.

She was "anxious to help." She spoke fluently of her father, explaining how she and her sisters had been brought to this country as children, of her mother and various stepmothers, of Papa's fantasies, extravagances and instabilities—all with ironic affection.

"An interesting background."

"Well, I'm at home now, here in Ireland. My birth and my nationality are just accidents. I suppose I remain Dutch, in various ways, but I have become a different, more complex person."

She enjoyed talking about the person she had become.

She seemed to wish to create a special relationship with him, in which they were both intelligent, informed, detached persons, collaborating in the scientific experiment devolving upon her father's death. Observing the geese together. Was she even moved, or touched, by this death?

"Why do you think your father was killed, Mevrouw?" lighting a cigar, being very obtuse, very literal, very Dutch.

"That seems impossible to answer—so metaphysical. People get killed. They cross the road without looking, or get attacked by criminals—why? Why are some so old, and some so young? I won't insult your

94

intelligence, Commissaire, with a lot of talk about destiny."

She was very forthcoming. He did not tell her that he had been reading her letters, but she seemed quite unsurprised at his knowing something of her life, and was perfectly happy to amplify. She spoke lavishly about her husband, "my poor Eddy," who she hinted was a bit of a drunk, of her sisters who had psychological problems with their men, of the difficulties of bringing up children, of anything under the sun; art, music, history, religion: she was unwearyingly fluent. She was compassionate, philosophical—and a good deal in love with herself.

She seemed in no hurry for him to go.

"Oh, there's my youngest waking up—no, no, don't take that as a hint to go. I'll make some fresh tea. I like company. I'm only a housewife, you see, and I'm stuck at home a great deal."

"But you have a lot of friends?"

"Oh, quite a few, I suppose. I like people to drop in; I like to keep open house. We have lots of discussions here." She waved an arm around; he looked about him. Pleasant room, shabby and comfortable: disorderly, welcoming. Vase of flowers, needing renewing: several reproductions of modern pictures as well as a Raphael: heaps of newspapers, magazines, and phonograph records muddled casually together. Intellectual interests right and left. It was very much like Arlette's living room at home. What was the difference? Was there even any?

"Do you, by the way, know a young man called Denis Lynch?"

Her answer was as easy and open as all her others. "Indeed I do. Dear Denis. A boy with a great many qualities—he'll be a valuable person, I think. In a difficult stage of development, of course; he's not very happy at home."

"You seem to know him well."

"I should think that, yes, I did know him as well as anybody." With a bland and cheerful innocence, and a note like self-congratulation, as though it were greatly to her credit to have such understanding.

"How did you come to know him?"

"How does one come to know anyone? He's just a student."

"I suppose that in Ireland, as anywhere else, people form compact groups and move in a restricted circle. One meets other people at points of intersection—a sports club, or a music society, or something like that."

She gave a supercilious little laugh. "My dear Commissaire, how Dutch you do sound. We don't have such tight little circles with those minute graduations of standing: Ireland is more democratic, more open. People are"—she sketched in the air with her hands—"more fluid. Less of these constipated little snobberies. Dublin's larger than The Hague, you know—and larger-minded." The tone was snubbing and he wondered whether there wasn't an area of sensitivity about Denis.

"But you don't know his family?"

"Heavens, no. Very rich and boring—politicians. I know a lot of it from him, naturally. Why all this interest in Denis, anyhow?"

"You must forgive me; I'm here to learn. Ireland is plainly very attractive—so much I've learned; from Anna, for instance."

"From Anna?" startled.

"She speaks of Ireland with affection—does that surprise you?"

"No, no, of course not. She lived here a while, true enough."

"She met Denis here?"

"Denis? Not that I know of—no, that's not possible —it's some years since she was here."

"But she knows him?"

"I've no idea. Since you brought up the subject, and she seems to be the source of your information, I assume she does; I don't know. I haven't seen Denis for some time."

"You knew he was in Holland?"

"I knew he had a plan for going around Europe," tranquilly. "Something about a possible job; it was rather vague, I think. You know, these students, how they make grandiose plans, but quite often nothing comes of them. I didn't know he was in Holland, but it doesn't surprise me to hear he was, if that's what you mean."

"He knew your father?"

"Well, again, you seem to be telling me he did, and I repeat I've no idea. I recall saying to him if he was in Holland why not look my father up. I suppose he did that, since Anna told you about him."

"Anna says she doesn't know him."

"Well, if she said that why ask me, since she knows more about it than I do. Sorry—but we seem to be going around in circles, don't you think? What is all this about Denis?"

"How long have you known him, Mevrouw?"

"Dear me; this is getting to sound quite like an interrogation."

"That worries you?"

"No—I suppose it surprises me."

"But it's quite natural. Your father was killed, Mrs. Flanagan."

"But, good heavens, what can that have to do with Denis?"

"I've no idea, Mrs. Flanagan."

"That sounds very queer in a Dutch mouth, calling me that all the time. You can't very well call me Miss Martínez—you'd better call me Stasie; I feel more at home with that."

"You don't want to talk about Denis?"

"I simply can't understand why you keep on harping on about him. What's he got to do with it?"

"That's what we're trying to learn."

"I only meant," with her little gurgle of laughter, "that all this sounds a bit ridiculous—we sit here so solemn. Of course, Dutch people do tend to be so solemn—I sometimes forget I'm Dutch myself. There—Father was the least solemn of people."

"You were attached to him?"

"Greatly. He had plenty of faults, of course, and I saw them, and suffered from them, too, being his daughter."

"You wish to know who killed him?"

She thought about this for some time, holding her cigarette up and turning it around, staring at it. "No," she said at last. "No, I don't think I do. It seems to me that it's part of his private life: he's dead, then leave him alone, in dignity and self-respect. Oh, I know you can argue the point, tell me it affects society and all that, but you're a sort of functionary with a vested interest in being nosy, if you'll forgive me; I don't want to sound rude. It's your job and so forth, and you consider it a duty—but I'm sorry, I hate it, all that raking over of people's lives and little secrets. I think it a frightful invasion of privacy, when one's dead, too, and can't stop it. I'm sorry."

"You don't have to be sorry: I quite agree. But you were telling me," blandly, "where you met Denis."

Her little laugh again. "You are persistent. I don't really recall, but I think one of my friends brought him here, originally."

"And you don't recall who?"

"Well, we've lots of friends, as I said. I didn't know it would be thought all that important."

"Yes, I see that. Well, thank you very much, Mrs. Flanagan."

"Stasie. But is that all?"

"Is there more?"

"Good heavens, man, I only meant I didn't understand why you go on and on about something trivial and then go racing off. I don't know if you're in a hurry, of course. I suppose you want to see my sisters. I don't think either of them are home, just now. Agatha's a nurse, you know, and at work. Agnes went into town, I do believe."

"I'd be interested to meet your husband."

"Oh. Well, he's generally here in the evenings, though not always, and most weekends—there are mostly quite a few people at weekends; friends, you know, dropping in."

"And you're generally at home during the afternoons?"

"At this time—mostly I go out later, for a walk with the child, and to do my shopping. Just like in Holland," laughing. "And in the mornings, of course, when I have boring domestic chores."

"I'll be trotting along, then," he said. "Many thanks for the tea."

"I haven't helped you much, have I? Elucidate, I mean."

"We haven't got as far as elucidation yet."

"No?"

"We're not scientists, so we do no predicting, and elucidating is a thing a court does—or doesn't, more likely. All we do is pick the piece of grit out of the machine, once we've found it—always assuming we're given the time to look. Goodbye, Mevrouw."

"Au revoir, surely?"

"It's quite likely."

He spent an agreeable hour exploring the seafront, and found a Martello tower, which would please Arlette, who went in for literature. He took a bus back into town, pleased with himself that again it was the other direction that had all the packed buses. It was nice being pleased with himself about this: there didn't seem much else.

"From the Netherlands Embassy," said the porter. A dinky little Olivetti typewriter, very nice except that, as he discovered at once, using it for a letter to Arlette, it had been dropped on the floor—or perhaps thrown at a diplomat—and had a strong tendency to stick. There was also a chaste envelope with a piece of pad paper inside, at which he made faces. He moved rapidly into a bad mood.

The message was brief and unhelpful.

Denis Lynch, we are told, has been seen in Rome, and on verification is staying with the Irish Ambassador to the Vatican, with whose son he was at school. No secret about this, nor anything odd noticed about his behavior. He seems to be in Rome for an informal stay of undetermined length.

Didn't seem to be anything one could usefully add to that. One could ask how many other Ambassadors' sons the boy had been to school with, but he did not want to: on the whole, he preferred not to know. He could get his own back on the Netherlands Embassy by writing in his turn a lot of stuff they would not want to know: he might have, if the typewriter keys had not stuck so. Instead, he went to the best bar in Europe, for sociological observation, taking his little notebook. Point acquired, wrote Van der Valk (very dear, the whisky here, and the Embassy will be scrutinizing the expenses: I don't care, went out to Monkstown and back by bus, and that's enough economy for today)— where was I? Oh, yes. Stasie knows Lynch, admits it freely. No attempt at denial: i.e., known about and readily checkable. It is now beyond question that Lynch knew and was with Martínez. Stasie seems to have no notion, perhaps quite truthfully, of his being involved in the killing (since he was, as far as is known, the last person to see M. alive). Query: what information has she received from Anna (who denies knowing Lynch)? Logical to expect Lynch had met Anna, but not inevitable; we have no evidence on the subject.

Two subsidiary points: Stasie does not ask outright what exactly the Netherlands Police is doing frigging about in Ireland, although (a) she's extremely curious, and (b) it's an obvious question. Does this show elusiveness, unease, or conceivable guilty knowledge, possibly indirect?

Nor does she ask what evidence the police has to link Denis with the death, since that, obviously, is what they're on about, or why keep asking about him. Hmm.

A presumption can be said to exist that Denis is not only connected with this death but is the author. Conclusion unchanged: in view of shaky grounds for any extradition demand, and probable diplomatic pressure exercisable by Senator Lynch, we simply need a stronger case, and that's what I'm doing here. We need either an admission by Denis Lynch, who is hobnobbing with the Vatican, and can't be just arrested anyhow, or, much more fruitful, some strong independent corroborative evidence.

On basis of conversation with Stasie, it is cons. op. that such evidence exists.

"Cons. op." means "considered opinion," which is jargon meaning the report writer can't prove it. Van der Valk, staring vacantly at the bar, saw he'd got something wrong. The not-a-drop-is-sold slogan isn't Power, but Jameson. Makes no odds, he decided; like all the detergents with different names, it's more than probable they're the same firm. . . . Where was I?

Two problems therefore exist. Getting Lynch back to Ireland, where one could possibly question him, and getting a handle on Stasie. She is not, presumably, an accessory. Technically she's not even a witness. But she is the link between Lynch and Martínez (evidence of gallery attendant and of picture), and she's probably more than that: to wit, a spring or detonator. It is postulated that L. killed M.: it then follows that something intensely violent set this in movement, and the simplest, most obvious thing is Stasie herself. Mmm, rather a lot of postulating there.

Questioning Stasie is not really much easier than questioning Lynch: i.e., she's an Irish citizen and while not as tricky as Denis we've even less grip.

Van der Valk sighed and ordered more whisky. He had been told to be very gentle, very milky, a study in tact; and very well, he would be all these things, but it would cost whisky and oysters in large quantities and the Embassy comptroller would jolly well have to put up with it, that's all. From somewhere his mind had resurrected a saying (army service, Hamburg, 1945) taught him by one of those mustached British officers in the Green Jackets or the Green Howards; green something, anyway.

> Exhausted nature for refreshment calls:
> Stout for the brain, and oysters for the balls.

Definitely. But where was I?

Can't just go round asking blunt questions, but ten quid to a brass farthing (we're picking up English, huh?), the boy is or was her lover. Possible explanation of his coming to stick Papa with the souvenir paper knife but slightly insufficient.

I wish I could seduce her, but one doesn't put remarks like that in written reports which go to the Embassy, the Procureur Général, and the Ministry of The Hague (he sighed for the good old days working for old Samson, who detested written reports which were "full of nothing but bullshit" and to whom one could say such things, and did). Mark you, Dublin—or so Stasie says—isn't as small-minded a town as The Hague. Still, we better not say such things here either, but we can damn well think them.

Back to point-acquired an instant, veux-tu? She is very curious. One could tease her. Have to view the other sisters, and interview, too, as part of a tidy formal operation, but this is definitely the one we want (it was her picture). Anyway, this minute she's busy briefing them, telling them to be vague on the subject of Denis. If we can establish by any tactical means (a chat with Flynn on this subject) that Denis is Stasie's lover, the point isn't just acquired; it's damn well vital. So we're going to hang her up by the heels and shake till things fall out, even if we have to bed the lady ourself to get so far. But he forgot about Stasie while looking at the people in the bar and listening to their voices: he couldn't get any further at present with her except in dirty daydreams. One could work in from the two opposite ends of the Denis problem: what about Mrs. Lynch?

Having studied the clientele of the cocktail bar with care the night before, he put on his good suit—what Arlette called his cavalry outfit. He was tall and, despite his big bones and clumsy features, looked good in a suit, but if it was a town suit, too light, too smooth, too narrow, too white-shirted, he looked too like a farmer on Sunday or, as Arlette said, like a boxer being interviewed on television. Since becoming a personage of dignity, he had acquired "squire" suits.

"But you mustn't look too horsy; your face is quite horsy enough." The bar last night had been full of talk about Fairyhouse and Leopardstown, Punchestown and Baldoyle (what lovely names Irish racecourses did have): he knew exactly what she meant. He spat on his shoes and took pains with his tie, as well as leaving his briefcase behind.

Downstairs he surveyed himself majestically in the glass, decided he was all right since the pageboys did not snigger, had the porter whistle for a taxi, and said "Ailesbury Road" with lordly nonchalance.

Ah, yes, the Belgian Embassy, brickwork nicely mellow, and the French Embassy, utterly hideous, built for a successful butcher. It was so very like Aerdenhout. He crunched across gravel, mounted portly stone steps, and rang a polished brass bell with a rich soft note. A uniformed maid opened almost at once, well trained; she said nothing. He took his hat off.

"I'm calling, if I may, on Mrs. Lynch."

She held the door, closed it softly behind him, and said, "I'm afraid Mrs. Lynch is not able to see you just yet," which meant she wasn't up yet.

"Perhaps you could give her my card." He had two kinds of card: nasty printed ones saying "Divisional Commissaire," which wouldn't do at all, and superior ones, engraved, with his name and address. The maid was experienced; she looked at the card, at him: was he likely to steal little silver boxes?

"I'm afraid you may have a bit of a wait; would you like to come in here?"

The hall had been stiff; cream paint, mahogany, gladioli, a soft bright echo up handsome red Wilton stair carpet. The drawing room, at the front of the house, was conventional but pleasant. There was a coal fire, a luxury surely now reserved to the few people with proper maids. It burned under a white marble chimney piece, a large gilt-framed looking glass flanked by rococo silver candlesticks. There were several large formal oil paintings, mixed with watercolor landscapes of somewhat self-consciously Irish simplicity. Polished parquet, carpet, Chinese silk hearth rug, Persian rugs in the bays. He thought it all looked very

105

gracious-living-from-Harrod's, pre-1939. None the worse for that, perhaps. (When in the dentist's waiting room, he always studied *House and Garden* and *Jours de France*.) There were two large cut-glass lusters, and crystal lamps by Lalique. In front of the yellow silk chesterfield was an occasional table, with, in a neat row, the *Irish Times,* the *London Times,* and *Le Monde,* margins lined up; he was quite carried away by this. Everything here was as it should be: glass-fronted cabinet with china, severely plain silver cigarette box—but the maid was coming back.

"Madame will be pleased to see you, and begs you to excuse her for keeping you waiting." He bowed. "Will you please make yourself comfortable, and the papers are there if you care to glance at them."

In the silence was a soft smooth-rubbed tocking; grandfather. He prowled about, puzzled. It all seemed very Forsyte—dear Irene has such good taste.

A lot of this stuff was antique, and had gone well at Sotheby, and would now go even better. Clock was probably Tompion, piano in one bay was certainly Steinway, writing desk in the other might well be Queen Anne, the curtains were a heavy yellow satin that had darkened agreeably. Yet there was something phony, and he did not know what. If he had ever seen a prewar West End comedy, probably featuring Gerald du Maurier and Gladys Cooper, with wisteria just outside the window where the lights were dimmed artistically for Act Two—an Hour Later, he might have thought this a pretentious effort at empire building. And yet at the same time there was something natural and simple—a genuineness—he could not quite decide about this, but the reverie was interrupted by the entrance of Mrs. Lynch.

She wasn't at all willowy, soft, or elegant: quite the contrary to dear Irene. She was quite small, round, and not quite fat, what the French call "boulotte." Her darkish springy hair was cut short and curled wirily round a plain, kind face like Madame de Gaulle's. She was dressed in a silk wrapper printed with white and yellow marguerites, which suited her, for everything about her was like that: fresh, bright, and simple. Her walk and her voice were rapid, direct, well-managed. (Not Gladys Cooper, but perhaps Yvonne Arnaud.) The professionally hostess smile was warmed by the fresh voice.

"How do you do, Mr. van der Valk? Do please sit down, and tell me how I can be of service to you. Have you forgiven me for being so long? And would you like a cigarette? No? And is it too early for me to offer you something? Perhaps a glass of sherry—oh, yes, please do."

"It sounds very nice, but what a lot I do drink here in Ireland."

"Nonsense, very good for you and I'll have one, too." She rang the bell.

"Annie, some sherry, please. Well, Mr. van der Valk?—I'm curious." She took him, presumably, for a politician or at least for someone with "a business proposal"—well, perhaps he had. But he mustn't sail under false colors.

He decided he had been right not to rehearse any freshness of phrase. Whatever foolishness now came out of his mouth would have to make up in spontaneity what it lacked in intelligence.

"You're going to find me a nuisance, I'm afraid. You won't be pleased; I may make you angry."

"Well, we'll see, shall we?"

"Put briefly, I am a police officer—from Holland, as you know—the Commissaire of a town where a few weeks ago a man was killed. An oldish man, a businessman, inoffensive, respected, a type of man it is difficult to imagine getting brutally killed. There are very few things that help us to understand this happening. One thing we learned was that a little before his death he was seen in company with a young man, whom we have since identified as your son Denis."

Mrs. Lynch picked a cigarette out of the silver box and held it between her lips; no hands, like a man.

"Killed? How killed? Like pushed-under-a-bus killed?"

"Almost exactly like that. He was suddenly stabbed in the street, with a sort of dagger. An unusual, puzzling death, which I for my sins have to try and account for."

"Ah, thank you, Annie. Will you tell Bessie?—I won't be going out after all this morning, but I may go out to lunch, and would she have that purplish suit for me? I beg your pardon, Mr. van der Valk, I was thinking over what you said. Perhaps you'll tell me why you come to me. I understand that, unless I'm mistaken, you have some reason to believe that Denis is concerned somehow in this tragic happening, but I should have supposed that the more usual approach would be to my husband, who is in Dublin, at his office."

"Yes," said Van der Valk. "The explanation why I haven't is so simple it doesn't bear telling: I was scared to."

She threw back her head to laugh. "That's really rich . . . scared to. Forgive me, but you don't look that scared."

"I don't know whether I ought to be scared or not, since I haven't had the pleasure of meeting Senator Lynch. But everybody tells me he's scaring."

"Well, perhaps so he is, sometimes, or likes to appear so. But I would think you'd have to grin and bear it, scared or not. Surely you should see him." Plenty of shrewdness in the round, pleasant face.

"That's perfectly true, and whether I should go to see him is something I hoped you would help me decide."

"Aha, I see, and how can I do that?"

"My superiors, the legal authorities in Holland, they're like most legal people very cautious, very scrupulous, looking at things from every angle—I daresay you know people like that."

"Very many, for my sins—which must be quite as bad as yours. But come to the point."

"The thing about Denis, who seems to have been on a little sightseeing trip in Amsterdam, is that by a coincidence he left the country that evening. We want to talk to him as part of the inquiry, since it is important to know what Mr. Martínez was doing and perhaps thinking. But there are legal difficulties. We can't question anybody in another country without, of course, their full consent. We felt a bit disappointed about Denis popping off so suddenly, and then we found out who he was and who his father was, and then everyone got in a state, because Senator Lynch, the Irish Embassy told us, isn't just anybody."

"True. But perhaps I am?"

"No, Madame. My idea in coming to see you was that you would know your son better than anybody." Saying which, he drank some sherry. Failing a good swig of Sister Crabtree's Tonic Wine (stimulates and fortifies; recommended for fatigue, listlessness, and convalescent states), sherry would have to do. She drank some of hers, too, without tasting it, staring over the rim of the glass.

"Not anybody. Than most, in the past, perhaps. I'm a level-headed person, Mr. van der Valk. Not conspicuous for brains, but a reputation for common sense. Somebody told you that, no doubt, and that's why you come." Smile, grim, showing lines around mouth and jaw, despite much careful work by Helena Rubinstein. "What you really mean, I think, is that Senator Lynch appears a formidable figure, and you decided I might provide you with a crack in these fortifications; a vulnerable point, as you might call it. Isn't that it?"

Level-headed was the word. "It's a lot of things, I think. Includes that, no doubt. But nobody really wants to pursue this. It's important, but it ruffles diplomatic feathers."

"So you got sent to do the dirty work. Ungrateful task."

"Lot of truth in that," grinning despite himself. "Honestly, Madame, we're poking about in the dark. Police work is very inexact—like meterology; I watch two clouds and wonder if they'll bump and, if they do, whether lightning will come out. As with the weather, any forecasts of what is going to happen are pretty inaccurate and the public tends to believe the opposite of the forecast."

"Perhaps it is to guard against that we have this basic belief about people being assumed innocent until proved guilty. You do the opposite, I've been told," stabbing out her cigarette and taking another.

Van der Valk lay back in the big armchair and

110

stretched his feet out. Conciliatory gesture against aggression, Dr. Lorenz might have called this.

"People do think that," he said softly, "with some justification. Comes from tidy-minded Officers of Justice popping people into jail and letting them stay there while their business is sorted out at great leisure—so handy. There's a lot of feeling against this, and it is being stopped—too slowly. But nobody's putting Denis in jail, you know: we haven't any right to, and anyway he isn't around."

"Sounds pretty sensible of him, not to be around," tartly.

"Only that this not being around does suggest—wouldn't you agree?—as though his conscience wasn't quite clear." This, he noticed, struck her. She reached over with the decanter and poured him some more sherry. Great stuff, making his English marvelously fluent, even if all these phrases had been given him by Inspector Flynn. "Nobody has suggested, at any time, that he's guilty of anything whatever. The fact facing us is that he knew Mr. Martínez was in his company that afternoon, and left abruptly that night, getting his ticket changed to do so. We want him to tell us what happened, under all the safeguards anyone can think of."

"Who is this Mr. Martínez—I mean what sort of man is he?"

"Was."

"I beg your pardon," nicely. "I do realize that you are concerned with the sanctity of human life."

"Well, there's a sort of relationship I don't begin yet to understand—it's another reason why I came to see you."

"Permit the terrifying Senator Lynch to offer you one of his cigars?"

"I think that's the right note—yes, please, I love them—I think we have to look at all this without too much solemnity. It's our difficulty and I do mean 'our.' Need a bit of levity."

"You have it."

"I hope enough to realize the absurdity of my position."

"I'll try to match that."

"How quick you are, and how grateful I am." To his relief, she gave her peal of laughter, not very ladylike but reassuringly real.

"Go on."

"We wondered how Denis came to know Mr. Martínez. He had interests in several countries, and used to have connections here. The commercial people at the Embassy are looking them up to see if there's anything interesting, which I think unlikely enough. What's more to the point is that he lived here at one time, and three of his daughters still do. Young women now, married to Irish people."

"But that is interesting—would I know any of them, I wonder?"

"It's unlikely, too, I'd think—I've met one of them. She does know Denis. I knew that already, but it was useful to hear her confirm it."

"And how did you know that?" she asked.

"By a coincidence—accidental eye-opener. Martínez lived in Amsterdam. We were trying to discover what he was doing in our town, which is some way outside, and found a witness who saw him in an art gallery, with Denis, at a picture which strangely resembles this daughter. You see, it's the kind of link

112

which without being tangible is real enough, and in the occurrence it was enough to bring me over here, expecting to have it confirmed, which I did."

"And in what way," cautiously, "does Denis know this young woman?"

"I'm wondering whether he could be her lover."

There—it was to arrive there that he had spent so much time on careful bricks and mortar.

Mrs. Lynch had been leaning back on the sofa, legs crossed in a negligent masculine way, as though to show she was indifferent and had no fear of him. Now she sat up, put her knees together, arranged her wrapper, and put her forearms together along her thighs, fingertips pointing at him in an instinctively defensive, essentially serious pose. "Have you anything—like a letter—to support what you say?"

"No. But I'm trying keys till I find one which can open a locked door. I've seen the woman. An odd woman—very attractive."

She was silent for some time. He tried again, wondering whether it was a mistake. "I came for that, too—wondering whether you knew anything about it."

She shook her head. "I don't. But I'm bound to admit there's no reason why I should. And would I tell you, if I did?"

"You don't strike me as the kind of woman that likes to delude herself."

She made no answer to that. "You realize I can't keep this from the boy's father," she said. "He will certainly want to see you—make no mistake; in his office, in daylight, openly. It isn't in his nature to have any underhand dealing— Oh, I'm not suggesting you would be a party to that, but I'm trying to say, very badly, that you can rely on one thing, and that is that if there are any explanations to be made, Denis will make them and his father will see to that. But who he will make them to—that's for Senator Lynch to decide."

"I accept that: I'm at his disposal."

She stood up abruptly and wrapped the morning coat tighter round her stocky body in another defensive gesture. "Where are you staying, Mr. van der Valk?"

"The Sheridan Hotel."

"Will you take me out to lunch?"

He was startled. "With the very greatest pleasure."

"I have things to do in the town. I must also talk to my husband. He has an official lunch; I won't be seeing him before three. Before then, I would like to see some more of you." She went over to the window, picked up a leather memo book, found a number, dialed it.

"Reservations? Mrs. Terence Lynch, for two, at a quarter to one. . . . Thank you. . . . Very well, then." She looked at him again direct, with a sudden lift of the head, as though she had had a doubt and dismissed it. "Sorry—a nice quiet restaurant, where we'll be undisturbed. Will you give me a quarter of an hour to dress? Sorry to be a nuisance." To that he had nothing to say.

She was not much longer than a quarter of an hour, either: she wore the "purplish suit," darkish burgundy red, a classic cut, skirt knee-length. The knees were plumpish, the stockings a pronounced pale tint, the shoes shiny patent leather. His eye getting all this must have been indiscreet, since she caught it straying.

"I hope you won't be ashamed of me, Mr. van der Valk."

In penitence for this sharpish smack, he took the coat the maid was holding—one of those short black furs, curly and glossy, with an Armenian look—and helped her into it. He had just realized that he had to pass an examination, and had failed the first question. Parked outside on the gravel was a small Lancia, chaste midnight blue.

"Will you drive, or shall I?" she asked.

"Whichever you please," not certain he had the second test right, either.

"Then perhaps I'd better—traffic in Dublin. . . ."

"It wouldn't do if you got a police ticket through my fault."

"We call them the Guards. Of the peace, but it gets left unsaid, which seems unfair." He held the door and she got in neatly: it was the four-door model.

"I don't much like sports cars; they're so indecent to get out of," she said.

She drove fast and very precisely, as women drivers do when they are good. He got innocent pleasure from being in nice cars, and said so, which got a good mark; she was amused.

"Senator Lynch," in quotation marks, "has a big black Mercedes—I hate it rather."

"Rich towns have them as police cars—the cheaper models, I hasten to add. They do smell so awful. I may as well say my town gives me a Volkswagen." She had a pleasant low giggle, not trying to be girlish, but unself-consciously being so.

"Now, I wonder where I'm going to park." They had stopped in a narrow, crowded street.

"Let me handle it; what are policemen for?" He gave her a formal arm, held his palm out for the keys, and played escort. The usual headwaiter hurried for-

115

ward; wheyfaced goose. Dr. van der Valk determined not to be bullied. He had the key ring on his finger, and a crumpled ten-bob note sticking out.

"Mrs. Lynch would like you to park her car."

"Oh. I'm not sure. . . ."

"Since I drove her, and since I'm a stranger, I am sure."

"But we've no doorman."

"Perhaps you'd like us to go somewhere else," nastily.

"Er—Stephen! Park Mrs. Lynch's car, and will you be careful not to scratch it, now. This way, sir, and will we be taking your coats?"

"Bravo," she said, grinning. He had got a good mark!

"No, really, I hate making a fuss in restaurants, but they need to be bellowed at a tiny bit. Are you a drinking woman?"

"Rather," smiling at his English.

"Then we'll have some champagne." Mentally, he was already writing out his expense sheet. "Giving lunch to Mrs. Terence Lynch"—he was looking forward to the Embassy comptroller's face!

Till they got rid of waiters she made social small talk. "Dublin is very small," she said. Even after the flapping ears had ceased to hover, she asked him about Holland. Eating cake—she had a healthy disrespect for her figure—she asked about his wife. It was only when sipping coffee that she suddenly said, "What's this woman like?"

"Not pretty—that is to say, yes, she is, very, but her looks are unusual. Exceptionally seductive; I feel it myself strongly."

"Old?"

"Something over thirty."

"Where does she live?" He hesitated a fraction too long: her direct eyes, clear pale brown, met him head on.

"You don't want to tell me because you're afraid I'll try and tamper with her."

He shook his head. "Monkstown. It's the police mind. Just like the meteorologist; they aren't able to look at a sunset and simply think it beautiful."

"I hate anything underhand as much as my husband does, but I can't expect you to take my word for that on a point like this."

He liked this scruple; she was awarding herself a bad mark!

"I know little enough about her, as yet. She has three children, her husband is in some fairly banal commerce, earns a good unspectacular living, has the reputation of a decent man but drinks."

"The description"—dryly—"applies to ninety-nine percent of Dublin. Have you been drinking with him?"

"Not yet. I hope so. I've only her word for it. She talks very freely."

"If she's as unusual as you say, how does she come to marry a man like that?"

"What I have asked myself, but he may not be like that."

"I suppose not. Yes, I would like some brandy, or is my nose red?"

"Not in the least."

"I come from humble origins," she said tranquilly, "and perhaps that's why I enjoy being rich, and why I'm sometimes crude in my manners. I make gaffes. Since Senator Lynch became what one calls an important political figure, I've had to learn not to."

"Except on purpose sometimes."

"I'm probably making one now when I say that I'll do what I can to make your job more reasonable—I won't say easier. Thank you for a very pleasant lunch."

"I hope I may see you again."

"If I thought that was for my pretty face! What have you in mind?"

"I'd like to know more about Denis."

"I see. Well, Mr. van der Valk, I look forward to returning your hospitality. I'll ask my husband to find a day that suits both of you, and perhaps you'll give me the pleasure of coming to my house for dinner."

"Yes."

"Will you be at your hotel this afternoon?"

"Yes." It was one more mark, a small one. He called the waiter.

"Will you get the car for Mrs. Lynch, please."

He wanted to work, all right, but had a suspicion it would turn into siesta. He had only had one glass of champagne, but she had drunk the rest, and left him to get through a whole bottle of burgundy. . . .

Exactly: he fell sound asleep, and the sudden bawling of the telephone found him cross and blurry.

"Van der Valk."

"Senator Lynch's office. The Senator is calling you; will you hold the line a moment, please?" Time to yawn, to look at his watch—four-twenty, oh!—and wish for cold water on his neck. Not a climate for lunchtime drinking.

"Van der Valk? Terence Lynch." The voice was deep, hard, unusually slow, saying that this was a man who spoke seldom and thought the more, and when he did speak that it was as well to listen.

"Yes, sir."

"I should like to talk to you. Does this evening suit you?"

"At your convenience."

"Try and be here by five. Ask for my secretary; she'll bring you in."

"Count on me."

"Good." Click. He leapt off the bed: cold water. Needed some inside, too.

"Have you any mineral water?" he asked the waiter.

"A tonic would that be, sir?"

"No, no." Damn.

"Nice cup of tea, sir?"

"Haven't time, alas; let it go."

"Very good, sir."

"Taxi, sir?" asked the porter outside.

"You know Senator Lynch's office?"

"The Senate, would that be, or the newspaper office?"

"Newspaper, I think."

"Is Senator Lynch in his office?"

"I'm not too sure now; were you wanting to see him personally, is that right? Oh, I see. I'm ringing his secretary now, if you'd just like to take a seat." His longing for a cup of tea, for a really Irish cup of tea, was becoming intense.

"Mr. van der Valk?" pronouncing it right. "You're lovely and punctual."

"I'm always punctual, but my longing for a cup of tea is practically uncontrollable." It was a girl, a kind of airline stewardess, but the kind one always sees in advertisements and never, never on planes; here was where they'd got to.

"Is that so? But sure that's no trouble; I'll make you one at once."

"You're a poppet." She was, too; a delicious object, in a frock like smashed-up raspberries spread out thin and holding on to salient outlines with pleasure, assuming raspberries know all about sex, which they ought because they're in the right place—mmm, oughtn't to have drunk all that brandy.

"I came down because you'd never find the way. Stairs or lift?"

"Stairs. What is your name?"

"Elizabeth." She looked even better climbing stairs than on the flat.

Senator Lynch's office was modern, comfortable, neither large nor small with a window behind him, the door in front of him, the wall space almost filled with bookshelves, and nothing but a desk in the middle, Senator behind, and a chair in front. A handshake as hard and clean as James Bond's.

"Sit down. I don't want to be interrupted, Liz."

"Understood. Mr. van der Valk wants a cup of tea very badly."

"Then bring him one. Bring me one, too."

Van der Valk sat down, and was aware of a menacing presence behind him in the corner. A gorilla? The I.R.A.? A Corsican gunman in dark glasses? He had to look. A large photomontage of W.C. Fields, in full Western gambler's costume, was studying him with satanic eyes from behind a poker hand: his blood, as the French say, turned over once. Senator Lynch,

120

immobile, was looking at him with the same expression.

"People," said the slow voice, like a blacksmith's hammer, "are seldom . . . what they seem. I like to be reminded of the fact."

"And sometimes pretend to hold cards?"

"It has been known. You showed some . . . to my wife. Not perhaps all. Hmm. I don't often meet . . . policemen. I daresay you'd like a cigar. Take one." Upmanns; he did, lit it contentedly, aware of still eyes. Smoke-screened, he looked back. Lynch was not striking-looking: medium-sized, more or less handsome, carefully dressed, silver-haired, but no shirt advertisement. Gray suit, gray tie, gray eyes. The self-controlled look was striking, but the man might be very intelligent indeed and he might be just another politician.

"Welcome to Ireland. We're not all . . . poets. Bricklayers. Or chatterboxes."

"Some people say the Irish have too much imagination."

"And I've heard said that the Dutch have none. So much . . . for what people say. We'll wait till we have some tea. Without tea . . . what would we do?" The door opened and tea came in.

"Without Liz what would we do?" offered Van der Valk, with a nice smell at his elbow.

"We would have to face . . . slightly more disagreeable aspects of everyday living. And get . . . a lot less work done."

"Fastening our own belts."

"And preparing, shall we say, to be . . . shaken about."

"And to feel sick."

"And to feel sick. I've seen my wife. Her judgment's good. But I want to see for myself. I'm not . . . mealy-mouthed. This sequence of events; you will have a dossier; I should like to see it."

Not much point in saying the dossier of an affair under instruction was thought of as confidential material, was there? "I haven't got it. The magistrate has."

"Your people in Holland: they will have made some . . . approach to the legal authorities here."

"Doubtless."

"Senators have a way of getting hold of classified material."

It was time to play a card. "The man you want is Inspector Flynn at Dublin Castle."

"Flynn . . . Flynn. I don't know him." The voice left little doubt that he pretty soon would.

"This crime in Holland," it went on, "you were yourself the investigating officer?"

"Yes, sir."

"Perhaps you'd be good enough to give me your . . . version of events."

He didn't want to give any version of events, but it didn't look at though there were much choice. There was a definite feeling of important man taking things into his more competent hands and running the show. While Van der Valk colorlessly explained how the Netherlands Police had been led toward curiosity about Denis Lynch, his mind thought about the familiar handicap of people wanting to get into the act. Not so very long ago, he had had a quiet domestic murder, just a bit melodramatic, turned into an international circus by D.S.T., the French security service, from where he had been standing an unmitigated pest by any name. Politicians were just another D.S.T., producing more melodrama. Vanity; an uncontrollable need to meddle, an infernal knowingness, a wish to be clever and to go about scoring points off people. Poor old Van der Valk; you hate melodrama, and has there ever been any affair of importance you handled that didn't attract melodrama like a jam pot attracts wasps—no, never. Well, hardly ever.

You bugger about with your son Denis and I can't stop you, he thought malevolently. But Stasie is mine.

"Hmm," when he had finished. "Hmm," again. Van der Valk respected the lengthy silence, which might be crucial.

"Hmm," for the third time. "My wife . . . would like me to help you. Never mind her motives. You needn't . . . mind mine, either. Like most people, I have duties . . . obligations; my . . . lights, you might call them. Nobody—including you—has any idea what . . . they are. I don't have them . . . dictated to me. You leave me to handle this. The boy . . . you know where he is?"

"In Rome, I'm told. Unless, of course, he's moved on since. He gets around."

"You seem to do your homework. He's in Rome, but he can move on. He doesn't have to account for his movements . . . to me . . . to you. He's over twenty-one: he's learning his way about. There's no ground whatever to talk of any extradition. To get him to come back here . . . and answer questions that . . . may be awkward might or might not be . . . my duty. That needs thought. There are ways in which I can conceivably help you. Putting . . . pressure on a boy of that age isn't as easy . . . as it may sound. How would you . . . go about it? Don't tell me, I . . . know. You'd

. . . bustle out there, try and . . . frighten him, work
. . . him up. Like herding a sheep. I . . . won't have
it. Let me handle him. A young man . . . of that age
. . . is an explosive in . . . an unstable form."

"Nitroglycerine." The Senator was not speaking stupidly. He was not pompous, and he was not foolish.

"That is correct. It goes off . . . when you drop it.
Now. About this . . . woman."

"No," said Van der Valk, unnecessarily loudly.
Lynch's eyes reminded him of the two faces of a pair
of tweezers, with which a possibly uninteresting and
probably distasteful object is picked up and put upon
the table for study. But he said nothing.

"Explosive in several senses," went on Van der
Valk, hoping it didn't sound too obvious that his burning ambition at this moment was to eat the horrible
boy raw for breakfast. "His position in moral law, international law, what you like, is apt to give a lot of
people nightmares, but that's not my job, which is
strictly to get an account of his sayings and doings on
a particular day. I have to ask him, and what his position then is depends on what answers he gives, and it
won't be my decision. I won't attempt to bully him:
I'll see him wherever you please and in your presence.
This woman is a different matter. I'm not suggesting
some kind of bargain, that you leave her to me and I
leave your son to you, since the position is altogether
different." Van der Valk was mindful of the poker-
playing eyes behind him. Should he go clutching his
"cards" tightly to his bosom, with a face of bronze,
aware that they were pretty thin but hoping that
Lynch's would prove even thinner? It was possible,
but altogether against his character.

"I'm trying to say," he said gently, "that I'm not trying to use this woman as a squeeze, as a sort of black-mail. I've nothing on your son; he was a witness to what may turn out to be an important moment in the life of a man who is now dead. I've nothing on the woman, who may or may not be able to shed some light on a state of mind. But I have an obligation to find out."

The tweezers had picked him up and deposited him on a table under a strong light. There was silence while the object was considered.

"I will not put pressure on your witnesses," said Lynch simply. "This woman . . . whatever she has to say, her words will be weighed . . . carefully. My wife trusts you. I was . . . unsure whether you were attempting to use this woman as a . . . threat . . . to put pressure on me. I accept your word. Hmm . . . I have said . . . too much already. We're in one another's hands, Mr. van der Valk. We each deserve to know the other better. I will keep in touch with you. And you will do the same? Very well. I'll ask you to . . . forgive me now. You'll perhaps leave word with Liz if you . . . change your base."

Van der Valk stood up. "What do you think I'll find?" he asked.

"I think you'll find a calf-love affair," said Lynch dryly.

"Which I need not remind you is also a potentially explosive thing."

"I don't lose sight of the fact. Believe me."

Van der Valk went and had a meal called in Ireland tea, which is to say fried eggs, and a lot of powerful bacon, and sausage, and tomato, and bread—all fried, and made more lethal still with tomato ketchup, very likely: as though drinking tea with this weren't lethal enough. Bread and butter: the clawky dough that is steamed and then labeled "bread" in Ireland, in England—and in Holland, too, alas. Experience told him that at this moment half Ireland was reaching for the soda bicarb. Which didn't stop him enjoying it very much. He was very leisurely about tea, and by the time he had finished, the rush hour was over and he could get a bus out to Monkstown without having to stand for half an hour in the gutter.

It had been raining while he was inside; the Irish drizzle that is gentler than that of Holland. The streets glistened black and smelt nice; it had cleared up a little but the sky was blanketed with the guaranteed pure virgin wool of maritime Western Europe. Minute drops filmed his face: under trees there were heavier, wetter drops that went down his neck, but it is almost a point of honor not to wear a raincoat in that soft September rain.

Astonishingly peaceful; scarcely a step behind him, the buses and cars were charging along the main road, but purringly, as though gentled and muted by a curtain of air. Twilight had fallen, of a pure Madonna blue. He was living in a glass bowl of peace, an aquarium, scarcely bigger than a jam jar, but enough to make him put off a tiresome chore for a few minutes. What did the fish's eyes show it, there under water?— he walked through Belgrave Square, down to the coast boulevard, to find out. Here, too, cars were running home from Dublin, but in supportable numbers. Night was falling on the bay; in front of him was the curve of Dublin, out to the big headland of Howth, a necklace of orange stars. He breathed quietly: California must have been like this forty years ago. Sea snored

126

gently; the sense of peace dragged at him with a sad, regretful seduction: he wished he had never come. Why had that infernal Martínez got himself killed—be sure, whoever it was killed him, that it had been his fault!

Out there where sea and sky had become entangled, Mrs. Lynch's face appeared, homely and comfortable, followed by Lynch's strongly forged and hammered look—both faces tested, reliable, able to stand a strain, face a storm. They were replaced by Stasie's features, undoubtedly beautiful but disquieting, irritatingly exotic: the sense of peace went away abruptly. He turned about and very nearly got run over crossing Seapoint Avenue. Civilized people, the Irish, but not in cars: no different in that from any other country in Europe—there is a strongly degrading element about the internal-combustion engine mounted upon four wheels. It has, a doctor friend had recently remarked to him, an amazingly powerful magnetism over persons of subnormal mentality.

Cars, in Belgrave Square, continued to preoccupy him. Men home for the night; nobody has a garage here, but what did you need one for in Ireland? It didn't freeze here, any more than it did in Brest. Cars in Ireland were mostly English, but quite enough German ones to show the English that Ireland was independent: all those Volkswagens made him feel quite at home. The not very neat and fairly dirty black Austin belonged no doubt to Mr. Edward Flanagan, whom he was counting on a bit as a weak spot. Not that one could tell anything from cars. A dusty black Austin full of bits of paper, like a dusty black Peugeot, meant as a rule the drearier kind of commercial traveler, but how wrong one could be: the way to find out was to ring the bell, so he did.

Mr. Flanagan opened the door, the light behind him, so that one could make nothing of a first impression. A voice that was soft and unaggressive—so were most Irish voices.

"Mr. Flanagan?"

"That's right."

"My name is Van der Valk: I'm an officer of the Netherlands Police."

"Was it me you were wanting?" perplexed. Being secretive, Stasie, dear?

"If it's convenient for you. I hope you've had supper. Can you spare me a few minutes?"

"I suppose so, but I'm afraid I don't understand."

"I had the pleasure of meeting your wife yesterday."

"Oh, I see." Light dawned suddenly, and so did suspicion. "Yes—uh—I don't quite know what it is you want."

"To talk to you. Nothing more."

"To ask me something, was it? I don't know. . . . Well—you'd better come in. I'm afraid the place is very untidy. My wife's busy just at present—oh, well, come in anyway. No, no, that's all right, I wasn't doing anything special." A mixture of politeness, unwillingness to be disturbed, curiosity, and uneasiness led the way to the room Van der Valk had seen.

"Sit down, then—you're not wet?—no, a nice soft evening." He seemed to want to efface the slight ungraciousness. "Please forgive all the mess—the children, I'm afraid. . . ."

"My own house is just like that." It was true, too. Arlette anything but a compulsively tidying housewife.

This room was homely; whatever else odd there was about Stasie, she had points as a wife. A cheerful fire was burning.

"I like a coal fire," said Flanagan defensively, misinterpreting an admiring look.

"So do I."

"Look—uh—suppose you tell me what this is all about?"

He couldn't help liking the fellow at first sight: good God, be getting a job as Santa Claus next. Getting so benevolent and avuncular, doddery old dear nodding understandingly at everything. He had liked the Lynch family: be prepared to start loving the Flanagan family.

"I am the Commissaire of the district in which Mr. Martínez—your father-in-law, isn't it?—was killed under unexplained circumstances, and I have made a visit here to—how do you say?—enlarge the scope of the inquiry."

"Oh, yes. Now you mention it, my wife told me someone called, and that was you—I understand now." Not a very good liar, but give the man time.

Outside he could hear a pattering and banging, sounds with which he was familiar and which he could place with accuracy; the noise made by a couple of smallish children in pajamas and bare feet (they never know where their slippers are) resisting, with great strength and ingenuity, efforts to get them to go to bed.

"But you said we could look at the television."

"I did my teeth this morning—that's today, isn't it?"

"My slipper's gone."

"Well, he took my book and he hit me with it, and

129

then I just gave him a push and he fell over and started to cry—baby!"

"Mama, I want a drink of water."

It was a side to Stasie that was important, that he could not disregard. Not only did he have to Love Her, Too, if he was going to get anywhere, but he had to understand. She was a housewife, apparently busy and contented, with three young children. She wasn't an aimless, unoccupied, bored, frustrated woman. What went on there inside?

Van der Valk went on explaining boringly: Flanagan listened with politeness, as though all this were quite new. The door opened a crack, propelled by juvenile curiosity: Flanagan handled it in a practiced way.

"Out. Daddy's talking business. And the door shut. If you please."

He was not as tall as Van der Valk but broadly built, good-looking with dashing Irish looks that might be getting a little gross. Topping the thirty-five mark, with big candid brown eyes, a massive jaw, curly brown hair that needed cutting badly, a neck taking a big size in shirts, and feet and hands to match, an unexpectedly soft small voice, the pushful beginning of a stomach. The eyes were clear and unlined; he did not look that much of a drinker but for the readiness with which one could imagine the pleasant voice saying, "How about going for a jar?"

Van der Valk had to exorcise the long white beard; his metallic voice acquired an edge. How did one cut into all this Irish mist? The Lynch family provided one with straight answers to a straight question, but he was rapidly getting the notion that the Flanagan family was sort of oblique.

130

"You understand that I have to learn more about this relationship between Mr. Martínez and the boy Denis Lynch."

"Quite; yes—uh—I'm wondering. I mean you seem to have talked to my wife—she mentioned it more or less in passing. It was only yesterday, wasn't it?" He lit a cigarette, puffing noisily. There was intelligence there, a lot of nervous tension, an elaborate wariness, and as well a faintly cocky, knowing air, as though he were well abreast of the police and their little tricks.

"You mean she hasn't had time to tell you? Or that you don't know Denis?" asked Van der Valk.

"Oh, I know Denis, of course; he's a bit of a family friend, then, perhaps. I don't know him well, of course; how old is he now, maybe twenty-two or so, and what have I seen of him really? I mean I don't know what I can usefully add."

"More your wife's friend? She told me she knew him well."

"That's right," agreed Flanagan calmly, almost with a sort of bland impudence. "He was going to go about and look to see whether he couldn't get some sort of job in Europe somewhere. Yes, I know that sounds vague but that's just the sort of vague idea one gets at that age, isn't it? I mean his family had plenty of money; he wasn't in any hurry, and if he wanted to find some agreeable kind of job, who'd blame him, then?"

"Yes," patiently. "About Holland."

"I think he asked my wife whether she could give him an introduction, don't you know, anybody in Holland who might be useful, and she said, I suppose, that she didn't know anybody much—she's lived here since she was a child almost, y'know. So she gave him her father's name, I think, and I guess that's just about all I know about it."

"You guess."

"I wasn't there at the time, myself," with disarming simplicity.

At this moment, on cue, as though to save dear Eddy some questions that might be embarrassing, exactly as though she had been listening outside—and quite likely she had—the door opened and Stasie came floating in. Van der Valk got up politely. She was relaxed and untidy in a brown skirt and sweater; there were wisps of hair coming down, and she hadn't stopped to comb it or repair her lipstick. Housewife "au naturel," who has just worked the children off to bed and reappears slightly disheveled, warmed by stooping under beds to find the missing slipper, sleeve finely spattered with soapy water from supervising a nail brush, just a tiny bit sweaty since suppertime. With some women—Stasie was one—this adds greatly to charm. Her unusually good looks were embellished, her magnetism intensified. She held a hand out with casual amiability, unembarrassed, unworried, unsurprised.

"Sorry—but I'm sure you understood. Give me a cigarette, then, Eddy." Out of politeness, perhaps, she spoke Dutch, which Eddy appeared at least to follow. She waved Van der Valk back into her chair, and curled up on a divan, arranging her feet under her, pulling her skirt modestly over her knees, puffing at the cigarette, screwing her eyes and blinking to keep smoke out, with a vague stare at the wall behind him. So much relaxation and casual composure, so easy a "take us as you find us" manner—was there a bit too much, was it defensive? And if it was? Natural: strange policeman coming moseying in, second time in two days; could get to be a nuisance. But she was all politeness. And plausibility.

"It must trouble you, Commissaire, to find me so, as you might think, unconcerned about my father's death. But he was an old man, though he didn't look it; he'd always lived a very strenuous fully packed existence and we've always expected—my husband, my sisters, all who knew him—that something in the end would give way suddenly and that he'd just die without any long-drawn illness or anything. And that's just what did happen. Oh, yes, I know he died by violence—and that is indeed very shocking and dreadful. We've had, though—saying this to you is absurd—to learn to live with violence; there's such a lot in the world. We all felt quite sure that he'd been attacked by some crazy person for no reason—oh, of course, to the crazy person there's a reason, obvious, and the need to do something about it quite overwhelming, but that is just typically psychopathic, isn't it. It is unexplainable in any other way—I mean, people don't stab one in the street, do they? I suppose it may have been someone he knew at best very slightly, and had some imagined grievance; thought he'd been outsmarted in some deal, I suppose, stabbed him in a sudden fit of rage like a child and then walked off into the blue without a care in the world. Those people don't have a guilty conscience or anything, do they?—and that's surely the reason why you don't find anything that makes any sense."

A fluent talker, our Stasie. Van der Valk felt in his pocket, found a crumpled box of Gitanes, put one in his mouth. Helpful Eddy jumping up snapping a lighter. Now he mustn't be heavy and Dutch being all sarcastic.

"Thanks. . . . What you say sounds perfectly plausible, yes." Very light and colorless.

Her eyes set in an oblique plane and flicked at him —she'd got it at once; nobody's fool.

Good old Eddy hadn't got it, and put his great foot in it. "Not only plausible, surely."

Van der Valk took the cigarette out to straighten it; got a bit bent in his pocket.

"A murder, Mr. Flanagan. Crime of blood, crime of violence. The escaped lunatic, the psychopath let out on parole a bit premature—oldest cliché in the business. Plenty of legal brains expended energy on this notion. If it hadn't been rejected, I wouldn't be here." Eddy fidgeted with an ashtray.

"I was down on Seapoint Avenue," went on Van der Valk peaceably. "Nice view there is. Very quiet. Holland's like that—we like to think we're very peaceful. No broken glass, unemptied dustbins, riots with Puerto Ricans in Spanish Harlem, police sirens wailing —we think of that as something on the television, hmm?—all the fourteen-year-olds able to buy guns freely. Or the pretty young woman, mother of small children—like your wife here—who goes to the shooting gallery after shopping and carries a thirty-eight in her handbag. But violence—as your wife says—is everywhere. Cliché to think it can't happen here. Cliché to think that I'm just a filler-in of forms because I don't walk about carrying a machine gun. This trouble with clichés is a handicap in police work. Like the policemen in books, who're all nice quiet guys with wives and children. Not a bastard among them. Like you—like me. Except"—blandly—"that I've a dirty mind."

"Sure, sure," said Eddy, disturbed. Stasie said nothing.

"I don't want to seem rude," went on Van der Valk, "but I didn't come for a cozy chat about psychopaths."

"Yes, but violence . . ."

"Violence is like the Good Housekeeping Seal; it comes in the package."

"That," objected Eddy, "sounds a bit cheap."

"You're quite right, it is a bit cheap, and I'm sorry. I think I should have said that lacking perhaps a good honest dirty war to exercise their muscles people do have a tendency to violence, even gratuitously—anywhere. We ought maybe to give them a little red book to carry."

"Dammit," protested Eddy, "I didn't know Denis —I don't know Denis—at all that well, but I find this pretty hard to swallow."

"So do I, and I don't know him at all. Why do you think I come to you?—for whatever light you can help shed."

"Stasie," in a cowardly way, "knows him, of course, better than I do."

"Well enough that I don't believe it for a moment," Stasie said. "Or perhaps I don't know him at all. But anyway, Commissaire, isn't all this the greatest nonsense? Just an exercise in rhetoric?" It was as though she wished to show him she carried claws and could defend herself; his eyes crinkled up with enjoyment, his "tiny little eyes all brimming with spite," as Arlette said. She saw this and was pleased with herself.

"You can't just settle on Denis simply because he handily happened to be around. Not unless my notions of justice are a great deal queerer even than American television."

"Nobody has 'settled on Denis' that I know of. He isn't accused of anything whatever; everybody is taking pains to be extremely fair, and he certainly isn't being harassed. He's a witness, and I'd like to see him: that doesn't mean there's some sort of dragnet out for him."

"If there is, it's a poor one," said Stasie mockingly, "because he's in Rome."

"If he's still in Rome," remarked Van der Valk.

"How do you know, anyway?" Eddy said to Stasie.

"I had a card from him this morning—it's on the chimney piece."

Eddy jumped up, studied a gaudy tourist photo card, and passed it to Van der Valk. It was addressed to "Signora S. Flanagan" and said in a slant, "Having a good time seeing a lot of new things as well as old wish you were here to share it love Denis."

"There's a proof he's not hiding or anything," said Eddy.

"Very conventional and reassuring," agreed Van der Valk politely.

"And hardly sounding like a murderer," added Stasie.

"Very true. Well, you've been very kind and cleared up a lot of doubt; I've bothered you long enough."

There were the essential perfunctory exclamations of regret that they could help him no further. Plus, he thought, a pleasurable feeling of sending him off with a flea in his ear.

He looked at his map under a street lamp: it was such a nice night that he felt like a long walk and made it, right out to Dalkey along the seafront. He wondered what had put him into such a good mood; he could see no real cause for such gullible self-satisfaction, but there it was, he was immensely pleased with himself and even found himself singing that catchiest of all waltz tunes:

"Mit mir, mit mir—
Keine Nacht dir zu lang."

—and guffawed, since this sentiment was addressed to the deliciously beddable Stasie, no doubt. Being Baron Ochs in a lecherous frame of mind amused him so much that he recalled another of those superbly complacent remarks:

"Hab halt so ein jung und hitzig Blut,
Ist nicht zum stillen!"

—and an old Dublin biddy going home from the pub took a look at this idiot figure laughing to itself and talking alone out loud in German, and made a significant gesture with her finger. "Sure these Poles are all the same, God help them," she remarked sympathetically, disappearing up a side street.

A small pale full moon, looking anemic and sorry for itself, appeared in the sky. Van der Valk looked at it, like Eugène de Rastignac gazing over Paris, but was not quite pleased enough with himself to say "A nous deux maintenant"—on the contrary, he was thinking that Baron Ochs had fallen with a loud crash through the trap door into the dung heap, and doubtless it would happen to him very shortly. He always did manage to get into the shit sooner or later.

Why was he behaving in so ridiculous a way, he wondered—he hadn't had any whisky for hours. . . .

Dear Arlette,

Have just had very large Irish breakfast in bed—coffee abominable natch but tea delicious here. This plus large amounts whisky would have horrible effect on liver, but I walk a great deal. Town center nicely compact, like A'dam walkable: this is nice. Today got to go to effing Embassy; job is pretty awful as usual but Irish v. amusing. Lunch yesterday with politician's wife in expensive restaurant: grub not up to much but drinks good, and post just brought invit. dinner private house of same—run to hire dinner jacket Moss Bros! His cigars are good.

All these fleshpots do not conceal exceeding trickiness situation. Nobody pulls gun on me, but getting arm twisted in variety subtle Irish ways. So go about being blunt & Dutch & unimaginative—have to or would dissolve into tangled webs of fantasy. . . . Have to do something clever, but no idea what.

Contact sound Irish pleeceman, bright but can't help me really, am pretty isolated. Thought of one indecent scheme unlikely to commend self to Embassy, whose one idea is to see my back, preferably falling over high cliff, by choice today but would settle for tomorrow.

Van der Valk was sitting at a little writing table in imitation antique style of the type loved by expensive hotels. Their spindly legs are never quite even; this is to be remedied by one of the books of paper matches with the hotel's beastly name written on it, which serve no other purpose. In the drawer of this horrible object, he had found writing paper and envelopes, as well as little brochures headed "This Week in Town,"

138

telling one all about the Flower Show and the Folk-lore Dance Festival, and laundry lists in four languages, helpful if one badly wants to know what the German is for "bra."

He was not washed and seemed to be wearing a mask of fried egg; it was nice to be dallying about writing a dutiful letter to one's wife, prefatory to a lavish splashy bath, luxuriously knowing that the chambermaid will clean up after one; this is indeed practically the only pleasure one has in hotels, and he made the most of it. He was preparing for a leisurely day, in the course of which he had to write his tiresome report, bring it to the Embassy, there no doubt to be asked several mostly foolish and all unnecessary questions, and then go for a quiet gossipy session with Inspector Flynn, which he enjoyed. After which one would do more work on his plot to squeeze the seductive Mrs. Flanagan till her pips squeaked. . . .

"That pipsqueak" was Flynn's word for Denis Lynch, but when asked what it meant he was vague. "Much the same as a whipper-snapper." Van der Valk, snared in the subtleties of the English language, was not much further. He yawned: high time he shaved (the combination of fried egg and bristles was nasty), but he would just finish his letter first. A knock came at the door.

"Yes?"

Pageboy, grinning—what was the pipsqueak grinning at? His pajamas, probably (chosen by Arlette, a bit psychedelic).

"Porter says he's very sorry, sir, bit of a mix-up sorting the mail, and he found another letter seems to be for you—that all right, sir?"

Van der Valk grunted, looked for sixpence, couldn't

find one, was damned if he'd give this horrid child a shilling, nodded vaguely, and was instantly absorbed in this letter. Aha, that explained the pageboy's grin. Extremely cheap envelope, ballpoint pen, illiterate handwriting of someone not knowing any Dutch. He handled it with some care, since there might be a thumbprint.

"Inspector Van Devalk, Sheridan Hotel, Stephen's Green, Dublin."

Postmarked Dublin late the night before. Hmm. Inside was a half sheet of cheap lined paper.

Get out, we don't want foreingers coming smearing our people, we know what to do with Them. You get 24 hrs to leave then you Get it stay away from the Gards they wont Help you annyway. This is the Last and Only warning.

Up the Rebels

"What d'you make of this?" Mr. Flynn examined the missive and smiled his crooked smile that made Van der Valk wonder just a little if he was being laughed at.

"Want it sent to the lab?"

"If you think that will help us."

"Mmm, midnight last night—General Post Office. Paper's Woolworth, so's the ballpoint, by the look of it. Irish handwriting learned at the Christian Brothers. Van De—that should be Van der, shouldn't it—not what a Dutch person would write."

"Could be faked, though. Common trick to put in spelling mistakes in an attampt to mislead."

"Surely. But look at the text. Inverting the 'n' and the 'g' in 'foreigner' is commonplace, means nothing

140

—but 'anny' is a Dublin fault based on pronunciation. 'Gards' is 'Guards' in English and 'Garda' in Irish and the feller got his feet crossed." It was the first time he had seen Flynn work—the vague joky manner had been discarded.

"You mean it could be faked, but not by someone Dutch, say."

"That's about it. Hardly your shiny new girl friend."

"Doesn't seem exactly Senator Lynch's style, either. Any ideas—sorry, anny?"

Flynn snorted. "Dublin humor," shrugging. "Might have nothing really to do with this job at all—just a loony. Dublin's full of loonies—if you were to put them all in Grangegorman, sure the queue would stretch from here to Athlone. I could probably find out, given time—it's hardly important."

"For the trouble you'd be put to," agreed Van der Valk. "What's these rebels?"

"A slogan, quite meaningless, like shouting 'Heil Hitler,' or that 'Ho, ho, ho' lark. We get thousands of these things—someone perhaps who saw you here, or with me."

"Seems to know something about me, though—this phrase about smearing: would that imply some knowledge?"

"Knowledge of somebody with nowt better to do than flap his ears in some pub—who maybe knows me. Quite a few people have reason to," with the rusty iron smile. "We might have made a remark or two what could be thought indiscreet; that is, if they hadn't been so general. Whatever, it's no great task to reason that you're here on some kind of job and not just for pleasure."

141

"If you're not impressed, I've certainly no reason to be."

"Certain amount of xenophobia anywhere, isn't it? —distrust of any outside influence or seeming interference—kind of thing a loony makes a lot of. We'll keep it, just in case, huh? I'll send it down the lab— do them no harm; bit of comic relief. By the way, got a bit of news for you; Senator Lynch took a plane for Rome this morning. Routine information from the airport: booked openly in his name, and there's nothing unusual in that; he's often away off to suchlike places and it won't even rate two lines in the paper."

"I saw Lynch, as you know. Made me promise hands off the boy but he'll see what's what and will have the honesty to tell me, and I took his word because if I trust him I hope he'll have no hesitation in trusting me. He said, 'We're in each other's hands.' "

"You don't surprise me a bit. That's his style."

"Got an invitation to come to dinner in his house day after tomorrow—by the way, that rebels thing came later, but it was in the same post; I checked with the porter. Got stuck under another envelope, he said."

Flynn touched the envelope delicately. "Slightly sticky," he agreed, nodding. "Fell in the jam dish or something." He bent down and smelled with his long bony nose, looking like one of those long sad dogs that hunt things. Beagles? wondered Van der Valk. Bassets?

"Guinness," said Flynn, grinning, "or, not to put a fine point, stout. Can conclude envelope is perhaps maybe been written on a pub table, like, where someone clumsy had slopped like with a jar. Loony. Who

142

in their right mind goes writing letters in a pool of stout? Nobody you know."

He was mistaken, though, because Van der Valk got slugged that evening in Seapoint Avenue.

He had had, as he feared, a boring day with the Embassy. They didn't think the situation quite altogether satisfactory (nor did he). They weren't very pleased with the rate of progress (nor was he). It was altogether unpleasantly vague, blackly unpromising, and decidedly disquieting (he quite agreed). He must be exceedingly cautious in any dealings with Mrs. Flanagan, since any suggestion of guilty knowledge or concealed information or whatnot could only be confirmed by this lad Lynch, who was in Rome, hmm; and anyway whose sayings now or in a hypothetical future were hardly gospel writ, hmm. So he'd better be exceedingly prudent, because if there were complaints about interference with the freedom of the subject, or false and malicious rumor, or God save the mark wrongful arrest (though this was prudishly and superstitiously referred to as "whatnot"), THEN there'd be hell to pay in the Netherlands Embassy— my God, it didn't bear thinking of.

He had a stronger desire than usual to tell them to go and get stuffed.

It was nightfall again when he got off the bus at Temple Hill and strolled down to get to Belgrave Square by the back door. He didn't have any ideas, and was strolling in an effort to concentrate his mind, which made him more oblivious than usual to immediate surroundings. Fictional detectives, he was thinking, made deductions. Real detectives got (or were supposed to get) most of their results from informers, meagerly paid for by a semisecret, somewhat squalid, and decidedly small fund appropriated by Authority for this purpose. That was all very well if one belonged to the more glamorous and publicized little clans with fancy names, like the Vice Squad or the Anti-Gang Brigade, but he was only a poor provincial policeman, and had no secret fund. What did one do then? Well, one did the best one could with petty jealousy and fear. With professional criminals one tried to maneuver the weakest of the group into splitting in order to receive preferential treatment. One tried to take advantage of a conflict of interest; hah. And with these family affairs what did one do? They were much, much, much worse. One got really squalid. One sank into a web of gossip, scandals, and pettiness, working on such promising facts as Uncle Henry's squabble with Tante Mathilde that grew out of bad feeling concerning the inheritance from Great-Uncle Charles (who had quarreled with Grandfather in 1910 over an investment that turned out sour).

He had still two of the lovely ladies to approach. What did they know, and what would they say? What had Anna written to them? What had Stasie told them? By now, they knew there was a Dutch policeman floating about, with an obstinate, unaccountable interest in Denis Lynch.

There was also Mr. Flanagan. What would his reaction be to a continuation of the hard-nosed tactic to which Van der Valk had pinned some faith—had to, because he had so little else—that of saying bluntly that, come now, there was some relationship between his virtuous and charming wife and this equally charming virtuous boy and what the hell was it, and

144

even more important what did Mr. Flanagan think of it?

He would continue to be simple, stubborn, and stupid.

He had been alone at the bus stop. Nobody had been following him that he was aware of. But somebody had been waiting for him in Seapoint Avenue who couldn't have known beforehand that he would go that way. Had someone in a car played hide-and-seek with the bus out from the town, dodged on ahead, lurked about in shadowy areas where the street lighting was thinner-spaced?

He had felt a sudden movement close behind him; too close, so that he dodged and side-stepped, a lot too slowly: as he began an about-face and parrying kind of movement, a heavy lump of something hit him a glancing blow on the side of the head, skidding along his jaw and descending painfully on to his shoulder. Heavy enough, and close enough to his temple to knock him silly for a second or two. He had had a heavy push immediately in the small of the back, gone tumbling tipsily into the roadway, tripping and sprawling in the gutter and hitting his head on the asphalt so that he had gone out for proper then, and known nothing else, heard no scream of brakes, never known whether a car hit him.

He had come round feeling beastly sick, with a helpful young man and his girl friend manhandling his limp knees clumsily into the awkward back of a small car. He had been too muzzy to answer any of their excited questions. They had driven him to St. Michael's Hospital Dún Laoghaire, heaved him into Outpatients, announced loudly that a gentleman had been run over, and left, mercifully, having utterly confused any subsequent effort to discover what happened.

Little he cared at the time. He slumped dully on a bench covered in plastic, where there was something sticky. Blood, possibly, or had a child been sucking a lollipop, or had somebody slopped stout, and a barman given a hasty wipe-round with a dirty dishcloth? No, this was a hospital, and a hard-handed nurse was cleaning his grazed forehead with cotton wool dipped in ether, horrid stuff. He couldn't think, felt vilely soggy, and had to vomit anyway; the stink of ether was overpowering.

"Sorry, I'm going to be sick."

"Here, be sick in this; don't try to walk." Sympathetic nurse holding him, seeing he didn't fall down the hole.

"Nothing too dreadful there," a male voice said. "Just a bump. A bit blurry in the head, a bit bluggy round the mental faculties; drink this."

Drink-this was sal volatile in water, nice old-fashioned remedy.

"No internal injuries." The voice got home to where it belonged, a brisk rugby-playing giant of an intern: his head had cleared.

"That hurt? No? Or that? Or that? Good. Or that? Or that?"

"Ow."

"Ah, yes, that's the collarbone. Fragile. Simple fracture, no need for an X-ray. Not too terrible, sure it isn't, all things considered. Stepped off the curb, I daresay, without looking to see if a car was coming; terrible the traffic is nowadays. Ah, a foreign gentleman; now, that explains it; you'll be used to the cars going the other way, isn't it, now? Sling, nurse, bit of

146

a pad under the arm there. Couple of codeines for the headache. Slight shock, nothing much; give us the wrist again a sec—hundred and five and steadying down; that's O.K., then, not to worry. You're a healthy great big feller; be right again in no time. Seen lots worse in a rugby match."

"Wouldn't you like to lie down a little now?" asked the nice nurse.

"I'm all right, sister, thanks—could I get a taxi to bring me home?"

"What happened you, then?" asked the night porter, full of sympathy.

"I'm afraid I stepped off the pavement rather stupidly and a car grazed me. It's nothing much." Nobody had noticed that his injuries were a bit oddly placed: the story satisfied everybody. Presumably, that had been the idea.

"Sure that's awful, now. Terrible the traffic is, terrible. Some of them bastards got no discipline at all, none whatever, tear along they do; should see them all parked outside here; 'Taxis Only' it says in letters as big as your head, and do they take a blind bit of notice: do they, hell, forgive the expression, sir; I'll work the lift for you. Goo' night, now: sleep well."

He did, but that might have been the codeine.

"Well, what do ya know about that?" asked Inspector Flynn; the question was rhetorical.

"Not a loony," said Van der Valk. "Or not quite as uncoordinated a loony anyway as you thought. As I thought," he added, anxious to be fair.

"I'll have him," said Mr. Flynn, touched in his honor, national pride, and sense of hospitality. "I'll have his ballocks for breakfast. So help me, in Seapoint Avenue. The goddam cheek."

"Somebody didn't want me to talk to Eddy Flanagan."

"Maybe that somebody's Eddy Flanagan."

"Maybe—I don't think so. Haven't any reason. Instinct."

"Instinct's no bad thing. What can't speak can't lie. You didn't get any glimpse?"

"I was far too slow. Too much whisky."

"Or not enough. Lunch is on me. A few oysters, now. And this gentleman will have my close attention and concern."

He felt wretched, tired, disheartened. He wasn't going to tell Arlette; she would get into a stew. Was anything more depressing than a hotel room in the afternoon? He was sore, he ached, but above all he was puzzled. This made no sense. He wasn't sure he really did enjoy Ireland all that much. He decided to go to bed, and not to do any thinking, since neither his head nor his feet went fast enough for anything so difficult. Somebody had better come along and knit up his raveled sleeve, preferably a blonde or two. He went to bed and slept.

He woke feeling peaceful, and prepared to bend an alert mind to major problems, like dialing a phone with one hand.

"Tara Printing Works," said a voice.

"Mr. Flanagan, please."

"Will ya hold the line, please. . . . He's not in just now, is there anny message?"

"When will he be back?"

"Sure he might be in any minute. Will I tell him to ring you back, then?"

"Do that; yes, please, if you would. Tell him it's

personal." He brushed his teeth, asked for tea, and received the sympathy of the waitress—what Inspector Flynn called "the lassie"—who brought it.

"Terrible the traffic is, terrible God help us." It was an Irish leitmotif. As Flynn said drýly, it had been terrible for the last thirty years to his certain knowledge and nobody had ever done anything about it yet. The phone rang as he was putting down his second cup empty, which made him feel he was going to be lucky at taking Eddy Flanagan by the horns. Fellow had horns, all right. Horns fit to knock holes in the bedroom ceiling, and if he was wrong, she, Stasie, was Santa Lucia the light-bringer in a long white nightie and he, Van der Valk, would take the next rowing boat home one-handed.

"Eddy Flanagan—who's this, then?"

"Van der Valk."

"Oh."

"No, I didn't ring up to pester you. I'm sick, I'm at home, I need a drink badly: come out and have one with me."

"Oh." Suspicions were lifted, but not quite dissipated. "Well . . . I daresay I could . . . I'm pretty near through. . . . Where?" guarded.

"Where you like. Here. Quiet. Pleasant."

"Well . . . all right . . . it's on my way . . . take me a few minutes. Tricky parking around there."

"Park in the bloody taxi rank," said Van der Valk: he was learning Irish rapidly.

When Eddy Flanagan came bumbling in, stopped dead and opened his eyes at the sling and the bruise, Van der Valk felt sure of innocence—and there's a big streak of innocence going all the way through this feller, he thought. But don't jump. Not at anything.

Step by step. He could hear old Samson, once his commissaire in Central Recherche Amsterdam: it had been one of his pet phrases.

"Step by step, like the Count of Monte Cristo." The only book the old bastard had ever read: so good, he said, he never wanted to read another.

"What in God's name happened you, then?"

"I had an argument with the traffic. Tell you about it. Whisky? Waiter, please. Two large Redbreasts in the pretty glasses."

"Yes, sir" said the waiter, used to eccentricity. "Water, sir?"

"Soda, Eddy, or Anna Liffey?"

"You're picking up the language," with admiration.

"I take lessons daily. Ice? No? Me neither. As she comes. Ice in whisky is putting a flag on the shit ship —sorry; Amsterdam expression, that." The less ice there was, the less he had to break.

"Will you pay, sir, or sign?"

"Sign," generously. "Left-handed. My God."

"What?"

"Nothing. Hurt a bit." He had only just tumbled. His right collarbone was broken, and he had been almost turned right round. Feller who hit him was left-handed. Eddy was clasping his pretty glass in an anxious paw—right-handed.

"Good luck."

"Up the rebels."

And this time he got an unbuttoned giggle; Eddy was relaxing rapidly. "Where did you pick that up?" John Jameson, ten-year-old, unbuttons the strait lace, thought Van der Valk. "I've met a few Dutchmen, and we do business with a few, but I've never seen— Oy, oy; I'll make a gaffe any minute."

"You didn't think a policeman—but given enough whisky we become almost human. Waiter, two cigars, Cuban ones, and not out of a lousy tube; bring the box. And two more of the same before the leaf falls off the tree."

"My, my," with another giggle.

Expense account—toward getting Eddy Flanagan a wee bit pissed. Poor old Eddy; he doesn't know about my conversation classes with Mr. Flynn.

"I was just coming up to see you last night." A rain cloud drifted across the sun. "These will do nicely," pouncing on Romeo and Juliets.

"Got to make up for this—no, it's not my arm; only a collarbone."

But the rain cloud was still there. "Look, it's really no use coming up to see me. I've nothing to tell you, and neither has my wife. If that's what you got me here for. . . ."

"Look, Eddy, relax. I'm quite prepared to hear you say it, and to believe it. But wait, now, till I tell you. So it was just night falling, and I was taking a bit of a walk along Seapoint Avenue, when a feller hits me on the head. I moved a bit, so he caught me here. Then here. Snap. Then pushes me in the road, to look like a car hit me. And if another car came along and did hit me, then good luck, that's just what the doctor ordered."

"Jaysus," said Eddy, much shocked, drinking whisky in self-defense.

"Now you know why I asked you over."

"But—but—you don't think it was me, surely to God."

"You?" as though it had never entered his head. "No. Of course not. Not for a minute. But who was worried about me walking along Seapoint Avenue? And who knew it was a direction I'd be likely to take?" Eddy's eyes were glassy, his mouth more than a bit open. Van der Valk exploited this.

"You get a lot of mugging around where you live?" he asked nastily.

"Jaysus."

"I should, of course, be grateful it wasn't a knife. Like your father-in-law."

"Jaysus," for the third time, but getting fainter. To fortify, he put down the second whisky in a practiced lump, and relit his cigar, with which he was less practiced and which was giving trouble. While he was thus distracted, Van der Valk changed the empty glass for his own half-full one, and wondered who had hit him on the head.

"You see, Eddy," confidential, "what could this feller hope to gain? What have I done, or what am I likely to do, that worries him? I come asking one question, which doesn't seem sufficiently poisonous to make anyone want to turn me into hamburger. That is, what is the relationship between Mr. Martínez, who is dead, and Denis Lynch, who's in Rome writing little postcards? Arising out of that, what is the relationship between Denis Lynch and Mrs. Flanagan, formerly Miss Martínez?"

"Look, you can't expect me to say something that sounds like accusing my wife of knowing anything about this. I tell you she doesn't."

"So your wife is being accused, is she?"

"I didn't say that."

"I'm afraid, you know, that that is exactly what you did say." Somewhat fogged, Eddy took refuge in the glass of whisky. The third helping was coming up already and Van der Valk took a swig at it.

"Look," he said suddenly. He was feeling tired again: euphoria had been very much a passing phase. He took another, longer swig, uncertain whether it would buoy him up, like Bovril, or hurry him faster still down the slippery slope.

"Look," again, clumsily. "Believe, if you can, that I'm not trying to be tricky. I know one always reads about policemen trapping people into damaging admissions, or exaggerating little scraps of fact, things that aren't conclusive in any way, into a horrible big overshadowing presumption of guilt. Well, such things do happen," dully. "They don't happen that often, that's all." Lamebrain; make an effort.

"There's one thing a policeman is frightened of"— rapid, if not incisive—"more than anything else, and that's a judicial error. Assuming a person to be guilty and acting accordingly is bad—in fact, it's criminal."

"How d'you mean?" asked Eddy, his eyes suddenly a lot more intelligent.

Done something clever at last, thought Van der Valk: this drunken Irish babble of mine might have moved the mountain of caution and suspicion. Been spontaneous! One side of his head was listening carefully, contemptuously, to the weariness and confusion of his tongue. But it is wrong to be contemptuous.

"I mean this." It had the ponderous overemphasis of a drunk, and yet he was not in the least drunk. In fact, he had hollow bones. Perhaps that was the trouble! He saw whisky trickling out of his broken collarbone, and settling in his bloodstream.

"I mean this." Sorry, said that already. "A court won't convict anyone, nowadays, on unsupported police evidence. But if a policeman gets a conviction that X is guilty of—whatever you like—fraudulent conversion—all the evidence starts pointing the same way. Everything adds to his guilt; in no time at all, he gets up in the morning and asks his wife for two eggs instead of one and it's an additional proof, and creates a judicial error. This is the position of Denis Lynch. There's no case against him: as far as we know, he's guilty of absolutely nothing, except maybe crossing the street outside the little black-and-white bands. But his relationship with Martínez—your father-in-law—is very important, perhaps crucial. He was in love with your wife—and what else? It's painful to you, but get it off your chest."

It so nearly worked. Eddy had his mouth open, and Van der Valk knew perfectly that it was to say that, yes, it was so, and he knew it, but he hadn't done anything about it because what could one do, but that anyway Denis had gone off to Holland. . . . But at the last second conditioned reflex was too strong.

"Well," Eddy said overhurriedly, in an overwarm, overfriendly voice, "I wish I could help you. You seem to think I can because I know Denis a bit; I mean he's an impetuous kind of young feller, it's possible he might have lost his head and done something silly—meantosay, suppose something happened where he got into a situation in which he thought he looked guilty, he might start acting as though he were, don't-youknow. I mean suppose he thought you were after him, he might hit you on the head—I mean only of course he wasn't there," in a very great hurry indeed.

"I feel bad about this, I do really—I mean it's a bit bloody much, that, and I'll do anything for you, honest."

154

"There's a thing you can do. Tell your wife to come and see me, here if she likes, quite confidential; there's nothing incriminating at all, and anything she tells me I'll treat in confidence." Oh, stop repeating yourself. "She's the one person, I feel convinced, that can shed light on some things that are worrying me. It's not a threat in any way, but otherwise, you know, Dublin Castle won't like this attack at all, and you may find them camped on your doorstep."

"I'll tell her," said Eddy. "I'll tell her. What about another—my shout."

"Another," said Van der Valk, "would put me in Granegorman."

"I'd be right in there with you," said Eddy with gloomy sympathy.

There are three lovely ladies of Belgrave Square, Van der Valk was thinking. Doesn't do to neglect the other two.

"What's this Châteaubriand thing?" asked Inspector Flynn, whom he had invited to dinner, and who had accepted with alacrity, once tipped off about the expense account: he had also been interested in the left-handed lurker, and was now enjoying himself. "Some French writer, isn't it?"

"That's all I know, too. Buried on a rock in Saint-Malo harbor, and I only know that from being there on holiday. I'm all for him, just the same."

"Did he eat this damn steak all by himself, then?"

"Maybe he left just a bit at the end for the girl."

"Good for him, the glutton. You're going to dinner with Senator Lynch tomorrow, too—ah, well, be in training. The idea, no doubt, will be to serve you up the boy Denis as dessert, like. I've told the airport to buzz me when they heave in sight."

"What makes you sure he'll bring the boy back?" Van der Valk asked.

"Me money's on him, that's all. Very persuasive, is the Senator Lynch. If he doesn't, he'll have a damn good reason."

"I'll have to pay a visit out toward Belgrave Square tomorrow."

"You must have a damn good reason, too."

"Yes—got to go to the hospital to have me arm looked at. If I push my plate across, can you cut this a bit smaller? Waiter thinks I'm a tiger."

"Sure. Yes—by the way, I looked up them two other jokers for you," pushing the plate back and producing a notebook even dirtier than Van der Valk's, which was saying a lot.

"Mrs. Collins and Mrs. MacManus?"

"That's right. Jim Collins," with relish, "an' Malachi MacManus."

"Old Polish aristocracy, those two."

"That's right. Neither of them married, by the way. Jim Collins isn't the marrying kind. Now, Malachi seems to be the opposite—been married more times than I've had hot cups of tea. Gas pair"—reflective—"the two of them. Real funny."

"Peculiar—or ha-ha?"

"Gas," decided Mr. Flynn after deliberation, "means in this case both."

"Anything known?" asked Van der Valk like an English magistrate, looking over his glasses down his nose at the shivering Collins in the dock.

"Plenty," through a mouthful of steak. "Jim we know all about. Biggest phony from here to Bray.

That's maybe an exaggeration; sure there's a terrible number between here and Bray. But a terrible phony anyhow. Great big feller like Charles Atlas." He swallowed and went on with enjoyment. "A national hero. Got a pension from the I.R.A. for his sufferings in the case against the oppressor. He goes about saying he knew Brendan Behan when they were in Borstal together. He's never done any work in his life."

"Is the pension so big?" with interest.

"Well, no; sure the I.R.A. hasn't a penny. But he does have a talent for getting given money. They give him a whole lot not so long ago to buy them from the Czechs or whatnot, and he come back with a few old gas-pipe Mausers what the Germans sold the Turks in 1915, and sure they all thought the world of him."

"A famous figure in Irish folklore."

"That's it. Once, we had him in the nick over showing pornographic films in a garage out in Rathmines; sure he was packing them in from all over, but we never got it properly pinned on him; feller owned the house went to jail instead. He's quite clever, is Jim," indulgently. "There's no great harm in him. All his brains is gone into them great big muscles. Spends a lot of time over a jar boasting about his exploits in a pub I know," negligently. "And a funny thing—Jim's left-handed."

"And the other?" working placidly through his steak.

"Malachi? There's no great harm in him neither. Nothing known—on the book, that is. The women"—it was an aphorism—"is a disappointment to him."

"What's he do?"

"He does be an expert on the native literature. Old Irish ballads and the like."

"No money in that."

"Not a penny. So he's in the oyster business, but he won't tell you that, because being a fishmonger has no class and the ballads has."

"Money in the fish," agreed Van der Valk, "but a lot of work, surely."

"Ach, not at all. Some poor silly feller down in Ballygobackwards does all the work. Belgium, as you'll know, is the great place to sell the oysters—what does Malachi do but nip over to Antwerp and tell them he'll give them ten million of the best straight from County Kerry by oxcart and half the usual price, and sure the Belgians'll jump at that even if there's typhoid in every goddam one. That way, Malachi's set for the whole winter and he can go home and muck about with his ballads. He doesn't want to make a whole heap of money—if he did, he'd be paying it all out in alimony to all the wives; sure there's dozens of them."

"Let's have pancakes," said Van der Valk pleasurably.

"With a lot of drink that the feller comes and sets on fire?"

"And coffee. And the special juice Napoleon put in the bottle."

"As long as he didn't piss it in the bottle. Even then, I'll love it," said Mr. Flynn generously.

"These people all sound a bit soft in the head— Eddy Flanagan is, too."

"Must be to be married to that one."

"Do all these loonies add up to anything?"

"Add up maybe to the loony what hit you on the head."

"But there's a terrible lot of left-handed people between here and Bray."

"Oh, it doesn't risk coming into any court. Sure Jim Collins was in the boozer and there's twenty witnesses to prove it. Nowhere near Seapoint Avenue."

"How do you know all this?"

"Sure Dublin's a small town," secretively. "Now, these girls of yours—they add up to a queer lot." He hesitated rather, as though regretting a few of these confidences. Van der Valk guessed he might be unwilling to say something about Dutch people in front of a Dutchman. He might not be very happy if it were me making jokes about the I.R.A., for instance, Van der Valk thought. "I mean all living together in a kind of colony like."

"From what I know of the father, I wouldn't be surprised at anything much. Why did he get killed like that? Because he's the kind of feller bizarre things happen to."

"Ah," said Flynn.

"You know anything about these women?"

"No—or very little. It's said—I wouldn't know whether it's to be believed—that they do be playing puss-in-the-corner quite a bit."

"What does that mean?"

"They never seem to know which of them's man belongs to which, if you get me. Now, a few years back, so they tell me—"

"But who's they?"

"Ah, people around town. Belgrave Square is a place where there's a good deal of gossip; they do tell me the young one—let's see, that's Anastasia, ain't it

159

—had a great big passionate affair with Jim Collins."

If he hadn't eaten all those pancakes, thought Van der Valk, he'd never have got into this confidential mood. Expense account justifying itself.

"Malachi," said Mr. Flynn, standing his coffee cup upside down on his nose, "started off with the big tall one. I don't know whether he ever married her, which is to say I've forgotten. They seem to get their lines crossed. And so do I," after a pause for thought.

It is his way of paying me back, thought Van der Valk. I got hit on the head and he took it as an insult. But he's found out he can't probe anything—it's all hearsay. So he gives me all this gossip and out of tact pretends that a good dinner has loosened him up enough to become talkative.

"All scandal," said Flynn. "Terrible ones for scandal, the Irish."

"Gas women?"

"Gas women."

"I can hardly wait to get into bed with all of them together."

There are days—which everyone has—that announce themselves as ominous through trivial signs of warning. These are not very significant: poor coordination, and a sense of being late for whatever it is, be it only an ordinary day at the office. Why did the alarm clock not go off, why does one knock over a coffee cup, drop marmalade on a clean shirt, and break a shoelace just when one is behindhand anyhow? Van der Valk, eating breakfast in bed, got one of those grapefruit that squirt juice in one's eye when attacked, exactly like an octopus, and then somehow got egg all over his pajama jacket. He decided to be

patient and tolerant about this, and on reflection he
remembered he had had rather a lot to drink the night
before. His shoulder was unpleasantly stiff and sore,
and he viewed the sling with distaste: it bore numer-
ous traces of lavish eating, drinking, and smoking that
in the early morning were just plain revolting. He
flung it pettishly in a corner, ran himself a very deep,
very hot bath to boil himself pink and mend the bat-
tered bones, and had just lowered himself into it with a
good many loud cries and moans of mingled bliss and
agony when the telephone rang.

Well, at least this was an expensive hotel, and
among its few advantages was an extension in the
bathroom. He pulled himself laboriously upright, sat
his weary bottom on the edge, and arranged a towel to
swath his wet top. As he reached to take the instru-
ment off its hook, the towel slid, he hurt his collarbone
grabbing at it, and the towel fell in the bath.

"Oh, bugger it," he said nastily into the phone.

"That's a poor start to the day," came Flynn's
voice. "How are you, then?"

"Lousy."

"Yes. I have an impression we both got a wee bit
stocious."

"Judging by all the things happening to me this
morning, we did."

"Yes. I was a scrap indiscreet, huh—about the
I.R.A.?"

"It's possible."

"The thing is, one would have great difficulty in
proving anything."

"One always has."

"The news this morning isn't too encouraging, either. Senator Lynch has just landed. Not very promising. I'm told he's alone."

"Ah."

"Indeed. He doesn't look happy, it would seem, and told a fool reporter at the airport to get away out of that, I gather in terms not as parliamentary as they might be. Sorry."

"Well—I'm due to see him tonight."

"I hadn't forgotten—the dinner party! So you'll let sleeping dogs lie for the moment?"

"My own dog's still half asleep. And I've a whole pack of bitches preoccupying me."

A snigger came down the line. "Quarrelsome, are they?"

"Well, this morning I've got to go to the Embassy."

"Yes, that's a bit rough."

"And this afternoon I've got to go get me arm fixed. I thought of dropping in on them. Only hope I don't get me other arm broke. They're maybe panting a bit, straining at the leash." There was another haw-haw sound of earthy mockery.

"Don't let them get in heat. Bye, now, for the present."

"I'll come and see you tomorrow—depends a bit on Tall Terry and what his news is." He got back into the bath, more convinced than ever that it was going to be a bad day.

He cooked himself pink, like a salmon in court-bouillon, and felt rather better. He was dressed in an undershirt when the phone rang again. Why didn't the stupid hotel have an unlisted number or something? He wasn't in the mood even for the delicious Liz.

"Porter, sir. A lady is asking for you."

"Lady have a name?"

162

"A Miss Martínez." Oh, blimey—Van der Valk rubbed his jaw like Humphrey Bogart being pensive. Things were happening too fast.

"Send her up."

"Yes, sir." It wasn't quite the thing.

"One moment—I've got to tidy up. Ask the lady to be good enough to give me five minutes."

"Yes, sir." He climbed into his clothes with great speed, kicked all the dirty clothes into the bathroom and shut the door on them, and composed his face with eau de Cologne into an expression of professional gravity. Eddy Flanagan had delivered his little message, and she had acted on it. The moment was perhaps ill-chosen, but today all moments were ill-chosen; he had to put up with it. He hung the "Do Not Disturb" notice on the door while combing his hair, and closed the window. It was bright, sunny weather. Should he take her down to a public room? No—the idea of this was to be informal, to chat her up, to get her to relax. The shirt-sleeve atmosphere was the right one. Anyway, it was too much trouble to put on a tie. Hell with what the porter thought.

A small discreet knock. He opened; Stasie stood there. Very dressed up and a strong smell of Lanvin enhancing her. "Come in," he said good-humoredly; she needed no telling. She looked fine; what had she got in that clever little head?

Formal leather gloves and handbag, hair carefully done, a silky suit, face painted, the good shoes, careful stockings. First time he had seen her out of her "housewife" role, and very nice, too. Hips a thought heavy, but very nice legs notwithstanding. What a good word "notwithstanding" is.

"Sorry if I disturb you. I know I'm a bit early: Eddy gave me a lift into town."

"You don't disturb me at all." The unmade bed bothered him—a hotel bedroom is so very full of bed. He had chosen the terrain—had he made a mistake? She perched on a small armchair, vaguely Empire in style, clutching her handbag and looking very demure for someone who had thought out a good way of neutralizing him.

"I thought it best to give another name," she murmured. "It's a bit of an embarrassing situation." Exactly; she was the one who was supposed to feel embarrassed. Really he was in a position of strength.

"I asked you to come here because it was neutral ground, so to speak." Yes, even though his English had got quite colorful, it was a relief to speak Dutch again. "You can speak freely—without bothering about the effect perhaps your words might have on your husband, let's say. You see, the position is a bit equivocal. Senator Lynch," offering her a cigarette, lighting one himself to give him more face, pushing the ashtray between them on the little writing table, "Senator Lynch feels the way I do, that the way to straighten things out is to suggest that Denis tell us his story, simply. He is, after all, the only witness known of the hours immediately preceding your father's death. Mr. Lynch has gone to Rome. Denis will be coming back with him." Denis, alas, wasn't, but Stasie need not know that. She was staring at him with a puzzled earnest air, as though she found Dutch difficult to follow.

"You see, this is very informal. I'm in my shirt sleeves—literally. Nothing taken down in evidence. You aren't even a witness, technically. You're not in a court and you never will be. You can keep silence—

but it's not very fair on Denis, who's in a difficult position. He may be worried, perhaps, about chivalrous feelings concerning you. Your keeping silence is a mistake. I—or a court—have no legal right to interpret your silence as any sort of guilt, or even a possession of knowledge. But we're human. We have a way of assuming that silence might mean there's knowledge there somewhere—not guilty, perhaps—but relevant."

"But why should I have any knowledge at all?" asked Stasie, pained.

"Put it this way. In talking to Denis, and questioning him, I have to take all the possibilities into account. A policeman must have a great many scruples, apart from all the devices that exist for protecting the liberty of the subject. But he can't be so scrupulous as to blind himself to the obvious."

"But what is obvious?"

"Denis, however unlikely it may seem, may be the author of your father's death." Why not cut through the whole thing? Why not say straight out, "You're involved and you know it. Everybody knows it. Even Jim Collins. Or he wouldn't have hit me on the head"? Prudence, my boy: remember what the Embassy said. And you've no proof.

"He'll have to answer a few questions based on that hypothesis," he added blandly.

"But how on earth could I know? You can't impute knowledge to me I couldn't possess. You seem to be suggesting that it—if it were so—that it would be in some way my fault. My father—it is so hard, so brutal, so merciless a thing to say—I was very, very attached to my father. We were very close." And that was all quite true. . . .

"Eddy isn't here, Mrs. Flanagan. What was the relationship between you and Denis?"

"I don't think you have the right to question me about my private life," in a tight little voice.

"You don't discuss it with anyone?" blandly. "Not with Denis, for example?"

"Certainly not."

"You realize that I'll ask him?"

"You're implying there was something untoward about—about this friendship. That's disgusting. Denis is a young boy. He had troubles—as boys of that age do—you know that, I hope. He didn't always find the atmosphere at home very understanding—that, too, is frequent, or hadn't you thought about it?" Lot of leaden irony.

"Oh, yes, I've thought about it." Equally leaden.

"So he wanted to get away. He thought of going to Holland. I gave him an introduction to my father. Why do you try to read more into this than there is? He found me—is it so dreadful?—a sympathetic listener. I tried to give him—I don't know—guidance, possibly reassurance. And you want to turn that into something filthy." Yes, thought Van der Valk; all that could be perfectly true, and I have no means whatever of proving it isn't.

"Let's understand one another, Mrs. Flanagan. There's an old cliché among doctors, when making a diagnosis—why look for a canary when there are so many sparrows? In other words, don't look for complicated rare diseases when the simple ones are so much more common. A policeman works on something the same lines."

She got up, walked over to the window, stood looking out of it, opened her handbag and searched in it, and said in a soft voice, not at all tense, "I've stupidly left my cigarettes behind—could I ask for one of yours?"

"But of course," getting up. He didn't want to sit while she was standing—this was not only the paragraph in the police training manual about politeness. She lit the cigarette at his match, facing him, jaw muscles set. Tears were beginning to come out of her eyes. And suppose it all is the truth, thought Van der Valk wearily. This is a bad day.

"I came to see you," in a low voice, "because I loved my father very much. I wanted to do whatever I could to help clear this up. Since you seem to think I can help you, I was ready to try. But you are bullying —and odious."

And I'd almost be ready to believe you, thought Van der Valk, if it hadn't been for Jim Collins's bright idea of clonking me. Or was it yours? He had just noticed that Stasie was left-handed. He wasn't going to mention the clonking. A policeman is like a dealer; he always tries to keep a little something in reserve.

"Don't get worked up," he said bluntly. "In Holland, I took the trouble to learn everything I could about your father. To try and understand, don't you see, why he should have been killed. One of the features about him was his attachment to women. That was an amusing technique—marrying them all the time. Your own resemblance to your father is quite striking. I noticed it in your letters—you told me as much yourself. Divorce here, of course, is unknown. Your sisters, interestingly, have not married. You yourself married Eddy. Yet your letters make no secret of it being a problem for you. I wonder why you married Eddy."

She looked at him with eyes gone wide and startled. "For somebody knowing nothing about me, you seem to read a lot into my letters." The tears had dried; she was more angry than anything.

"Once, you mentioned a physiological cross you had to bear. What is that?"

She flushed, furiously, up to her hairline. "Eddy drinks a lot, that's all."

"And is he sometimes unfaithful to you?"

"Ask him!"

"And have you been sometimes unfaithful to him?"

"Ask him that, too!"

"And if I asked Denis?"

"What would you expect him to say?" sarcastic.

"I'd expect him to say no."

"So would I," bitterly.

"But the point is—will he be believed?"

She walked a few steps without looking at him, turned toward the bed, and suddenly threw herself down on it, hammering it, and going "Oh-h-h-h," in threatened hysterics. Tiresome female. Why had she come? To clear herself. Eddy had not said anything about the attack in Seapoint Avenue, surely. He had simply urged her to go and have a chat with the feller, and get things straightened out. And she had found herself pushed a scrap further than she had expected to go. And was now having a fit as a consequence.

He went over and shook her shoulder lightly. "Come, Mrs. Flanagan, you must surely see that this is an obvious conclusion until something shows otherwise. A young boy at a starry-eyed susceptible age, forming an emotional friendship with a young pretty woman—it's a foregone conclusion that he would fall in love with you."

168

She wrenched herself round on the bed, staring up at him with eyes drowned in pain—or fear. "You're merciless," she whispered. "You're a horrible, dreadful man. You think these things—you think yourself clever. Simple things you can't understand. You don't know what my life is. Yet your one wish is to torture me. You're a sadist."

It took him aback a bit: was he a sadist? It hadn't occurred to him. Bastard sometimes, certainly. Bending over her, his arm hurt. He felt foggy and not very clever, and not at all convinced he was handling her right. With his good arm he shook her feebly, like a small dog that only wants to play. Suddenly she threw her arm up and gripped his wrist. Her other hand shot out and clenched on his bad shoulder, so that he felt a sharp shock of pain. At the same moment, he felt a sharp shock of desire, and had time to think that he shouldn't have let her go sprawling about on his bed.

Her eyes had turned up, showing the whites. Van der Valk lost his head.

Stasie got up suddenly, snatched her clothes, and pattered with rapid feet into the bathroom. He sat on the bed, his collarbone hurting. He had been an exceptional fool. And now he was in the shit.

Was she really very clever? Or was she out of Flynn's queue, the one that stretched from here to Athlone? He was about to open his mouth and say "Oh, Jaysus" when he recalled that she was in the bathroom and would hear.

He dressed, clumsily.

While dressing, he thought that, no—surely—she could not realize he had understood that, whoever had hit him on the head, it had been her idea. Perhaps he wasn't in the shit, after all.

What would Arlette say if she knew about all this? How right he had been to conceal the clonk on the head. . . .

He had underestimated this woman.

Stasie came out repainted, fresh, tranquil, no cloud in the sky. She gave him a tiny timid smile, like a very little girl.

"I'll come again," she whispered. "Whenever you like."

"That might be difficult. And tactless."

"Hire a car," she said. "Come and pick me up. I know places. Eddy's often away—he'll know nothing —nothing." His head reeled slightly. Need a big whisky.

"I'll phone you," he managed to say. She nodded, wisely, and whisked out. Don't know about being be-mused, he thought. Sure am bebitched, though.

St. Michael's Hospital felt his bones with expertise, made him say "Ow" mildly a couple of times, said "Knitting nicely now," and turned him over to the nurse, who rearranged his padding, added a few arch jokes about falling under cars, gave him a clean sling, and safety-pinned it into neatness. She wiggled her little bottom away under its starched apron after tell-ing him to come back and see Doctor on Friday, and left him feeling vulnerable but refreshed. With some notion of getting up on the horse he had just taken a fall from, he buzzed round to Belgrave Square, but none of the lovely ladies were in: pity, that—he won-dered whether they knew all about Stasie's little ways. If you can't beat them, join them. If you can't join them, there are even simpler verbs. He wasn't altogether happy about all these Anglo-Saxon monosyllables. What could one say to the Procureur Général —"Well, she hit me on the head, after all"?

He would go to the Embassy. Whatever they did to him, it wouldn't be that.

Mr. Slavenburg raised his eyebrows a wee bit over the car accident, prudently said nothing, and was unexpectedly forthcoming on the subject of the I.R.A. In fact, he came quite close to being funny.

"Well, I suppose I had better not ask what relevance that has to your inquiry—tangential?"

"Wasn't quite as tangential as all that—but you could call it so."

"Quite," said Mr. Slavenburg with very nearly a grin. "Quite right to ask me—your man Flynn would be evasive, no doubt, because it's an embarrassment, something of a hydra. The Irish government has been chopping off its heads assiduously for fifty years now, and it did appear to have been reduced to total impotence. Difficult to go on being excited about the border, you know. Recent events have given it a new lease of life. It goes in for rather senseless acts of violence."

"Quite," said Van der Valk primly.

"It's extremely difficult ever to get at the truth of anything in Ireland—they possess a highly sophisticated technique for confusing one, known generically as The Brother. Let's say you hear something—that income tax is going up. You ask your informant who told him. The answer will be that the brother was mentioning it. Where is the brother? He's in the States, or in England, or 'down the country.' What does the brother do? Here in Dublin, he has generally an excellent—you might say honorary—post in the civil service. In the country, he's generally an auctioneer, or a cattle dealer, of course—or both. He knows things for certain and tells one in confidence. He's in with the clergy, and the only place one can be sure of finding him is on a Sunday morning 'catching half-eleven mass in Clarendon Street.' Now, if you ask about the I.R.A., you'll be told to apply to the brother, because he's in it. He," said Mr. Slavenburg dryly, "is the only one who is. You will no longer be surprised to hear that when a Minister was involved in a most obscure tale concerning fifty thousand pounds supposedly devoted to gun-running, the Minister himself was not, of course, directly implicated. But the brother was."

"I see perfectly," said Van der Valk, and indeed he did.

"Things have been happening," he told Inspector Flynn. "By the way, don't bother about my being hit on the head. I'm told it's knitting nicely. It was the brother did it, of course."

"Well, that was obvious all along. What worried me was that you'd maybe want to go collecting evidence, you know, pin it on him like. That would have been difficult."

"Yes, I realize that. However, there is now a different tactic afoot."

"Of the brother's?" with interest.

"No, of hers. She climbed into bed with me this morning."

"Jaysus," shocked at this Dutch ebullience. "Jaysus. You mean it." He suddenly started to laugh. "You are a right one, though—oh, you are a right one. A proper one."

"Wait till she has you in a situation like that. It all happened pretty fast," apologetically.

"I wouldn't be asking the lady up to my bedroom, now—would I, then?"

"Don't go for any walks in the fields, either."

Flynn shook with silent laughter, though plainly a bit scandalized and almost alarmed. "Well—you won't have to swear to it in court—but you better watch out. That'll bear saying again, too," added Flynn as the enormity sank in.

"I can't fathom it at all," said Van der Valk, lighting a cigarette and breaking the match very carefully into four equal pieces. "What d'you make of that, then?"

"That she's in a flaming fearful frigging panic, that's what."

"Yes, but why? I don't menace her, there's nothing I can do to her. . . . All I can suppose is that I brought her bad news, it put her in a flat spin—she's certainly highly neurotic and unbalanced—she tried to kill me, you know."

"It shows that the boy killed her poppa, that she knew it, that you started connecting it up, that the notion frightened her, and she runs to your man telling him to see you fall in the river. You better ask for police protection, haw-haw." Mr. Flynn was pleased with his wit.

"But then why would she rush to get into bed with me?"

"Well, you know what happened to Denis. She likes the men."

"What'll be the next thing she tries?" wondered Van der Valk aloud.

He went for a walk along the river, a good deal more upset than he gave himself credit for. He didn't come terribly well out of this! Had she come with some deliberate notion of seducing him? That was too preposterous, surely. No, something he had said or done set her off. He had told her he knew—in as many words—that she was in trouble, that she was responsible for the attack made on him; was that it, was it some screwy way of trying to whitewash that, to cover it up? Too crude, too simplified, too absurd. He had told her he had Denis in a bag and would shortly be questioning him, upon which her relations with the boy would be established. . . .

Well, she's complicated, dotty, anything you like, thought Van der Valk, admiring the massive proportions of Guinness's Brewery. What would old man Freud make of her?

Clue there somewhere. She is very attached to her father, very like him. Now, if we grant that Denis killed him, never mind the how or the why, but assuming that his little affair with Stasie is the link, which seems certain . . . could this amazing upheaval inside Stasie be caused by her somehow getting hold of the notion that she was responsible, that she was even guilty? . . .

Wait; take this step by step. She learns that I have made the link between Denis and herself, and goes off the deep end. She cooks up a plot to suppress me. Jim Collins is involved with that, and how? Flynn suggests that he's an ex-lover of hers, and he's anyway her sister's lover. Too many people involved; he sighed gloomily—I've quite enough trouble sorting out

Denis Lynch; let's not bother about Collins, the more so as we'd never get anything proved.

And then suddenly she comes to me and chucks herself at me—now, is that another elaborate plot? Or is that quite spontaneous? Don't tell me the whole gang of them there in Belgrave Square are sitting brewing up these conspiracies. First they decided to suppress me. That doesn't work, so they decide to discredit me—and that might have worked except she's in the same position as me with Big Jim—she can't prove anything. . . . Or is she now going to try and maneuver me into a position where she could prove something? In which case, it's up to me to maneuver a wee bit my own self, huh?

Let's go and see the sisters, and find out what they think about all this.

It was a very Dutch woman who opened the door. "Mrs. Collins?"

"No—I'm Mrs. MacManus—who are you?"

"About your father."

"Ah." She knew all about him. "Well—I suppose you'd better come in. If it's Agnes you want, she's inside." Fine pair of legs, he thought, following. Look good in her nurse's uniform—his mind had gone back to the little nurse with no legs at all who had tied his sling that morning. Suppose I'd got this one—he was grinning, and she didn't like him grinning; there was a hostility.

There was even more hostility from Agnes, the eldest sister, not as tall but with blonder hair. They looked very like, and yet unlike, and neither very much like Stasie, but what did that mean? Agnes was sitting knitting and looking at the television: she wore

175

glasses, which she took off to look at him with dislike, as though disgusted that big Jim had not done a better job. Did they know anything about that?

He didn't know what he could gain by this visit. He had never felt much interest in these two. Their letters had been boring, and nothing now contradicted this impression.

Agnes echoed his thought. "What you hope to gain by this I can't imagine."

Why did the lovely ladies live so close to each other? What was it that they had in common?

A family feeling, of course. Nothing strange there; it is a Dutch phenomenon. Dutch families are very clannish: grownup children go on dropping in on each other, so that the next generation lives in a most intricate network of aunts and uncles even if half of them are in-laws. They take pains over one another's birthdays and wedding anniversaries; they spend evenings together playing cards. There are constantly fights, changes of alliance, temporary bouts of not speaking. No reunion passes without at least one yelling quarrel, but the deeply knit ties of family are never snapped: if anything, they are enriched.

Agnes, he saw at once, was a tiresome woman, brainless and aggressive, with the quarrelsomeness of being opinionated without being informed. One of those people who argue for hours whether it had been Thursday or Wednesday a fortnight back that something happened that had been trivial even then.

Her voice, her looks, her manner were harsh and overvigorous. The room was dark, she had the light on to knit by; electricity made her looks even more striking. Her hair was so ferociously blond that one would have gone bail it was artificial, but after a quarter of an hour he knew it was natural, just as he knew she hadn't been in any conspiracy: too outspoken on the subject, and saying too many silly things.

"Well, Father, of course—just an accident—like yours. Yes, we heard about that; guessed it must have been you. Stasie told us you'd been coming pestering her."

"I heard at the hospital," said Agatha more placidly; she was knitting, too, in a less violent style than her sister. "They were full of the Dutch gentleman who stupidly got himself run over in Seapoint Avenue." Not without malice.

"Just the same sort of thing," said Agnes almost gleefully. "You see, these things happen. Like scaffolding falling on someone's head. Coincidence, that's all."

"We've thought about it," said Agatha. "Coincidence isn't quite the right word—more kind of wrongheaded. Like these student riots where an innocent bystander gets hit on the head. Probably by the police." Quite spiteful, though she was more tranquil than Agnes, who knitted as though in a rage with the wool. More coordinated. Came from being a nurse, perhaps. "Somebody unbalanced—look at the Boston Strangler, or that young man who got up in a tower and shot a whole lot of people for no reason at all. If you worked in a hospital, you'd understand that," she told him kindly.

"If you had known Father as we knew him," Agnes said thoughtfully, "he was always getting mixed up in odd situations and weird people; the house used to be full of them, artists, all quite cracked, with grudges and grievances—what d'you call them?"

"Psychopath," supplied Agatha-the-nurse. Weren't they odd ones, apparently convinced that a police officer in the criminal brigade has less experience than a nurse in the accident ward. Lack of imagination.

"Not necessarily anyone we'd know," Agnes went on, "or that Anna would know. Since he'd become poor, he was too proud to bring people home. This theory you've apparently got about Denis Lynch is just too idiotic for words."

"You know Denis?"

"Of course I do; he used to come to me for German lessons—we have our living to earn, you know. Nice boy, considering his background—that so-called Senator is purely and simply an offense to humanity." It sounded like one of Jim Collins's political opinions.

"*I* think it was a stranger," said Agatha. "People carrying daggers; I've known them with the weirdest things in their pockets. Somebody Father spoke to or maybe snapped at for treading on his toe—he was very sharp, you know, and had a very sarcastic tongue. And very little patience with fools," she added, rather cleverly: Van der Valk felt like getting up and bowing.

"Just like you," said Agnes, who plainly had heard of his adventure with much pleasure. "*You* couldn't say that the car which hit you had killed you or tried to."

Agatha took the needle full of knitting, tucked it under her armpit, and with the empty needle scratched unself-consciously round the clip of her bra, quite unconcerned about the presence of a stupid policeman going on about her father's death. This absence of tenseness struck Van der Valk.

Figures danced meaninglessly across the television

screen; Agnes had turned the sound down out of perfunctory politeness, but had left the picture to show him clearly how little he was wanted. He didn't like the room much. An ordinary room in a small Victorian house, but furnished with a garish ostentation.

"Of course," went on Agnes, "Denis met Father, who was probably showing him round Amsterdam. But if you really can't find anyone better than that to suspect—well, you must be pretty incompetent is all I can say. As for coming snooping round here, well, Jim—my husband—wouldn't be best pleased is all I can say." And all these people can say always does include such a very great deal. . . .

Agatha was a bit more conciliatory. A nurse—tactful. "It does seem an awful waste of time. I simply can't imagine what you go wandering around Dublin for. Even if Denis could tell you anything, he isn't here. He's in Rome, by the way," to her sister. "Stasie got a card from him." Agnes made a pooh sound; what was that to her?

"Did your husband know your father?" he asked Agatha.

"Met him a few times—no, not when he lived here —not for a few years now. He was here on trips, a time or two."

"I'd be interested in his opinion." No reaction.

"Well, he's not here—he's gone to the pictures. He goes often; it rests his nerves."

"No real importance," he said vaguely. "Well, thank you for the courteous welcome and your patience." A whisky bottle was standing on a tray with glasses, but he wasn't getting offered any!

"Don't mention it, but if you take my advice you'll be getting back to Holland. There's nothing here to interest you. Our private lives are our own—and you don't get away with invasion of privacy here." He got the message! They knew, of course, about Denis and Stasie; they must know. But they didn't, he thought, know what big Jim Collins was up to in his spare time. Or their little sister! So much for the conspiracy theory.

The lovely ladies of Belgrave Square are either very stupid or . . . No, they can't be that stupid!

He left, with an impression that the moment his back was turned the two of them would be having a violent quarrel.

"They don't know anything at all," he muttered. "I wonder if even Stasie really knows herself."

Inspector Flynn had had a sudden idea. "Did you maybe bed her a tiny bit on purpose?" awed at so much wickedness.

"Not really on purpose. Kind of half and half. Like her a bit. One decides to—or not to—and then one wavers, because of—oh, fear or shame or scruple, or anything you like, maybe worry at being found out, and you end up doing or not doing it because you just can't help yourself."

"The cork theory, is it, now? Floating along according to the whims of the current?"

"More or less," vaguely. What did it matter what you called it? He couldn't explain—he didn't need to, either; this fellow was quite bright enough to see for himself: he wasn't a fool. What will Stasie do next?

He had wanted to get closer to her. Well, he had. Right up against her. There was a nick in his finger-nail that caught irritatingly on his pullover; he opened the small blade of his knife, cut a smooth edge carefully, and flipped the knife at the table, where it stuck for once, quivering in a nervous, sensitive way.

"Destroying the good government equipment," said Flynn. "I'm wondering now whether perhaps this wasn't a clever thing to have done."

"I've no idea," retrieving the knife, flipping it again, and spearing an empty cigarette packet.

"Saint Sebastian, that's who you are. All stuck full with arrows. The Senator Lynch will be shooting a few off at you, too."

"I wonder what's happened to Denis."

There had been about five occasions in his life when he had had to put on a dinner jacket. The fancy dress did not irritate him: this was a carnival; very well, dress up. The dinner jacket fitted well; the secret of these hire places was to have good stuff, well cut, standing up to the cleaning. One paid a high price—as for most things, including understanding. No difference really between Lynch and Stasie. One had to obey these people's "rules." The Lynch world —the more important, perhaps, to obey its rules since Denis had slipped outside them. And it was a test, again. Lynch's confidence depended on himself being house-trained, as the civil servants put it.

The sling was too white and too smelly in a nasty hospital way. He threw it out, and tried a black silk scarf instead. Better. Hurt my wrist playing polo.

The formal invitation had said seven-thirty for eight, so he made it seven-forty-five precisely and the maid took his trench coat without disapproval. Being tall and big-boned had been some use when he'd been a rookie trainee on the streets, and it still served a

181

purpose. But he needed a little cord, a tiny little Legion of Honor or something, really.

There were several guests. There was an old gentleman in a monocle from the Belgian Embassy, who spoke a few polite words in careful, formal Dutch, like a District Commissioner addressing the natives. Van der Valk, with no wish to get caught in linguistic problems of the Brussels suburbs, answered in French, whereat the old gentleman smiled and began a series —which lasted all evening—of rapid, brilliant, devious comic stories. There was also a Dublin surgeon and his wife, both covered in what Arlette called les marques extérieurs de la richesse. He was a big, fat man, interested in criminology and the reform of the penal code: Van der Valk was found wanting, slightly, here. There was also an old lady in petunia satin who began over the glasses of sherry by asking him whether he had read Proust. He did not come too well out of this, either, but it made the old monocled gentleman chuckle.

"When the Duke was on his way to an evening party, and met by agitated female relatives announcing the death of his cousin—a piece of news he had been dreading all day, since he was greatly looking forward to this particular party—he climbed resolutely into his carriage saying, 'People do exaggerate so.' "

"An answer I've always wanted to give when told about people's deaths," said Van der Valk, winning back a bit of ground.

During dinner, which was grand enough for him to eye all the little trinkets and be grateful it wasn't the asparagus season, he was told a good deal about the Common Market, about which he knew little. Everyone was a mine of information, including himself. The food was good, the wine very. The soufflé might have had too much sugar in it. Mrs. Lynch took the ladies away—he had wondered about this phenomenon—and port was produced. It all went on, rather. Did one have to tell dirty stories? He never could remember any. He was relieved to find it wasn't Lynch's style.

But was it going on all night? He was beginning to wonder whether he was being made a fool of, fiddling with a little gold cup holding two drops of lukewarm coffee, terrified that somebody would begin talking about art, when he was suddenly liberated by the old gentleman taking polite leave of him. It was a signal; the old lady went off to read Proust in bed, the surgeon had to operate at seven-forty-five next morning, a very pretty young American girl (fancied, distinctly, despite Stasie) had a whole sheaf of lecture notes to go through, and he was still bowing politely, more or less, when both Lynches reappeared suddenly in the drawing room and said, "Please take another cigar." It was, he realized bemusedly, his cue.

"Denis," said Senator Lynch as he slowly passed the cigar cutter. "Denis," he said again, striking a match. He blew a long symmetrical plume of smoke as though he were a bronze Renaissance fountain and said, "I haven't seen Denis at all."

Van der Valk blew smoke back. We're like two old battleships, he thought, at Jutland or somewhere, firing away like mad even when there's nothing to be seen. It was important not to get flustered. He had got flustered once that day already, and was still none too sure what it mightn't lead to.

"But I don't think you brought me here to tell me nothing but that. My wife has read Proust. She knows, too, a lot more than I do about the Common Market. And myself, when I hear of somebody's death, I'm in a poor position to say that people do exaggerate so. It might be misunderstood."

"I haven't finished," said Lynch. He turned suddenly to his wife. "You tell him," he said abruptly.

She had been looking very good. Dark blue velvet, a sapphire-and-diamond necklace, earrings and eyes to match. But as he turned toward her the sparkle went out of the sapphires.

"He has vanished," she said.

"Completely?" asked Van der Valk with adrenaline whisking into his bloodstream.

"Completely."

"He knew you were coming?"

"I can't turn up totally unannounced," said Lynch simply, "even in a friend's house. I gave very little notice. I rang from the airport, saying I had unexpected business in Rome—expecting and getting an invitation to lunch."

"Yes, of course. But then?"

"I could hardly ask my friend not to mention my arrival, could I?" The voice had lost the mannered, pompous inflection. "My host—I need hardly say he is considerably upset—noticed nothing untoward. Denis received news of my coming at breakfast, apparently unperturbed, remained tranquil. Said little. Did not appear at lunch. Has been missing since."

"Took no clothes or luggage?"

"No—well, there's a certain confusion. The day before, he was at the beach, and had a bag. This morning, he had beach things with him. The bag is missing. His other clothes are untouched. The infer-

184

ence seems to be . . . that he went toward the beach."

"The police?"

"Have been informed," reluctantly. "Have . . . so far . . . found no trace of him."

"And now please forgive a brutally professional question. Mrs. Lynch—do you think . . . ?"

She faced him with firmness.

"That he drowned himself? Does one ever? I mean accept such an idea, without a fight?"

"Go on."

"I mean that one says—I suppose without thinking of it—that a person is not capable of such-and-such an action. And then—when one comes to think of it . . . It's not in his character. He doesn't run away in front of difficulties. It's not like him—I can't believe it."

No, thought Van der Valk, looking at her and at Lynch in turn: nor do I. Except that one never knows. When there is an unknown quantity, and that quantity is called Stasie . . . I better keep quiet, he thought.

"You came straight back here," to Lynch.

"I wished in the circumstances to be with my wife," staring into Van der Valk's face. "Not entirely abnormal, that. And . . . what could I do, anyhow?"

"And since then—no news?"

"You understand, Commissaire, that this is being handled . . . diplomatically, if you follow me."

"I'm only too aware of it," not without bitterness.

Mrs. Lynch got up suddenly, came over, and sat down beside him. "Please, please don't be angry. We are doing our best. We will do our best. We won't try to hinder you; you must do what you think right. Try and be patient, try to believe—we haven't hidden Denis or encouraged him to hide. Whatever lies be-

185

hind this awful story—one faces things when one has to."

Lynch had seen that Van der Valk was exasperated, and had understood. "You saw Monsieur de Coninck here tonight," making his mind up. "The gentleman with the monocle. He looks an antiquated dilettante. It's a mistake to think that. Well, be that as it may, he is acting for me in this affair. He is an ex-diplomat—he has great experience, and—and considerable influence," he went on hurriedly, flustered for all his command over himself by the bleak stony eye. "He is acting for me in this affair. He has been in touch with Rome—with the Embassy, with the Ministry of the Interior—with the police. My wife is right —I intend to see this business through. I have nothing to hide from you."

"Very well," said Van der Valk abruptly. "What do the police say?" He suddenly realized that he was stone-cold sober and badly in need of a drink. Mrs. Lynch, whether she read his thoughts or not, made no offer, but picked up the decanter and gave him a slosh.

"Coninck heard from them tonight. They say they don't think the boy was drowned, because they would probably have found him by now."

Quite so, but could one believe them? He disposed of the slosh and got another right away. His face must have been showing his skepticism.

"Well—they're formal: what can one say? Try and understand that if I had not contacted you earlier, it was in hope that the boy would turn up."

Helped by the slosh, Van der Valk made an effort. "All right, there's been time lost; it's too late to worry about it. You realize that I have to make a report to my superiors. I hope that Monsieur de Coninck has good relations with The Hague."

"He has," said Mrs. Lynch. Van der Valk did think of saying "Oh, Jaysus," or possibly "Janey Mac," a euphemism Mr. Flynn seemed fond of, but he was past it.

"Why did you give this party tonight?"

"Several reasons," quietly and slowly, "not all of them bad. I planned it. I wished to gain some distance, some detachment, to impose a balanced frame of mind and to mature my thoughts. I wished to get a grip upon my self-command, and, ridiculous though you may find the notion, these conventional patterns of civilized society are a considerable help to me in forming judgments. It is also true that Coninck wished for an opportunity to meet you—for God's sake man, don't take offense," for Van der Valk was again beginning to bristle.

"Nobody is going to interfere with you, Commissaire," said Mrs. Lynch's soft voice. "You are on the spot. You will judge. You do not yet know that Monsieur de Coninck is not an interfering old busybody. He is an old, trusted, valued—proved—friend of ours. That is nothing to you and of course I understand that. But he has unusually clear judgment. He agreed at once that you must be given a free hand but what is of more importance to you is that he can be of considerable service to you."

Van der Valk shrugged his shoulders. "You don't see that this affair goes beyond the little local framework—it's going to explode. The moment The Hague hears about this, I will be called back for what the press calls consultations and what I call getting my orders. I won't have any free hand. This piece of news

—this disappearance—will mean a lengthy panic. After which somebody will have the exceptionally brilliant idea of sending me to Rome. I'm nothing but a goddam tourist."

"I think," very gently, "that if Monsieur de Coninck were to have the good fortune to be taken into your confidence, he could persuade your authorities—The Hague, as you put it—that you were the best judge of whatever steps needed to be taken. Is it pardonable to ask what your—what's the word?—your ideas have led to? I mean it isn't just Denis. There's a—there are other factors; isn't it so?"

He took his brandy glass and moved it from side to side so that it caught the light. "Perhaps," at last, "you've been wondering why I ate mostly with my one hand."

"Not particularly," politely. "Americans always do."

"I have a broken collarbone. My arm should be in a sling, strictly speaking, but I took it off because it's healing well, and because I thought it seemed a little ostentatious. But this scarf isn't so formidable."

"And how do you come to have a broken collarbone?" asked Lynch with careful courtesy.

"Somebody tried to hit me on the head."

There was an appropriate silence.

"Coninck," said Lynch at last, "lives just two minutes from here—I could perhaps give him a phone call."

"The Irish police can hardly be left totally in the dark—perhaps you'll leave that to me to handle." Everybody wants to get into the act, Van der Valk was thinking wryly, wondering about the old gentleman with the monocle.

"Coninck has your total confidence?" he went on.

"As I assure you."

"And you're prepared to give me the same?"

"Yes."

"You mean that?"

"I mean that," said Mrs. Lynch.

"Then, yes, I'd like to talk to him on the phone. I suppose your line's not tapped?"

Something of the old Terence Lynch reappeared around the lines of the Senator's mouth. "Make yourself easy. I know how to protect myself. It is my son, apparently, whom I have failed to protect," he added.

Monsieur de Coninck would be more than pleased to have a little talk with Monsieur le Commissaire. Yes, that little affaire; he was au courant. . . . Why, yes, he did think perhaps he could be of some use: to talk of influence . . . but he was fortunate in having the ear of various people. . . . In the morning? My dear fellow, he was good for nothing in the mornings. If the Commissaire was not too tired right now, there was no time like the present and he had a cigar on which he would value an opinion. . . . Just around the corner. My dear fellow, I will be expecting you.

It was only in the street, in Ailesbury Road, that Van der Valk was struck by an idea that was now of increased importance. That the gap between Senator Lynch's world and, say, Eddy Flanagan was pretty wide. Flynn had made the point; perhaps neither had given it enough weight. The Lynch house, the Lynch life—a carefully constructed machine in which standards—old-fashioned use of the word—were important, and were respected. Dinner jackets, formal manners, and place settings, well-trained servants, silver boxes, courteous diplomacies, the elaborate code that belonged at first sight to a world of before 1939—these had their use. Lynch had decided that this was the way to lead one's life. The man was far from ridiculous.

Denis had been part of this life. The boy had been trained in polite conversation to old dears like the Proust lady. He had known how to ring for the footman, had grown up with the poise and the polish, and the confidence. And then he had fallen into the world of the lovely ladies, and the table talk of Jim Collins. What effect this had had remained to be seen—but the change in his thinking would have been massive.

Monsieur de Coninck lived in a ground-floor flat in a somber, heavy brick house with many laurel bushes masking the windows, a flat which lent a new dimension to Van der Valk's thought, for this was not just a world before '39 but before '14. Light from heavily shaded lamps gleamed on his own lapels and his white shirt. The old gentleman's shirt had one of the antique bosoms that had to be starched. He had undone his tie and put on a quilted dressing gown that had been bought from Hildritch & Key forty years ago. The monocle, on a broad ribbon of black watered silk, gleamed on the faded sage-green satin.

There was a musty smell of dapper old bachelor. The place was full of furniture and bric-à-brac; books in their shelves climbed to the ceiling, and if their owner wished to climb, too, there was a mahogany stepladder with a padded leather seat at the top. There were pieces of china, of faïence, of Venetian glass, and a silver inkstand. There were things only to be seen in the Army & Navy Stores catalogue—smoking stands of great complexity and a tantalus with heavy cut-glass decanters. There were beads, bobbles, and fringes; there were faded water-color paintings of Swiss Alps made by whiskered Victorians in knicker-bockers; there were framed autograph letters from heaven knew whom—Bismarck and Count Metter-nich, probably.

The old boy was very spry. He pottered in and out of tables, cleared back numbers of the *Connoisseur* off for Van der Valk to sit, produced some astonishing whisky—straight malt unblended, apparently as old as he was—lit a Balkan Sobranie, sat in a nest of manu-script notes—diplomat's memoirs, or a monograph on the hundred and sixty kinds of tobacco ash?—and said, "I give you, my dear Commissaire, my closest at-tention."

Van der Valk spoke for perhaps twenty minutes without any interruptions. When he did get a reaction, it was brisk.

"An excellent synthesis. What it lacks in lucidity, here and there, is more than compensated by the little imaginative touches—illuminating, that, very. Will you permit me to add something, conceivably, to a point or so you find obscure. This man Flanagan—you are puzzled by his attitude."

"I don't follow his indifference—it can't be ignor-ance; he must have known about it."

"You've never read P. G. Wodehouse?—perhaps not your generation, no, but mine, my dear fellow. He illustrates an attitude most useful in diplomacy. When faced with an unpleasant or embarrassing situation, merely to pretend it doesn't exist is insufficient. One must maintain firmly, positively, that it does not and cannot exist. Most useful in matters of adultery," with relish. "Attitude known as 'stout denial.' I should sug-gest that Mr. Flanagan is not such a fool as he looks—

191

whether, by the way, the process of stout denial is conscious or unconscious is of small importance, n'est-ce pas?"

"What do you make of the attack on me?"

"I don't think I've much to add. The very frightened person—that goes without saying. The confirmation of your certainty of guilty knowledge is more dubious. Intrigue for intrigue's sake, violence—there's a certain relish—a pleasure taken in the heady mixture of violence and intrigue. Sexual satisfaction?—we mustn't look too closely. As for the astonishing stupidity, *that* causes me no surprise. In any kind of crisis, behavior of staggering crassness is commonplace: everyday in diplomacy, that; it flourishes most rankly in little closed groups—ministries, secretariats, all crying examples. Insufficient fresh air, insufficient contact with everyday common sense. This little family group, so oddly turned in upon itself, belongs, I should say, to the category. . . . This woman coming to seduce you," chuckling with robust Edwardian glee, wishing it had happened to him—or perhaps recalling when it had, "she sounds great fun."

Van der Valk enjoyed the antique phrase.

"Blackmail will be the next step, no doubt," as though it were the most natural thing in the world.

"Ah," said Van der Valk. "I'd been wondering about that."

"Has it, by the way, occurred to you that Denis has vanished rather suddenly? It strikes me as being a little pat. Explosion—puff of smoke—trap door—pantomime demon . . ."

"I hadn't thought about it. His father's arrival caused a panic, I suppose, and precipitated him. You mean that she tipped him off in some way? Too deliberate and conscious an act, I should have thought. I may be reading her all wrong, but I think she's trying to make a stout denial, as you put it, that her father's dead at all. It doesn't work—keeps blowing up in her face. Hence her very unbalanced reactions."

"Anastasia," said Coninck reflectively. "I like her coming to the hotel like that . . . great fun. Now, let me see. There's bound to be an uproar; my dear friend Betty Lynch has enlisted me. . . . I take it that your immediate authority, for administrative convenience, will be the Embassy?"

"A man called Slavenburg—a counselor of some sort."

"A man called Slavenburg. . . . I'll talk to the Ambassador, I think; I know him well." No dogsbodies.

"But the decision, I should think, rests with the Procureur Général in Amsterdam. From the political angle, Lord knows who—The Hague. . . . This boy Denis must be found."

"Quite. The Procureur?"

"Yes, Mr. Sailer," Van der Valk said.

"Not Tony Sailer?"

"That's right."

"What is it that you want, Commissaire?"

"Not to have the boy chased, I should think. He'll turn up—or perhaps I should say that we can probably find him quickly enough when we really want him. More urgently, *I* don't want to be chased. I don't suppose I'm telling you anything new, but the problem for a police officer is that he's practically never left in peace to get on with his job."

"The problem is fairly familiar to me," dryly. "Suppose I say to you, in confidence, and I use that abused word literally, to mean that I will trust you

193

and that you can trust me—suppose I say to you that I
I can take Tony Sailer off your back. I add, in the
hope that I cause you no offense, that I am concerned
with a highly valued friendship, with persons I love
and esteem, more than I am with the adventures of—
ah, this eccentric young woman of yours."

It took Van der Valk a moment to sort out this diplomatic syntax: he said he would be very happy.

"I was thinking of asking him," he said to Inspector
Flynn next morning, "what he thought about Denis
when he took the words out of my mouth. Don't know
anything about Denis, he says. I'm eighty years old
and I know a lot about men, but I know nothing
about adolescent boys. After which I got told it was
my bedtime and I'd better pop along, which I did.
Have you ever read Proust?"

"No."

"Nor me. Maybe he'd teach us to understand the
adolescent boy."

"Don't want to understand the adolescest boy,"
said Flynn. "Too many fellers doing that in the world
as it is."

"Source of this whole trouble."

"Yes, yes, but eff the adolescent boy—only figura-
tively, that is," he added cautiously. "I mean I've
enough on me own plate right now. What are these
Italians doing?"

"Been instructed to drop it. Got the fellow at the
Vatican to say that if the boy indulges in a fugue it's
better not to hunt him. Leave 'em alone and they'll
come home. Wonder where he's got to," reflectively.

"Shouldn't think it much matters. Be more inclined
meself to ask where he'd turn up."

"You're a man in my own heart."

"After, it would be," automatically.

"What's that mean, after my heart?"

"No idea; the English is a loony language. Why we use it is anyone's guess."

"Like where Denis turns up."

"Right here, my guess would be."

"You think so? He's just run away blindly, no? Why did he go to Rome? To gain time, no? Put your head under the sheet and hope the nasty men will go away. These people always do that. Say they want to be alone to think things out. Boy must realize he's in trouble, but it's like getting out of bed on a cold winter morning; he's going to count slowly to fifty first. Do you think it possible that Stasie tipped the boy off? Doesn't make sense to me."

"Why not? We've no way of controlling it. If you're right about her, she's too dotty anyway to worry about being accessory after the fact or aiding a fugitive or whatnot. Because there isn't any fact. Anyway, why shouldn't he have contacted her? He sends her a card saying 'Having fun,' but why shouldn't he phone, say? I'd think he feels bewildered and looks for reassurance. . . . Oh, damn it; I don't know."

"Nobody loves me neither."

"What are you doing about that?"

"Going to make Stasie love me," said Van der Valk, grinning.

Mr. Slavenburg was perplexed, but not showing it.

"The Ambassador would like to see you," careful to sound neither menacing nor disapproving.

Monsieur de Coninck was spry, no doubt about it.

"Good morning, Excellency."

"Ah, Van der Valk; sit down, sit down. This Lynch affair. I gather you are aware of this recent development—mmm, precipitates matters, hmm?"

"I just hope it won't go precipitating me."

"I certainly don't think you should do anything hastily. I am not myself fully briefed on your activities: not my fish, shall I say?—see no need to concern myself with the frying of it: however. I am aware that in such circumstances you will be seeking fresh instructions: I wished merely to tell you that your view of the matter—I've had copies of your reports under my eye, naturally—that your handling of the matter seems proper, and that I should be disposed to endorse any eventual approval of the way you see fit to conduct your—uh, investigation. In the event of an adverse decision, of course, I would not feel called upon to criticize the Ministry's judgment. I wouldn't be exactly discontented, either," with a pleasant smile. "Am I clear, eh?"

"Yes, Excellency."

"As for calling the Irish judicial authorities into consultation, I should be inclined at the present to—to leave the door open; in fact, uh, not to put too fine a point upon it, to do nothing. Your liaison man—he's au fait? Good, and he gives you no cause to believe that they view your activities as, uh, undesirable? Very good, very good, we'll say no more. You will continue, of course, to keep Mr. Slavenburg informed: I need hardly say that from our standpoint the fullest possible reports are the essential feature of your work here. We'll take it all as said. You're comfortable? Looking after you all right? Yes, well, so they should; lot of money being spent—however, long as it's all properly accounted for. Very good, Van der Valk, I needn't keep you."

Amiable enough. Feeling his rear comparatively secure, he bought a large map of the environs of Dublin and spent a pleasant hour studying it. Around lunchtime, an Embassy messenger brought an envelope containing a telegram that had—knowing Mr. Sailer—probably been succinct enough to start with but had been translated into jargon by some diplomatic code clerk.

INSTRUCTIONS UNCHANGED STOP. YOU WILL TAKE ALL REASONABLE STEPS CONSISTENT WITH PRUDENCE FOR INTERVIEWING WITNESS AT LARGE STOP. SHOULD CONCLUSION SAME ABUT ON DESIRABILITY OF APPREHENSION SAID WITNESS YOU WILL CONSULT EMBASSY WHO WILL CONDUCT NECESSARY DÉMARCHES IRISH JUDICIARY STOP. NO STEPS TO BE TAKEN WITHOUT CONSULTATION IRISH POLICE STOP. ESSENTIAL ALL FORMS IRISH JUDICIAL PROCEDURE FOLLOWED STOP. DISCRETIONARY POWERS CONFERRED SUBSEQUENT EXTREME PRUDENCE ENJOINED ENDS. ORIGINATED PROCURER GÉNÉRALS OFFICE PROVINCE NORTH HOLLAND SIGNED SAILER.

He had lunch alone in the corner of a corner table, in the hotel restaurant, both flanks anchored like Ernest Hemingway.

Since getting hit on the head, he had had his eye open a good deal. He did not know much about Mr. Collins, but felt fairly sure nobody had been dogging his footsteps. Still, so far, he had strolled around on foot and used public transport. His expense account having been passed absolutely without a murmur by the Embassy comptroller, he was now thinking of hum, enlarging his scope of action, and approaching the invaluable Mr. Ryan for a little self-drive car. Nothing can be done in Dublin without one Mr. Ryan or another. He found that Dublin traffic took a bit of practice, but he passed a comfortable afternoon and nobody followed him.

"Hallo?"

"Oh, it's you."

"That's right. I promised to ring you. Things to talk about."

"So you did. That would be nice."

"Can I talk?"

"Yes, but not here."

"Oh, I wouldn't want to compromise you."

"No harm done. As it happens, it's good timing. Eddy's going to Liverpool—oh, that happens quite often. The planes don't suit, so he takes the night boat. So that I'm at a loose end, a bit. Perhaps we could go out somewhere."

"That sounds nice."

"Have you got a car?"

"Yes."

"Why don't you pick me up at the top of Temple Hill where the road branches off to Bray—you know? Not at the house, I rather think."

"No. What time?"

"Around half past seven?"

"Understood."

Darling Arlette,

Wound up in a most involved intrigue, which would amuse you greatly; impossible woman going to extraor-

198

dinary lengths to throw confusion and embarrassment into the Martínez business. Her latest gag is to implicate me in a kind of complicity—the workings of her mind!—and there is a seducation act going on—there, the subconscious of my typewriter has produced just the right word. She is at the bottom of the still-unexplained behavior of the boy, and now perhaps it will be my turn for some of the sentimental seducation! Damn, there's the phone again. . . . My laddie Flynn waiting for me downstairs. I'll get this finished tomorrow—we've got to plot a bit of tactics, and then I have a dinner date with the lady. . . . Full report then! À tout à l'heure . . .

PART THREE

ROSEMEYER'S CAR
WAS WAITING

Van der Valk had always had a taste for risk. Arlette
was fond of saying that it was bad taste. . . . He had
a Nordic streak of sentimentality, too, which she didn't
like. It tended to come moistly out at melodramatic
moments. Like the time he had been in hospital, im-
mobilized in plaster from the waist down, after an
adventure that had finished rather badly for all concerned. Arlette had been with him all evening, for
the next morning the plaster was due to come off, and
one was not quite certain how much movement there
would be. He himself was wondering whether he
would walk—whether he would ever walk. . . . He
started talking about his childhood, in broadest nos-
talgic vein.

"Must have been just before the war—'38, '39. I
was about sixteen, I suppose, going through the
racing-car craze. It wasn't like now, everything so cut
and dried, so dull somehow. The drivers, too, seem so

drab nowadays—serious, dedicated little technicians, just like astronauts. Then there was a human element: drivers did extraordinary things—the cars, too, sometimes; things exploded, or the tires flew off. My big hero was Nuvolari, Tazio Nuvolari, the Mantovano Volante. Once, his motor caught fire—he got out on the back and steered with his feet till the car lost speed enough for him to jump off.

"It was beginning to get dull, because the German cars out-classed all the others—oh, there were Alfas still, and Talbots and Maseratis, but Mercedes won everything. Caracciola, and Lang, and Manfred von Brauchitsch—and an English boy, too, called Dick Seaman. . . . I remember his getting killed on the Nürburgring, on the humpbacked bridge."

Arlette didn't at all like this talk of getting killed: she was rather bored, too. But if he wanted to talk . . .

"Most of the other drivers joined the only team able to keep up; Auto Union, another German lot—funny cars; you sat in front of the engine, and they were tricky to drive. Nuvolari, of course. And there was a young German boy with a great deal of talent, good-looking boy, all very romantic, called Berend Rosemeyer, who became a popular hero."

"Not mine," said Arlette, who had been ten, skipping a rope, very carefully brought up, forbidden to see Walt Disney's *Snow White* because it was both vulgar and frightening.

"Hitler was very keen on all this; you know, enjoyed winning. The car firms got given lots of money, and of course won more and more easily, and looked for other fields to conquer, and they started building very low streamlined cars—painted silver, rather pretty, very spectacular—and began breaking speed records on the Autobahnen, which were new then—all adding up to a fine bit of national propaganda, you get it?"

"I do recall how terribly cross they were over Jesse Owens winning everything."

"Yes, but he wasn't a car, alas. Mercedes and Auto Union, ding-dong, and it developed into a sort of personal match between Caracciola and Rosemeyer. Old and young, plain and good looking, the Rudi and the Berend."

"Sounds a bit one-sided."

"Oh, no, the Rudi had tremendous prestige. He'd won everything, and he'd been in dozens of crashes, broken his legs so often that he limped in a funny way . . . like me—I hope. . . ."

"Not like you," firmly, "but go on anyway."

"It wasn't like a race—only one car went at a time, measured along a special stretch, fantastic speeds, I don't recall, but getting on for three hundred kilometers an hour. One day there was bad weather, strong gusting wind, I think, and everyone said oh, well, no racing today. But Caracciola was hanging about, and said the hell with it, and got in his car and made the best time yet."

Silence; the man was remembering excitement. Heroics: it was 1939; heroics had still a couple of years to run.

"A bit like a ski competition—you know, Jean-Claude or whoever still at the top and word coming back an Austrian has made the best time ever."

"I do see." Arlette was getting interested despite herself.

"Next day there were huge newspaper reports, very highly colored journalese—but what I remember is the photo of the car standing there, and the caption underneath: 'Rosemeyer's car was waiting.' "

But she had not understood. "But what happened?"

"Sorry, of course you didn't know. He got killed. The moment he heard that Caracciola had broken the record, he got in and went off. He was going faster still, and the side wind caught him, veered him straight off the road into the woods. It's near Mannheim somewhere, you can still see where; the Germans put a little plaque, saying, 'Here he laid down his life,' or something. Word to that effect."

"But why did he do anything so foolish?"

"But he had to."

And what put that in my head, thought Van der Valk, I just can't think. He wasn't much of a Rosemeyer bumping out along Leeson Street in Mr. Ryan's rather smelly, very dreary, not quite new Ford. Not even much of a Caracciola, except of course for the limp, and perhaps the face a bit. The hammy face of his youth, the beaming chubby look of Baby Cadum, had been gone a good while now. As for the lines, he shaved them every morning and was used to them, but now and then, when pain or fatigue got the better of him, he did notice that an innocent idealistic Dutch face had acquired a few claw marks. It could be worse; he was not yet embittered. The face looked out still jovial enough and—he was a little astonished—quite kind. Not as big a bastard as all that.

Nor as clever, he said nastily to the driving mirror. You enjoy playing the part of crafty old Rudi: Schranz the super skier, that's me; wily Karli the Old Fox of the Arlberg (except when journalists forgot and called him the Old Lion). But have the courage now to admit that just for a tiny moment back there you weren't the old fox of any damn berg, not even a Dutch one—not by a very long stretch of virgin snow you weren't. In fact, Stasie took you for a fast ride downhill on your face. You may have pretended to Flynn that you knew where you were going, but in fact now you're just trying to get your own back, you're playing her a filthy trick, and in short you're not detergent-white one bit, one bit; you're a chewed dog biscuit.

Good old Rudi drove soberly out through Donnybrook, cut across Ailesbury Road to the seafront, and trundled along to Temple Hill, feeling more ashamed of himself than triumphant, and well he might.

Lovely fine warm evening, would be a lovely sunset, pity to spoil it. Stasie wearing a coat of some rough cottony material, an attractive pinkish gray, looking, he was bound to say, very pretty. Huge appealing grin that would have been more appealing still if one hadn't suspected it of being well practiced. But it was appealing all the same; an immense glee at skipping school, a great big happy laugh at playing such a fine trick on all the good bourgeois. The grin was so naughty—and the coat so enveloping—that he had a suspicion she hadn't anything on underneath, and was relieved when she took the coat off: respectable skirt and an Italian print shirt. Hair was loose today, falling informally to shoulders. Looked young and vulnerable, and he was not convinced that it was altogether put on. On the contrary, he thought that she was genuinely—spontaneously—out just to enjoy herself and found himself wondering if he wasn't, for the second time in two days, due to make a horrible great ass of himself.

Need a few quick drinks, he thought, rubbing his nose furiously with his forefinger.

"Where are we going?"

"Stepaside."

"Oh, good." She burst out laughing, possibly at a memory. "Well done you. But how do you know about Stepaside?"

"Found it on the map, and who could resist that? Seems there's a place one can eat."

"There is, too. And a very nice view, all over Dublin."

"They know you there?"

"No, no, have no fear; I know how to be discreet. I've hardly been there in ages; knew it well once, but then it was just Doyle's pub. You know the way?"

"Well, if I go wrong you'll be able to put me right, won't you?"

"Yes. I used to go to school around here. Will you give me one of your nice cigarettes? No, don't bother, I can light it for myself."

Stupid to be caught lagging behind all the time! Stasie was a very agreeable companion. Why not? She was an intelligent, educated woman. And moreover Martínez's daughter. Had it not been the progressive unfolding of a rich and intricate character that had first captivated him, back in Holland? Had it not been apparent that of his children Stasie was the one closest to him? In sympathy with his theatrical manner, understanding—and practicing—his little tricks and subterfuges? He thought of the fine white hands, the very good gold signet, the casual play with the Mercedes ignition keys.

Familiar, too, was the adaptability. There is nothing to be surprised at, he told himself. The petty suburban background—the world of knitting, sitting small children on the pot, and getting the dishes washed—had not seemed in the least jarring in Belgrave Square. Stasie shopping in the supermarket, pushing a pram, a tatty scarf disguising the hair in curlers—no sense of shock there. Dutch housewife! Stasie Number 2, who came to visit him in his hotel room—well, yes, a shock. But not a huge shock; he had at least suspected that one's existence. And this one . . . very poised, quite the sophisticate, ordering expensive food and plenty to drink in the languid way of someone who does so every day. . . . Martínez had been just the same. It had been, no doubt, this many-sided charm and vitality that had delighted Denis.

No, what got Van der Valk was her ease and fluency, the unself-conscious confidence with the policeman investigating her father's death. Who suspected her of complicity. And whom she had calmly climbed into bed with. Now, that was dotty, surely. A bit simple, that. Stasie was not that simple.

"Do you mind if I give Agatha a buzz? She's at home this evening. I like someone to look in on the children from time to time." The simplicity of this was engaging in such a devious woman.

"Of course. Give her my love." Tickled, she laughed. As with Mrs. Lynch, he had earned a good mark.

The sunset, and the twilight over the hills, and the sweep of Dublin Bay below him was all that he had hoped, making up for the meal. They had three cups of coffee, and another go of cognac: plenty of time to get their respective troops into position. Her eyes were promising that he wasn't wasting his time and he hoped she was right!

In the car, she snuggled up, a mouth tasting agreeably of herself, flavored with cognac, Gitanes, and fresh lipstick: she had drunk a great deal, and showed no sign of it at all.

"Lovely dinner."

"Marvelous view," he corrected.

"But now I want to drive. Fresh air. And a change of view." Yes, darkness was growing. In fact, darkness was there. Couldn't tell one car from another car.

A little uncanny, almost making the back of his neck prickle, how closely the scenario followed the script he had written! Stasie disposed with artistry, the backs of cars quite the natural habitat of the species. Bits of clothes scattered around—she would have made quite a good impression, too, in the Crazy Horse Saloon. And he himself, hardly able to move at all: not a bad thing, wouldn't be able to make any sudden jumps that might spoil the camera angle. Trying to take this light-hearted view of matters did not prevent its being among the vilest half hours he had spent in his life. In fact, he could only remember one worse: waiting, at the age of eight, with an abscess on a back tooth, in the outpatients' clinic of a busy hospital, knowing that he would be gassed and the tooth extracted. His mother sitting beside him, grimly clutching her handbag, suffering worse than he did. Gassing was like guillotining, quickly over: it was the waiting that was unspeakable. And now, as an adult, he had the keener and more exquisite torments of degradation and humiliation, of conscious knowing hypocisy, of stimulating passion, of artificially inducing desire—of making a hearty meal of gall. I paid there, he thought later, for my moment of lechery.

Even when the flash bulb came blinding in, it was

no relief: it was an anticlimax. He had waited too long for it. No congratulation at having been right, no sense of liberation. He felt he had pulled off the trick the way Sherlock Holmes got out of the Reichenback Falls—by cheating everybody.

Stasie gave a most convincing scream and groveled on the floor. Laboriously, Van der Valk fumbled with the lock and heaved out into grassy-smelling darkness inhabited by a man taller and broader-shouldered than himself, taking attachments off his camera and tucking them busily into pockets.

"Cooked your goose, I think, friend." Native Dublin notes, perhaps blurred by watching the adventures of the cops from the 99th precinct, on the telly. Very cool, being not only bigger but not having any broken bones.

"How do you do, Mr. Collins?" said Van der Valk mildly.

The man was jarred, enough to step backward and go further into his role. Lacks imagination, thought Van der Valk, looking at a large nasty nine-millimeter pistol. "It is a dangerous habit," he said coldly, "to finger loaded firearms in that flustered way."

"No false move, chum." And banal.

"It's not original, either, Jim boy." A hand as big as his own and Jim's put together—or so it very properly seemed—came reaching out of the gloom and took the pistol away.

"It's not even polite," said Inspector Flynn. "Luckily for yourself, I know just how dimwitted your ideas are—creeping about in the dark there like Dr. Fu Manchu—you breathe too heavy."

"I'm afraid that gave you a lot of trouble," said

Van der Valk, grateful to Flynn for being so tactful and not looking at him.

"Sure we're right up to date, then," comfortably, "and when 1930 dawns we'll be there with the very latest technology. We do have the inconspicuous old Chevrolet with the infrared headlamps—picks you out like daylight, it does; read all about it in *True Detective*. These boys are always doing things like this, attacking stagecoaches and the like in the middle of the night. Now, Jim, the hands, please. What are you going to do, then, with your girl friend?" Stasie, wooden, was sullenly smoking in the back of the car. Something else unraveled in that complex person, Van der Valk was thinking. Not only was she getting a considerable kick out of her games, but she was considerably sharpened up by the idea of being snap-shotted playing them. Been let down on both counts.

"I think we all go home to Belgrave Square," he suggested; "one of the few positive points about all this is that Eddy really is away."

"Saw him on to the boat myself, so I did," said Flynn, "the idea isn't bad. Act Three by the cozy fireside, like."

Flynn opened the camera with careful sausage fingers, held the film up to the light, and said, "There, now. Disposes of what we might call the evidence. Needn't mention it again." He sat down heavily.

"No," said Stasie sarcastically. "Doesn't show your pal in a very creditable light, does it?"

"The Commissaire isn't proud of himself," unemotionally, "and neither am I. But don't be too hasty, now, Mrs. Flanagan. Holding the scrap of film up to the light doesn't clean the slate, and I don't much like this situation of yours. You'll be thinking maybe I can't prove anything, and if you did I'd answer you that I don't have to. Jim here—now, we don't have anything on him, of course not. But he goes up, being a stupid man, for illegal possession of a firearm, carriage of same, proffering menaces with same.

"So all we know about you is you're out too late at night. And I take things into consideration, shall we say? I think about the children, maybe, and about Eddy Flanagan, shall I say, and about the Commissaire here who provoked you kind of and isn't too proud of himself. But there are arguments—yes, serious arguments—for charging you with a few things, too. Don't have to cast around, you know. Attempted corruption of a functionary in the course of his duty. Corrupting a functionary isn't a very grave crime in my eyes, because they expect it, shall we say. Withholding material information is, though, and willful misleading of a judical inquiry, and attempt to shield and conceal a fugitive. No, I'm not making threats. I'm suggesting to you you do a bit of serious thinking. I don't want to know anything, and as a consequence I don't ask you to come down the Castle tomorrow and make a written statement."

"If I may suggest," said Van der Valk, "I'll come down the Castle and make the statement. Now that I'm no longer embarrassed by the private eye there, I've got an interrupted conversation to continue, about an accident I had."

"Very good so," agreed Flynn. "You two have a nice cup of tea, while your man and I here will keep one another handy company as far as the Castle. The boys were thinking it was time he did something to earn that great big pension they pay him."

210

"You," said Mr. Collins, "can go and get yourself effed. And you, too," he told Van der Valk.

"But don't say it to your sister-in-law," said Mr. Flynn. "She might take you seriously." Crude, Van der Valk thought; the kind of thing I say, too, sometimes —and yet under the circumstances I couldn't. He was looking at Stasie's face, at once so falsely and so genuinely pathetic.

"The nice cup of tea is a good idea, you know." No answer. "Here, have one of these cigarettes you like." Still no answer. "Understand me, I haven't come to crow over you. What the man said is true; I don't feel pleased with myself. I don't even want to twist your arm, any more than Flynn did. He could have arrested you, you know."

"I've committed no crime," she said angrily. "All the rest is moonshine—imaginary. It's all imaginary. You're just trying to blackmail me."

He had to laugh. "Ah, yes? As you did me?"

"That was just self-protection."

"So was hitting me on the head, no doubt."

"No, no—good God—no—that must have been Jim."

"Must have been," dryly, "but wasn't. I only caught a glimpse—but now that I've met him, it wasn't anyone nearly as big as Jim. Also, Jim's a fool, but not that much of a fool. You have no trouble getting him to follow me tonight, the less because you and he have been pretty pally once upon a time. Jim—or one of his cronies—may have written the little note: he's boastful enough when a bit drunk for that. But he didn't hit me. Without knowing it, maybe, he has a really good alibi, which it took Flynn a day or two to check. You, on the other hand, did."

"You seem to think me capable of any kind of crime," wearily.

"Except that of killing your father." Her tears this time, he thought, were genuine. He himself was feeling the drag of fatigue that told him, with ominous frequency now, that fifty is double twenty-five. He was so sick of it all sometimes. . . .

"Listen, Stasie, listen just for once to another voice instead of that tricky little imp you have there in your head." He was tired, too, of talking English: he wasn't even talking the polite, polished Dutch that Stasie had learned as a child—it had now a stilted sound, with turns of phrase which had almost a prewar ring —but the rough and pithy Dutch of the faubourgs. "Paste it up on your board—there's no way out. You're between the lorry and the wall, and that lorry isn't going to stop. You hadn't succeeded in realizing that if you had got rid of me you'd never have shaken Flynn off. A man in public affairs—I needn't say who —wants the truth. He's going to get it; nothing else will do. His integrity as a man and as a politician means that he'll want it in an open court. A Dutch court. You may not have to go before that court yourself—it's a legal point that neither concerns nor interests me, but you'll have to make Flynn's statement. Now, if you want for once to think of your family, and I mean your husband and not the Martínez family, you can ask me to try and keep your name out of the press. Give me the truth, satisfy me that it's the truth, and I'll do what I can."

"What is it you want?"

"Sooner or later, Denis is going to get in touch with

212

you. He wants to be reassured; he wants to hear your voice. You have to tell him to come to me and say what he knows. He has no choice; he must understand that. He loves you."

"Yes."

"And he trusts you."

"Yes."

It was with some difficulty that he bit back the phrase "heaven help him."

"What did you get out of Jim?" asked Van der Valk, trying not to yawn and failing.

"Didn't get anything out of Jim," said Flynn peacefully. He was cutting his fingernails with a little pair of folding scissors he had searched for and found in his breast pocket. A litter of strange objects had come to light in course of the search, at which Flynn stared with a sort of indignant surprise, as though they had no right to be in his pockets.

"Jim's lips is sealed," he went on tranquilly. "What he calls his honor—you'd think he was in the Mafia or something." It was never any good trying to hurry Flynn. "Whereas, on the other hand, he didn't need to tell me what I knew already. What I think happened is that she got on to him to push you in the canal like, reckoning maybe Jim knew how. He was too fly for that—wasn't having any. But he got a bit loose-mouthed, and this much I know. One of his pals in the boozer wrote that note; they maybe thought themselves funny. What good it was supposed to do is what we call an enigma, but I'd hazard the guess they was both footless at the time."

"Footless?"

"Ach, here in Ireland we wouldn't say a feller was

in a state of intoxication, then: we say he'd drink taken. Now, then, I'd hazard the further guess that Jim went back and told her, still thinking himself funny, and she gets pretty easily into a hysterical state. Set her off to clonk you, like? Don't ask me to explain these women's ideas, but we'd say maybe hearing about this she got mad, reckoning it would lead you straight back to her? Depends what interpretation you want to give the word 'mad.' "

"Right the whole way," said Van der Valk. "She coughed it all up, admits everything. Denis, too. He was dotty about her."

"They were sleeping together?"

"Of course. For a year. Under Eddy's nose. Eddy refused to see it or do anything about it, reckoning that would just be humiliation all round."

"Good for him," said Flynn. "So now you can go back to Holland in a deck chair, with four pretty girls fanning you. What more d'you want? Denis is loose somewhere in Europe. Sooner or later, he'll come back here. I, eejit that I am, will pick him up and give him to you."

"Yes." Unenthusiastic.

"What's bothering you now? She told you the tale, didn't she? What did she do to the boy?"

"That's just it. Genuinely, she hasn't the faintest idea. She can't understand it, she refused to believe it; it sent her into a spin and now"—dryly—"she believes it, but she can't explain it."

Flynn shrugged. "So what? When you have the boy, and put the stories together, you'll explain it—or, rather, the psick man"—pronouncing the *p*—"will do it for you. No crime at all; what they need us for, I ask meself."

214

"Having once done something unbalanced, he's likely to do so again. He must be in a state of uncertainty that would put anyone off their rocker—I don't see him just wandering vaguely round Italy."

"I do. I'd say his idea was to get away from something he only realizes very vaguely, but which presses on him: he knows there's something pretty badly wrong. He bums about—times he forgets all about it. One fine morning, his da turns up and that brings it home all right, and he just bunks. It's so easy. Grow a beard, get in with this hippie crowd; they slop about aimless anywhere. You won't get him yet awhile, but when the cold weather comes there's kind of an icy blast in Italy then; that winkles them out."

"I don't know," said Van der Valk. "I'd say more his one idea was to get home to Mum—Stasie, rather —irrespective of what's happened. Tell her all."

"How he felled her da with the stroke of a loy."

"What?"

"It's the English," said Flynn apologetically. "It's a hell of a difficult language."

"How are you, then?" asked the delicious Liz, managing to make it sound as though she really cared. She was in tobacco brown this morning, eyes greener than ever, hair cascading voluptuously; he was ready to swear it had grown another ten centimeters since he saw her last. "You're looking a lot better."

"Looking at you that does it." She laughed as gaily as though she had never heard this atrociously feeble gallantry before.

"No, genuinely, you looked tired when you were here last, not really sick or anything, but harassed— what the French call emmerdé, you know?"

"I do indeed," heartfelt. "Will the Senator see me, do you think?"

"I'm quite sure he will; in fact, I needn't even ask. Would you like a cup of coffee?"

"Nes?" with remnants of suspicion.

"Certainly not," reproachful; how could he think such a thing? "I grind it myself."

"Then, yes, please."

"We'll all have one." That girl—he followed, much cheered by her behind—she'd be selling Manhattan Island back to the Indians any day now.

Lynch sat at his desk, carved out of stone, like the Lion of Belfort but sharper round the teeth, which were holding one of his little Upmanns. He signed to Van der Valk to sit down, pushed aside a sheaf of papers, offered the cigar box, and said "Good morning."

"Less bad morning, at least. I've some news, anyway. Before I tell you, have you any news—or Monsieur de Coninck?"

"Coninck," lighting both cigars, "has had conversations with half of Rome," not smiling. "There is no news of Denis, but I am told that this is normal; there are still very large numbers of foreign visitors and they need a little time. I suppose we do have time. Some, anyway. What have you got?"

"A surmise, no more, but based on my dealings with the lady in question. If it is accurate, we may not need all that laborious work from the Italian police. We may need time, not perhaps a lot; I've no idea. Can you tell me, do you—or perhaps does Denis—know people who have a yacht?"

"I suppose I do. So does he, I should think. In fact, two or three. I see what you're driving at—that he might have joined up in some way with friends and gone somewhere by sea? Isn't it pretty improbable?'

"I don't know; perhaps. It seems possible. The universities open in only another week or so, Europe is still full of students sculling around; sailing is a very popular sport, the weather won't break up before the equinox—it seemed worth inquiring into. And it seemed to me at least likely that he's headed back here."

"After avoiding me deliberately?" said Lynch, frowning.

"Instinct," with tactful vagueness.

"What would he do here? He must realize that if he has . . . permitted himself . . . some grave action . . . irresponsible or not—here he'd be expected to face the consequence." Lynch rubbed his eyes, took his reading glasses out of his pocket, put them on, changed his mind, pushed them up on his forehead. "I'm not exactly making myself clear."

"Responsibility—never easy to assign. This woman —she's been tremendously upset by her father's death, and frightened—she's neurotic and over the last few days she's done some astonishingly foolish—irresponsible—things. I've managed to persuade her to say what she knew."

"Persuaded her how?" with sudden shrewdness.

"By not very creditable means, and I'm not going to tell you about them. Put it that I'm satisfied at present that she is telling the truth and let's leave it at that. She and Denis had a love affair for several months. That I expected—I virtually knew. I had thought they had a fight then, but, no, she staged a dramatic resignation, stuff about not ruining his life and so on, and he went to Holland with an idea of breaking. A peaceful break, to which he was emotionally keyed up."

217

"What sort of woman is she really—a bad woman?" touchingly.

"No, not a bad woman. There are few really bad people, no? Nor sad—she's a naughty woman, a maker of mischief. She has what she finds a dull life, and she needs to create excitements, thrills, risks—she wants to be on the trapeze all the time—none of this perhaps would be dreadful if she didn't have a nasty habit of manipulating people's lives. I don't pretend to understand her fully. A complex character, not very different from the father, whose life was full, too, of fantasies and pretenses, little intrigues and theatrical gestures; these people never can forgo a gesture. That is their undoing and, I think we'll find, is at the bottom of this tragedy. What actually happened we'll only learn when we find Denis—and then it's doubtful." And unlikely, he added silently. Lynch was following with narrowed unhappy eyes.

"What has she done to Denis?" pathetically.

"Nothing very much, I suppose, when you add it up —not that would cause him harm, or not permanent harm," stumbling. "Filled his head with unrealities. He may—must have tried to say something to the old man, who perhaps lost his temper, said something insolent or wounding: I don't know."

Lynch suddenly became Terence, putting his cigar in his mouth, staring bluntly straight into Van der Valk's eye.

"What is a court going to make of this?"

"I hope that you won't be disappointed, but myself —I'd be fairly optimistic. Courts have got a lot better —judges, assessors, prosecutors: they're much better trained. Homicide is a crime that they make a real effort to be sensible about. Breaking jewelers' windows is a thing that gets less sympathetic consideration—Sorry, I don't mean to sit here being comfortable about this. I only wished to tell you that prosecutors no longer shriek and bang the table. The other day in France, a woman who had killed her husband got two years' suspended sentence. She had children, so a home to run and a living to earn, but that's not really the point; the court made a real and successful effort to grasp what went on."

"You reassure me," said Lynch, "a little."

"Could you inquire about the sailing-boat possibility?"

"I can. The result . . ." He shrugged.

"Of course. But if it were so—one could assume that they were headed back here. How long that takes. . . . I suppose it could take a week and it could take two months. Sounds like working out the cost of entering the Common Market."

Lynch permitted himself a thin grim smile. "Which happens to be my subject."

"That's why I chose the illustration. So many considerations—political, economic, plain human—all police work is like that, past the stage of robbery of hen-runs."

The door opened.

"Can I come in? I've cups of coffee."

"Liz," said Lynch in his heaviest voice, "you do a lot of sailing, don't you?"

"Maybe it is a daft notion, like you say"—Mr. Flynn's voice was indistinct because he had his front teeth propped against a large wooden ruler—"but I like it."

"I'd asked Mrs. Lynch about—you know, what his interests were, about his friends, stuff like that."

"This feller is a feller he's been to school with, and that's a possibility. Boat's out there in Italy, what makes it a better one. But, hell, it's giving me trouble. I understand the pleece out there can't check everybody; people all look the same anyway in this sailor getup, but, hell, they can't even check the boats. This one, now"—he tapped a large glossy photograph—"I've had checked out in every harbor from Genoa to Gibraltar, and they all say they can't be sure. Don't they keep records? Isn't there a harbor master or something, port dues or whatnot?"

"I don't do much yachting, either," said Van der Valk regretfully. "I'm vague. I suppose it's like everything else—they should, but they don't."

"There's customs declarations, and quarantine and stuff. You're supposed to hoist a yeller flag or something—feller in the office was trying to explain."

"Well, of course, nobody does."

"And the pleece is too busy sucking up to Greek millionaires, I suppose. Well . . ."

"But we'll find this," said Van der Valk, studying the photo. "Can't hide a thing that size. Forty feet schooner rigged steel hull, built in Ijmuiden—funny, that."

"What's a schooner?" inquired Flynn: luckily at that moment the phone rang.

"Flynn here. Yes . . . yes . . . yes . . . Of course I'm holding on but don't be all day about it. . . . Can't make out who it is," he grumbled to Van der Valk. "Coast guard this and port authority that and police maritime the other, and I can't tell them apart. . . . Yes, this is Inspector Flynn. . . . What? Try and speak up. . . . Well, that's a little something, anyhow. All right, many thanks. . . . Where's Vigo?" he asked Van der Valk.

"Spain somewhere."

"They're there?" Like several of his phrases, it didn't sound like English.

"Better still. *He's* there. Police checked the passports. Once they were told what was expected of them, they got quite efficient. It was all those ones who might have seen something last week who didn't want to know."

"They've been pretty fast—the boat. I mean the boat went fast," looking at Vigo on the map. It was still a long way from Ireland, but it was a long way from Rome, too. "I suppose if there is a good wind, a thing like that can travel. How many on board?"

"Assuming the Spaniards know how to count, six. Janey, it's about two thousand miles," laboriously measuring with his ruler.

"Depends if they go on up the coast or cut straight over. Depends on the wind—phone the weather bureau. Might end up absolutely anywhere along here," with his thumb on Valentia and a finger on Kirkwall. "Not only the wind—a little mistake in the navigation at that distance would create a big variation."

Flynn studied the atlas, muttering. "Need an atomic submarine or something. Sure if we was proper pleece, we'd be organized. That countryside there's nothing for miles. One Guard; and when he noticed something he'd have to get to the telephone, and first he'd have to find his bicycle clips and have a cup of tea. Just think, when the General came, for just a quiet holiday, there was more radio vans and helicopters and whatnot. Janey, what a situation. How do you make arrangements to meet someone what might turn up in the County Clare next month?" Flynn hit himself accidentally with the ruler and looked at it with disgust—it had been so plainly activated by malice.

"Couldn't get a helicopter, I suppose—not by twisting someone's arm?" asked Van der Valk hopefully.

"What a hope. Let's go and have a jar."

Over the jar, Flynn decided that the helicopter was a bad idea anyhow. Indiscreet, making a noise, setting the whole countryside buzzing. Be quite as bad as the General's visit, which had been, God save the mark, like nothing but the discovery of the Abominable Snowman living right there next door to MacGillycuddy.

With the second jar, he had made a simple flexible plan. He would get a radio car and a driver. He himself had no authority for any such thing outside the Dublin area, but he would use Senator Lynch. Then he would get on to the fishery protection service. They had routine air patrols to keep an eye on them saucy French lobster poachers. They would not find this unusual, being frequently asked to look out for yachts blown off course or whatnot, and a plane flying over attracted no attention.

"The plane gives us a rough fix, tells us how far off they are, and what direction they're going. Then they have a sloop or a cutter or something, I don't know what it's called." This had a radio telephone, which would tell him where to go. And if they were stuck in the wilderness and there were delays, he would fix it with the customs-and-excise people to hold the boat up.

"Very severe is the customs and excise," said Flynn

happily, "and if there isn't any alcoholic beverages, they can keep you there till kingdom come with the foot-and-mouth disease."

Van der Valk was impressed with this simple program. "If I wanted to do a thing like that in Holland, I'd need about ten different government departments, and there'd be a long legal worry about misuse of official communication facilities, and at the end you'd get sabotaged along the road somewhere by little interdepartmental jealousies you didn't know existed."

"In Ireland," said Flynn grandly, "you can do anything—bar, that is, getting the Pope to throw the ball in at the All-Ireland Hurling Final, and even that they never give up the great expectations. Now we've nothing to do, isn't it wonderful?"

"We could go to the Hurling Final."

"You're through to Dublin—speak up, please."

"Hallo. Hallo . . . hallo, that you, Stasie? This line's pretty poor."

"Who is that? I can hardly hear. Oh, my God, it's you. Dear—you mustn't phone."

"What? I can't hear properly. Thought I'd ring to hear how you were."

"Oh dear—darling, listen—where are you? No, don't say—are you in Italy?"

"Italy, nothing. Off the coast, but we're only just in range; that's why the line's bad."

"Where are you—for God's sake tell me, where are you?"

"Well, you just said don't tell you. This is ship-to-shore. I just thought I'd ring to hear if everything was O.K. your way."

"Hush, listen to me; the police have been here. God —I don't know, I can't possibly explain. It's taking a frightful risk—listen, I'll try and contact you somehow. Let's hope that— No, tell me where you land— Cork, is it? Try and understand; they're watching for you—the airports, too, I'm sure of it."

"No, no, we're on a sailboat; you don't understand."

"Oh, I see—well, maybe—but don't come here, whatever you do; try and land as quietly as you can and lie low, and I'll try and get in touch somehow. Where will you land?"

"Don't know yet, we're too far out still. Know this evening, I should think."

"When you know—ring me back this evening—or, no, ring Agatha's number, that might be safer—have you understood?"

"I don't know."

"I'll try and get a message to you—but ring off, this is a frightful risk; oh dear, I can't talk, bye."

"So far, so good," said Mr. Flynn, clanking his phone down. "That was the fishery people at Cork. Plane picked them up, all right; I mean they haven't got lost, or decided to go the other way, or something." He scrabbled on his desk among pieces of paper. "Weather bureau says gentle swell, good visibility, wind west to southwest force four. But they're still a long way off. Feller says course set for Fastnet, but he don't know for sure. White hull, schooner rig—that's them, all right. Now, the Fastnet is here— Janey, all them little ports. Skibbereen, maybe, or Castletown Bere—won't know until this evening. We got plenty of time—car's in the yard. You got no police authority here, of course, but I fixed it for you to come along as United Nations observer. Whatever that may be."

On the schooner, there was a certain hilarity. The boys knew one another well—three, in fact, had been to school together. Running up against Denis had surprised nobody. He could make himself useful on a boat, too—wasn't sick all the time or something. True, he had been a bit moody and cranky, but this was put down to a troublesome girl friend, a hypothesis confirmed after the phone call.

"That Denis and his girl—what was all the panic about, then? Never a dull moment there. What's for grub? Don't tell me it's beans again or I shall run amok."

"Take a sun-sight, I think. Too far to the west. Lot of current making with the tide—four knots and I wouldn't be surprised."

"Well, the day you were cook we had beans, too. Why didn't you think of something else, then?"

"Watch the chronometer, then, and when I say stop."

"There was a whole goddam sack of them, that's why, and I wasn't the silly prat that bought them, either."

"Stop."

"Wait till I work it out. What did I tell you? Fastnet, how are you?—Rockall, more likely. Gimme the protractor. And a half north to allow for drift. New course, helmsman."

"Made a good passage, though; be in easy this evening."

"These beans are taking a hell of a time to cook."

"Sorry, no tins left but those awful pomodori."

"She's all right. Any more wind, you'd have to take sail off because she'd start tripping a bit. Wake up, Denis; you're steering the way Leary's cow got home."

"What's the matter, then; won't she be at the pier-head waving her hanky?"

"Not pregnant, is she? Look, watch the pennant and then look at the sail—can't you see you're starving her of wind?"

"Yes, well, stop shrieking like that and stamping about like Genghis Khan."

"Sorry, Denis, a boat's not run by a committee; only one skipper, you know."

"Sorry—I don't seem able to concentrate."

"All right—take the helm over, Tim. Mainsheet, Denis, ease her a scrap. You got a problem—spit it out. Tell Auntie Maeve, son; don't forget the stamped addressed envelope."

"I was wishing we were in, that's all."

"If he was in that much of a hurry, he should have taken the plane."

"Shut up—stop thinking yourself witty. What would you do if you got a message saying the cops were after you?"

"They are?"

"Can't you see he's serious? Look, Denis, leave this to us. Get the coast chart, James, would you? Bantry Bay won't do—like the main road out to Bray. Heave her to—we'll run in after dark. Foresheet, James—ready? Shove her straight up into the wind. Right, down below, all; we've got to work this out."

The police were also having trouble with their navigation.

"Those fish people seem to have lost all trace."

"No new plane sighting?"

"Say they can't keep sweeping the area; they're using too much petrol."

"Look fishy, anyway, if they kept on going over."

"Feller says the wind will likely drop around nightfall, and the tide will then be going that way."

"Wouldn't worry them—that boat's got an auxiliary diesel."

"But what if they turn that way—left—that's port, isn't it?"

"Could be South African sherry, for all I know."

"Then it would be a harder beat in. Bantry, or Kenmare. But if they turn right . . ."

"We'll hold on when we get to around here. Currents and tides and things. Who does this boat belong to, anyhow?"

"Feller called Bailey, Bill Bailey—that's not the won't-you-come-home feller, but an awful lot of money, so he has."

"On second thoughts, don't tell me," said Van der Valk. "You've lost me already."

"Lost the ruddy boat, too."

The boys were being very tactful. Nobody had asked what the police could possibly be after him for, nor would any of them dream of asking. The one idea they all agreed upon was to save old Denis getting pinched, and in this they were being alarmingly helpful. They saw he had gone a bit numb, sinking into a lethargic kind of passivity as though he didn't much care what happened, and they weren't having any of that!

"I say turn around and run for France. This wind would serve. Concarneau or someplace."

"I say not—it's just what might draw attention to us

—and him. Remember those nosy bastards in Vigo—
I didn't think anything of it then."

"But they weren't after you in Italy, Denis, were
they?"

"I don't know, don't think so—everyone knew
where I was."

"So there's a good chance they don't know where
you are now. Near certainty, in fact."

"But if they're after him in Ireland . . . The girl
friend said they'd been out talking to her."

"Well, that's in Dublin. They watch airports, but
they won't be watching for him in Dingle Bay, for
Chrissake."

"Don't know for sure."

"Wait till dark, and bring up behind one of the islands. . . ."

"Land Denis with the dinghy; we go on to make
port next morning, and we've never even seen him."

"Slip in quiet without lights . . . like Roger Casement."

"But this is damn silly—put him on shore, and then
what does he do?"

"Get into Waterville or somewhere he can catch a
bus. He's got to find somewhere he can lay up."

"But in another country they can't get at him at all
—unless it's extraditable or something."

"Maybe it is—and anyway what would he do for
money?"

"We ought never to have come north—if we'd
stayed in the Med and dropped him there, they'd
never have found him in all winter."

"Don't talk so wet—you've never been in the Med
in winter; that's obvious. We can't stop the police getting him, maybe. But we can delay them. What he

228

needs is a damn good lawyer. How about your old man, Denis? No? Well, once we're in Dublin that's easy found. I say find somewhere he can lie up a day or so, while a lawyer finds out how tough it's likely to be, what they have on him—give him advice, help— what else are they for? Thing is, does anybody know a good place down in the country where he could rest up quiet for a couple of days?"

"We've got the ship-to-shore. Couldn't we phone someone to come down to meet him? We've got a few hours to spare; it would be easy done."

In Belgrave Square, the three lovely ladies were in conclave and arriving in their own way at conclusions.

"Whatever Denis has done, it's what he will say that counts. It's a pity about Jim."

"You saw exactly what happened with Jim; because they knew all about him, they were able to pick him up straight away. I'm sure they're watching every move I make, laughing to themselves. I felt sure they would leave a man hanging about to watch—not that I've seen anyone, though I kept a careful lookout— but that might just be cunning, the trick of luring one into a sense of security—anyway, if the phone is tapped we're sunk, because they already know."

"Well, of course, it's the kind of terribly naïve thing Denis would do, but one wouldn't really expect it. I don't think they can tap the phone that easily, anyway; it's illegal. I recall Billy Roche telling Jim that the circumstances were special because the organization had been outlawed, so they got away with it in court."

"Billy Roche would be the fellow to get hold of— he'd know what to do."

"He wouldn't do it—he had some sort of bust-up with Jim."

"We couldn't ask him, anyhow, to go and find Denis and tell him to keep his mouth shut. You needn't look at me like that; I'm only saying what's in all of our minds."

"We don't even know where Denis is, anyhow."

"I did tell him to ring back here if he could—Agatha's phone won't be tapped."

"Well, that is pretty cool. It doesn't make any sense anyway."

"I don't know what you could think of that's better on the spur of the moment."

"Well, if your phone's tapped they know, so it's useless, and if it isn't tapped it's as safe as mine."

"And since arresting Jim they would have an excuse for tapping this one, too."

"Well, obviously, there's a lot of risk any way you look at it. But we've got to take it."

"Yes."

"Yes."

"Billy Roche had a soft spot for you, Agnes."

"No, that won't do—but I agree we need a lawyer. I'm not standing for the family getting dragged into this by that twerp Denis. What about that one who defended Gorman?"

"Hennessey—but he's so sly, he'd never stick his neck out. Somebody's got to stop Denis—he's such a fool he's liable to come storming up here, and if that Dutch bastard gets him he'll just blurt everything out. Someone's got to meet him—and not one of us."

"Of course not. Someone inconspicuous."

"What about Malachi? Nobody need ever know, then."

"Easy said, what about Malachi? He's not going to do anything that would compromise him like that. A lawyer gets paid for it."

"Who by?"

"There is that."

"Now, look, Agatha, surely Malachi can be made to see that if Denis starts talking we're all compromised much worse—There's the phone—you take it, Agatha."

"Hallo. . . . Yes, this is Mrs. MacManus. . . . Yes . . . yes, I'm still holding on. . . . Yes, I am . . . . I do, yes . . . . Yes, I see. . . . Listen, don't explain so much . . . Look, I won't talk but I'll listen, and you tell me exactly what you've got in mind, right? . . . Yes, that's sensible. . . . Well, I can't promise. I mean we'll do what we can. . . . Well, I mean there isn't an awful lot of time. . . . Yes. Yes, we thought of something similar. He'd never come down there, though. . . . Yes; quite. That's understood, then; you'd better ring off now. . . . Yes, thank you, yes, I understand. . . . All right; goodbye."

"What did he say?"

"Well; it wasn't Denis—some boy, some friend of his. Really, that puts a different color on things altogether. It looks much better."

"Well, tell us."

"This boat—students, friends of his—that man Bailey, who has the big factory out by the airport, his son, I think. Denis seems to have had the sense to tell them. Not what the trouble was; he was very sensible, said he didn't want to know—this boy, I mean—but that they'd worked a plan out; the funny thing is they thought of Hennessey, too."

"Everyone would since that Gorman business—but go on."

"Well, the plan is to stay quiet behind those islands and slip in at night in Baltimore Bay, and if possible we find someone to meet them there. Rendezvous just before dawn at a pub called Henry's. The idea is that if someone could go down with a car and pick Denis up, he could hide out somewhere in Dublin and Hennessey could go and see him there."

"The thing is, we must get Malachi."

"Malachi must start straight away."

"He'll have to drive all night."

"How long does it take to get to Cork, anyhow?"

"Pity we can't ask Eddy," said Agnes dryly. "He's a perfect mine of information on how long it takes to get to Cork."

None of the lovely ladies were in any further doubt about it—even Agatha had been infected by enthusiasm. The essential idiocy of all these dramatics did not strike them, or if it did, it sharpened their determination, if anything. The element of risk, and the wonderful notion that the phone might be tapped, was just what appealed to them, really, though none of them were taking any risk. If there was any, Malachi was supposed to take it.

Of course their phones were not tapped. The idea would have occurred to Mr. Flynn without any trouble at all, but he would never have been tempted to use it, being an honest man. But he would have agreed with Van der Valk if he had known about this. "Whores at heart, basically, all three of them. It's classic—power without responsibility."

The funny thing was that none of them had any doubt about being able to "get Malachi to start at once." Hard to imagine any sensible man taking on a job like that; tiring, boring, difficult, and silly. One can only conclude that the lovely ladies knew their Malachi. They had married him, after all.

"The thing is," they all said, practically in chorus, "to make sure Malachi understands exactly what it is he has to do."

Both the policemen had gone cold on the prospects of the operation.

"Damn silly, really, running about like this." Both of them had thought it privately, and neither had said it for fear of upsetting the other. It was Van der Valk who finally said it, hoping he was not being tactless and not really caring any more. "The trouble is, one never can rely on people behaving sensibly. If only we knew that the boy would go quietly back to his father and tell him he'd got into trouble—and of course he won't: they never do."

"You don't think I enjoy pretending to be eighteen again and in the ruddy Resistance or something," said Flynn a bit snappishly. They both looked at each other then, and two grins flowered unwillingly. "Waiting around all night like this for these idiot adolescents to do whatever they've thought up that looks clever. But the fact is we were right." Around three in the morning, both were a bit red-eyed. Both jaws were getting stubbly and scratchy, and so were both tempers.

"Fact is the boy behaved in an unstable way right at the start, has gone on doing so ever since, and it was quite logical to suppose he wouldn't stop now."

"Think they're gunrunning, probably, so they do," agreed Flynn. "The curse of the Irish is the romantic imagination."

"But I wish to heaven they'd hurry up with it."

"The funny thing is I said to the boss that this was all bullshit, and why not let them get back to Dublin and then hang a pinch on the boy quietly like, and he said no. Said he wanted the boy intercepted as soon as he was on Irish soil, because the boy looked capable of unbalanced behavior and he owed it to his old friend Terence Lynch, so he did."

The night was long; the two men had had leisure for much meditation, and a tolerant philosophic acceptance of their position. Both of them had been kept up so often all night, on errands every bit as ridiculous.

They had started getting tetchy quite early the evening before. Van der Valk could not say so, but being shut up in a car with the blither of a shortwave transmitter-receiver was enough to drive him round the bend. Such were the servitudes of the pleece, as Flynn said, but it had been several years since he had had to spend hours on end with the foul thing. Nothing changes, he thought dolorously: everybody still has their mouth far too close to the utterly fouled-up microphone; everybody still shouts far too loud; nobody has managed to suppress the beeps and burrs and clouds of static, magnified by very-low-fidelity-indeed loudspeakers into road drills, demolition squads getting to work on a pyramid, and close-ups of the sound track of Atlanta burning in *Gone With the Wind*. Even in Dutch, he had the utmost difficulty understanding that succession of hawks and grunts (every police shortwave is afflicted by chronic bronchitis), and here in Ireland understanding one single word was a forlorn hope if ever there was one. And Flynn himself was showing signs of being exasperated with the object: he had given it several bad-tempered smacks and twice declared he could not understand what they were all talking about.

"Everybody's behaving like an imbecile," he muttered nastily, "including me. Those fish people with their corvette thing keep buggering about there outside Kinsale, and it's three hours since anybody saw that boat. Can't make it out—to a plane, you'd think picking out a white yacht with white sails would be like following a black beetle across a fresh snowfall, so you would. Ought to be off the Fastnet by now for a couple of hours or more, and now it's bleeding nightfall and nobody can see a thing."

"Changed course, maybe."

"What the hell would they want to do that for?"

"No idea except, after all, that way maybe they're a bit off the road—whatever landfall they'd planned, I mean."

"All I know is they aren't where the flaming fish people said they would be."

Van der Valk understood that Flynn was nervous, pardonably, about complex military maneuvers. As usual, C Company has got lost somewhere. Coordination is a word that sounds peaceably reassuring back at headquarters but out in the front line tends to become complaints about "Well, there's a river here that isn't on the map."

"What we need," reasonably, "is dinner. And a rest from that thing." This was a good idea: they got salmon—alas, Van der Valk had discovered that in Ireland it's just boiled cod mysteriously gone pink as though a fervent reader of the *New Statesman*—and tough steak, which paradoxically put Flynn back in a good mood. He sharpened a matchstick and picked

235

his teeth with more of his familiar placidity. Freed from the tyranny of in-flight movies—his driver had been left with ham sandwiches and two bottles of stout to keep the morale up although chained to the thing—he could forget about the tactical dispositions and meditate about the strategy.

"Have they got wind of us in some way, now? Dodging about like that. Can't be far away, and anyhow they can't give us the slip, properly speaking: I've the pleece alerted all along the coast. I mean look at it from their angle. Nothing queer at all. That boat's been mucking about around Italy for a month. Bill Bailey told Lynch he took it out himself to Positano for a holiday. He had to go home, and a group of his son's friends were sailing it back. They didn't go to Rome special to pick up Denis, so he's just a casual passenger, like."

Van der Valk suddenly got an idea. It was so long since he had had one that it had an effect as of many star shells bursting.

"Hey!" he shouted. "Could they have any communication with the shore this end?"

Flynn stared. "Nobody knew where they were."

"No, I mean a shortwave radio—like yours. They may have been listening happily to everything you've said," maliciously. He could not resist a grin on seeing Flynn's open mouth. It was a bit like getting his own back for having been caught in compromising positions with Stasie, and lecherously photographed by Jim Collins. But, really, someone ought to have thought of it before. "Expensive yachts like that always have them."

"I'm sure as hell going to find out," said Flynn, rushing to the car.

"Holy mother of mercy!" he screamed, coming back furious ten minutes later. "O, what an eejit; oh, what a right eejit. I don't know anything about these damn boats, but I'm learning, I'm learning. Well, of course, I did ought to have thought of it. A heap of guff I've been told—all them fishing boats do have these transmitters. They all talk to each other—it's natural. They're all registered, got a call sign and Lord knows what. Nothing easier—this benighted packet's registered, too, got a special number; a hundred miles or so offshore she can pick up the phone, call the signal station at Valentia, and what's more they can get switched into the phone circuit, international line or anything—phone up Uncle John McCloskey in Cambridge, Massachusetts, if they care to pay the freight. Ludicrous, so it is. And I didn't think of it."

Van der Valk, who for a long time hadn't thought of it, either, and hadn't anything he could usefully say, said usefully nothing.

"Why not?" said Flynn resignedly. "It's just like what we've got. The one dispensation of generous Providence is they can't hear us—not the same wave length and a whole heap of stuff I got my ears banged with, all technical about VHF—and eff me, too, while you're at it. Here, lassie, get me a cup of that stuff you call coffee."

When it came, he put in several spoons of sugar, stirred it for a long time, and then said in his usual mild voice, "Thing is, we can ring that telephone exchange, too. What do you know, two calls put in by Mr. Bailey to Dublin numbers."

"Stasie?"

"Flanagan and MacManus, too. No, nobody paid no

heed to the talk, of course. But Master Denis will have been tipped off, and what does he do then?"

"They change course, I take it. They're all that age —their one idea will be to run rings round the fuzz."

"Just my conclusions," said Mr. Flynn, gratified. "All looking up what to do in the little red book."

Around eight, the boat was sighted a few miles off the Kenmare River, having apparently drifted up with the tide. Before it became too black, she was glimpsed again, moving down, it was thought, toward Mizen Head. What Flynn described as "all the perspiring pleecemen in the County Cork" had been mobilized.

"Lovely cruising ground for yachts, so it is," said the local sergeant.

"But hide-and-seek inside all them islands in the dark isn't what you'd call, now, a sinecure."

Like other effaced-looking people, Malachi MacManus had a restless streak, or perhaps only reckless. This did not mean he was Dr. Crippen, either. He did have rimless glasses and a beginning of baldness, which gave him a great deal of forehead towering over tiny little eyes at the bottom of a cliff, and a very small curly mouth was surrounded by lots of pudgy jaw, but there was nothing stooped and scholarly about the stocky, compact body and an upright, resolute way of moving. The mouth could set into obstinate tenacity, the little eyes could become still and stony: he was more formidable than a diffident manner suggested. In fact, the ladies of Belgrave Square knew that he could be a handful. He was younger than Jim Collins, and more mobile than that warrior, whose

238

Tarzan looks were running to seed if you looked closely. He was an old flame of Agnes's. How he had come to hitch up with Agatha nobody knew; mistaken them in the dark, perhaps.

He was clever. All Dublin intellectuals long to have undemanding posts in the customs and excise, where the rent and the milk bill get paid, and there is peace and quiet and an official desk in which one keeps literary efforts, and two hours' work a day and three of procrastination leave three for Letters—and there is even a pension at the end. Malachi had the shell of the civil service wrapped round him like a particularly able hermit crab, and was much envied. He did polished witty pieces for weeklies, reviewed books with lapidary phrase and the right touch of erudite one-upmanship, had three rejected novel manuscripts (referred to as his juvenilia), and was rumored to be chiseling a masterpiece that would open the eyes of those that could see to Joyce's real merits.

A streak of quixotry or romanticism, or just something soft and wobbly in the character—or a taste for overripe pheasant?—hard to say: he had got wound up with the lovely ladies in his ardent youth and never got unwound. He had a genuine affection for all of them. He had a taste for intrigue, certainly, and a relish for diddling the police over small regulations, which he called "showing up bumbledom." All in all, he was a good choice for rescuing Denis from the clutches of the law, especially as he had no opinion of Jim Collins, and allowed a faint ironic gleam of enjoyment to play round his neatly shaved chops when he heard of Jim's discomfiture.

The night was dark, not rainy but cloudy and moistly

stuffy, like a damp eiderdown, thought Van der Valk after having it explained to him all about the Gulf Stream and why the palm trees grow in the County Cork. Very little visibility, and it was eleven before the yacht was discovered at anchor, at the price of agonized efforts and confusion caused by some innocent English people in a ketch. What now? Divergence of opinion. Fed up with wait-and-see, Van der Valk was all for a bold attack on the *Hispaniola*, Ben Gunn style, demanding to know why a boat arriving from foreign parts had not declared itself free of rabies and psittacosis. The local pleece fancied this approach, too. But Flynn, whose accent was getting thicker all the time ("Isn't a patch of cow dung between here and Tralee I couldn't put a name to"), vetoed it.

"If Bill Bailey were to make complaints about his boat being boarded in the middle of the night by a lot of quare fellers masquerading as the Special Branch, there'd be hell to pay in Dublin. He's done nothing illegal. They don't have to know Denis is in any trouble. There's no warrant out for him. Nothing but this mandate for interrogation you brought with you, on the basis of which I can ask for a bit of cooperation. There's no immigration problem; in fact, it's all as blameless as Baggot Street Bridge on a sunny Sunday morning, and the pleece better not go exceeding its powers or the magistrate throws the whole thing out on a legal kink; and after all the trouble took, we'd look pretty silly then."

Van der Valk saw the force of this argument.

Despite some stocking up before the pubs shut, the night was absolutely interminable.

So much discretion almost ended, fatally, in anticlimax. The radio car had been kept out of the village

240

to avoid creating gossip among the locals, and when the pleece arrived breathless on a bicycle to say things were happening at last, both Flynn and Van der Valk were cross and somnolent, but woke up at the news that a dinghy with three people was landing on the foreshore. They had agreed that if it came to this the pleece were unwanted.

"Don't want any publicity," said Flynn. "This is Terence Lynch's home territory, and it's even possible that the boy might be recognized. Having him pinched by the local cops is something Lynch hasn't deserved, seems to me, and I haven't named any names."

The three persons advanced quietly, not furtive but as though avoiding noise out of consideration for everyone being still asleep. The two large figures looming out of the dark must have looked alarming.

"Mr. Lynch," said Flynn. Conversational, but undoubtedly official. The little group huddled.

"Yes," said a surprised and shaky voice.

"I am a police officer from Dublin. This gentleman is a police officer from Holland, officially authorized to ask you questions about a matter for judicial inquiry. It is thought your evidence may be useful."

"That's a lot of nonsense," said another, sharp voice, practiced at challenging campus regulations. "What d'you mean by sneaking about in the middle of the night like that? We've landed peaceably after a long passage; nothing illegal in that, and nobody obliges us to go answering questions—it'll do another time, if at all."

"Nobody stops the rest of you going where you please," politely. "Besides it is none of your business."

"Well, whatever it is, I know nothing about it," said

241

Denis more boldly, "and I don't see why I should answer anything anyway."

"I'm sorry, I must insist."

"What gives you the right to be so high-handed at four in the morning?" said the other voice. "We said some other time."

"You did leave Holland rather suddenly, didn't you? And Rome. I can't take any refusal: you'll oblige me to take you into custody."

A third voice broke in, impatient with shilly-shally. "Chuck them in the harbor," it said bluntly.

"You'll do nothing so foolish," Flynn said, wooden. "It would be very serious, and you'd be in considerable trouble."

At this point, Malachi entered the picture. He had been a bit delayed, held up in Dublin by Jim Collins's damn car having a flat battery, and losing the way a couple of times, so that he had nearly arrived too late. Walking discreetly through the village, he had been perturbed by the sight of a policeman pushing a bicycle: this at four in the morning looked ominous. He had arrived down at the little harbor in time to catch the end of the interchange, and a demon of irresponsibility took hold of him. Three and one made four —against two. He glanced cautiously behind him and saw nobody. What he did see was a large plastic dustbin. Empty, but for a pronounced flavor of pig swill. He crowned Van der Valk with it neatly, and with a good shove sent him rolling on the uneven ground. No direct animus, he claimed afterward; just happened to be nearest, that's all.

Indistinctly, from inside his bin—like somebody in Beckett; just what *would* happen in Ireland—Van der Valk heard thumps and heaves and muffled grunts.

"Handkerchief—tie it tight." Up the rebels, he thought, struggling against middle-aged spread and slight dizziness and general four-in-the-morning feelings.

"Rope in the dinghy."

"Any more of them?"

"Not here, anyhow—but there are police in the village."

"Put them in the dinghy. Quick, Denis."

"Calm down, boys. Just to get him to a lawyer is all. Otherwise there's trouble."

"But them?"

"They jumped on you in the dark, didn't they? All a misunderstanding."

Van der Valk was irritated, both by the pig swill and his still-sore collarbone. He was still only half out of his bin when a figure loomed over him; he kicked it somewhere in the middle. Later he found it was Malachi, and felt soothed. He got on his feet and found Flynn with someone's knee in his back, and two healthy boys closing in on himself. He felt that the position was much too melodramatic. They stood still but carefully well out to each side. To yell was not helpful; to be rushed unpleasant. He was not, just now, at his best.

"I'm nearer fifty than forty," he said as quietly as he could. "I have one collarbone recently broken, and I've an old rifle bullet makes my leg stiff in damp climates." They listened; this was all that mattered.

"I also live an evil life of too much whisky. I'm a bit slow." They were still listening, which meant they were beginning to think of what would happen later. "A serious matter. You heard what the man said. Help Mr. Flynn up, Denis; this won't do. At sea everyone is free, but here on land, I'm afraid, we always catch up.

You better come with me, Denis, because we have to have a talk about Stasie."

"About Stasie?"

"And the rest of you go back to bed quick, and Inspector Flynn will feel more tolerant in a few minutes. You," to Malachi who was getting up by degrees, "stay quiet or I'll throw you in the harbor and it'll be a pleasure."

The three boys looked at each other.

"Don't be a fool, Denis."

"I'm sorry," draggingly.

"Well, you've got to make up your own mind."

"I don't really have much choice," with simplicity.

Flynn had got to his feet rubbing his behind, which he had been sat upon without ceremony. "I don't want to appear vindictive," he said quietly. His eye rested on Malachi. "Who are you? I seem to know you."

"I wasn't going to stand by and see people intimidated. I've done nothing to reproach myself with."

"Handy with a dustbin, aren't you?" mildly.

"I came to see that the boy has some protection against being tricked and trapped, and that's my right. I'm not at all sure of your right to question him, and I'd like to see your authority."

"Aha. MacManus, isn't it?" He looked across at Van der Valk and made a little gesture as though to say "You've really more cause of complaint."

"Busy fingers of the lovely ladies," said Van der Valk, "serving as usual to confuse everyone. Forget him."

"You buzz off home," said Flynn, "and don't come talking law to me. Conduct unbecoming in a government servant, especially one with a cushy job. Vanish."

Those women, Van der Valk thought, looking at Denis, who was standing staring at nothing, utterly uninterested; they can make a fool of anybody. Including me.

"Denis," he asked with lumpish stupidity, "who was it killed Mr. Martínez?"

"I did," the boy answered, exactly as though the question had been "Who left the window open?"

Now that he had got the answer for which he had come such a long way, Van der Valk felt totally dissatisfied with it.

The journey back to Dublin was largely silent, marked only by the morosity of the two policemen. One never does have much to say on these occasions, as Van der Valk had many times remarked: there is a sort of post-coital sadness. By a tacit agreement all policemen accept, arrested people are handled gently. Their persons are respected and it is apologetically, almost humbly, that handcuffs are put on; it is a diffident finger that presses on the arm. Denis behaved with dazed sleepiness: neither Flynn nor Van der Valk had any wish to break in on this. The bright gay sunshine that had accompanied him almost unbroken from the start had abandoned them at last. The sky had clouded heavily over under a limp dragging westerly draft, and every now and then a few drops of rain spilled languidly against the windscreen, giving up the effort almost at once, showing a fainthearted unwillingness, a lack of perseverance.

Van der Valk stared out of the window at the landscape of central Ireland. Mournful, but he had to make an effort at last to be unemotional. All the worry about crime and punishment that afflicts earnest little left-wing intellectuals is rarely a burden to professional policemen, and to call this callous and hardened of them is superficial. They see all that is needed to feel pity for the victims of crime—strangely undeserving of pity as these are so often. They know all about prisons, those medieval hospitals where you or I or anyone has to go, once we have picked up the contagion of crime, to be disinfected, made into useful members of society by being, in Conrad's phrase, stuffed with fattening food in an airless cellar.

A policeman is able to feel pity for the criminal, too, though he shrugs at cant about the poor misunderstood highwayman. He is so nearly a criminal himself. He sees a bewildered poor devil, to be sure, lopsided with grievance, eaten by inadequacy, but he sees plenty of people exactly the same who have not committed crimes. He has no use for the hang'em and flog'em brigade, because he is not infuriated—he is not even repelled—by the mean-minded selfishness, the insensitive vanity, the self-pitying egoism of the average bandit.

He is distorted by the immense pressures of hypocrisy, and becomes, save in rare instances, as blunted and stunted as the man shut up in prison, for both his dignity and his self-respect are under constant attack. A policeman has a good trade put to poor use, like a painter commanded to put a coat of glossy enamel over rusty corrugated iron, shrugging, and doing as he is told.

Van der Valk was thinking that someone had once told him that when you are being given the Legion of Honor you are sent a little form to fill in, reassuring the government that you won't do anything tactless. Like saying you wouldn't be seen dead with it, or that you won't run away the following week with the petty cash. There are questions to answer, yes/no: strike out where not applicable. One of these is: Has a court ever handed you a condemnation? Most people can still say no, with a quite clear conscience of course. But how many can say with honesty that they have never deserved it? But there, he thought, humanity's capacity for self-deception is bottomless. So is my own. If I were offered the Legion of Honor, I'd say that I deserve it—have to, wouldn't I, or I'd lose my nice job, and the pension I've worked for all these years (and been shot for, shot at for, and hit on the head for—and gone to bed with Stasie for).

It's a bit like "Who Polluted the Environment," he thought, grinning—no, no, whoever it was contaminated the water it wasn't me; or, well, maybe it was me but it wasn't my fault—I was on government contract, making napalm.

Looking at Denis, sitting quietly there between himself and Flynn (trying to read an Agatha Christie paperback and yawning his head off), he was aware that he had an unsatisfactory criminal on his hands. Not good-looking in a conventional sense, but a handsome boy, tall and slim, with a wiry well-built frame and pale skin, much freckled and tanned to terra cotta by sea air. Smooth dark red hair, rat-tailing where it needed cutting, and a pathetic effort at a beard; the boys had skipped shaving while at sea, and a beard doesn't come quickly at the age of twenty-two, an age when Humphrey Bogart also looked mighty callow.

They were back in Dublin by midafternoon, nicely in time for tea at the Castle, where Denis was put in a waiting room full of obstinately optimistic army-recruiting posters. Flynn sat down with a sigh of relief, looking at his four walls with content; Van der Valk knew the feeling well: rosy gold instead of dingy beige. Flynn sipped tea from a large and hideously willow-patterned cup; how nice is being home and having one's own cup, and Van der Valk wished he was home, too.

"Well," he asked, "what are we going to do with him?"

"All nice and simple now, ain't it? Nice, uncomplicated, straightforward pattern. Technically he's under arrest—I mean he admits homicide so he damn well has to be. Got to be locked up. That makes your extradition claim a simple formality. Got to get an order from the magistrate here, so we put him up, five minutes, gabble-gabble, out again, reserve defense for assizes—you know, what the Americans call the due process. Get'm good lawyer, of course; not that abortionist Hennessey—applying for bail for Jim Collins is more his speed. Don't know what goes on in Holland, but we can leave all that to the Senator, sure we can. Poor feller, now's the time when the nasty part starts for him, because we've managed to keep all this quiet, but now the press will start poking in that long wooden nose like Pinocchio, but sure theirs stays the same however many big lies they tell. I leave that to you, since if I know anything, yattering at the press is what Embassies is for."

"Exactly," with feeling.

"But now I got to book him formally and observe regulation precautions because—well, would you say he was a suicide customer? No, neither would I, but until we find what really did go on . . ."

"We never will," said Van der Valk gloomily.

"Will what?"

248

"Find out what went on."

"No, I see—you mean now that he admits killing yer man we got no further right to interrogate."

"Lynch's lawyer," predicted Van der Valk with total accuracy, "won't let me get near him. Nothing left for me to do but write another long, boring, bullshitting, perfectly accurate, utterly untrue report. Dichtung und Wahrheit, as Bismarck said." He couldn't quite recall who it was said it, but chances were Flynn wouldn't know either.

Technically, his job was finished; please, might he go home now? Surely they wouldn't be so dense as to keep him hanging around another ten days just to bring Denis back to Holland? Surely they could see that it would be easier, cheaper, and more suitable to send an elderly flatfoot with an excursion ticket? He wanted to go home. He even had a department of his own to worry about, back there in Holland. And what about his expense account now? (But the Embassy, vastly relieved by the turn of events, and handling lawyers, press, and Senator Lynch with dazzling disingenuousness, beamed upon him and signed the lot.)

And of course he was kept hanging about. He was, too—as Flynn had warned him and as lawyers confirmed at a matey conference over cigars in Lynch's office, and again over coffee and brandy in Mrs. Lynch's drawing room—inextricably involved in affidavits, subpoenas, sundry other sharp and subtle quillets once learned in painful law courses but long since mercifully forgotten.

"But don't think for a second," said Mr. Matthew Dillon, Senior Counsel, tenor of the Dublin Bar, "that I can possibly consider leaving this woman sitting

249

there in peace. I intend," demonstrating with an imaginary but villainous hatpin, "to winkle her out."

"Despite everything? You think that wise, Matt?"

"Despite everything. I'm sorry for its being her father; I'm sorry for Eddy Flanagan, who is a decent man even if he drinks; but despite myself."

"You must," said Mrs. Lynch very gently, "recall that the woman has children."

"It was not, in my opinion, Denis who put her home, children, reputation, and household's happiness and stability at risk," retorted Mr. Dillon, punishing the brandy.

"I could not allow myself to make the suggestion," said Lynch slowly, "but if anybody should be on trial she should be on trial. Van der Valk?"

"I could avoid answering," blandly, "by saying it would be improper in a policeman to express any opinion at all. I have to say—I'm on record—that I found nothing to show she knew or understood anything about her father's death. Since you ask me, I agree she's in some obscure way responsible. I can't understand how—neither does she, I'm convinced—neither does anyone."

"But we intend to find out," put in Dillon briskly.

"Am I right," asked Van der Valk slowly, "am I right in thinking Denis refuses to implicate her at all?"

"You are, alas, perfectly right," said Dillon.

"Good for him," said Mrs. Lynch gently.

"Yes," said Van der Valk. "Good for him. But the examining magistrate in Holland might not admit his refusal. I don't know; I think he could have her attached as a witness and brought over."

"I'm quite prepared," said Mr. Dillon ferociously, "to have all the lovely ladies, in your delightful phrase,

250

as well as Collins, Old Uncle Tom Cobley—the whole boiling swept up and produced in court in Amsterdam. If that's what it takes."

"I would hate that," said Lynch softly, "and I will go on hoping that it won't be necessary."

In the end, it would be Van der Valk who, without meaning to or even really knowing much about it, would make this decision. He wasn't going to get his peace of mind back quite yet.

Getting home after "being abroad" was a notoriously apt occasion for terrific uprushes of chauvinism: it was not a vice of Van der Valk's, but, without exactly being pleased to see the horrid place, he felt more sympathy toward Schiphol than usual, though most of this delight was due to Arlette (reseda-green trousers and a chic new pullover) waiting at the barrier. That was what made home—not the familiar smells and sounds, not the sight of scrubbed red brick and bright white paint—so different from sloppy Ireland (a place he had much enjoyed and greatly liked). Home was Arlette's house and making home her great talent. She was an intelligent woman, if alarmingly obtuse at times; charming, though she knew how to make herself extremely unpleasant; a balanced person, if with a good many tiresome and violent prejudices; a good cook when in the mood, which was most days, luckily. But above all she generated love and security around her: her loyalty was total, her warmth and affection had an explosive quality, so wholehearted was she. When one came back to it, even after no more than a day or two of absence, one could be sure of finding everything furiously polished, furniture all changed around, and a great many flowers, as well as a new phonograph record, a "party meal," and something eccentric to drink.

"And what is Ireland like?"

"Very individual—you'd like it." Being individual was her chauvinism, at once an assertion of her Frenchness and a protest against the conformism of Holland.

"The tourist literature is marvelous—I've been studying it like mad. You can see they've taste—such a difference to the English, who have none at all, poor dears, but there's obviously a fearful snag somewhere; the climate, is it, or the food?"

"Yes, the grub's on the bleak side," with his mouth full. "Weather was lovely all the time I was there, though."

She was indignant. "Most unfair; it's been beastly here. The famous whisky—I hope you've brought a lot."

"Yes, I was in fear and trembling and the customs just smiled amiably, and I was quite ashamed of myself. Is there still some sauce left?"

At the office, things were quite placid, so that he was displeased when he found how smoothly it had all gone without him, and he had to have a tour of petty faultfinding which was on the whole pretty artificial. Everyone seemed to have been working hard, too, much harder than he, and there were tiresome proofs of zeal all over his desk. Bit by bit, as always after a holiday, emerged a lot of stuff that had been quietly shelved until he reappeared, so that he cheered up. Indispensable after all. He forgot all about Mr. Martínez for a few days. But it was too much to expect that the examining magistrate would leave him alone.

"Ah, it's you; come in and sit down. Pleasant trip? Bit of a holiday, what? You quite enjoyed yourself, by the sound of it, but the mystery tour is now, I fear, over." He did sound spiteful. "This dossier is monstrous, and now that I've seen the boy—oh dear. . . ." Indeed!

"One simply can't get to any firm ground. His relations with Martínez . . . can't talk about motive because there plainly isn't any motive, and that's the crux of the whole thing. Admits killing him quite freely, as though it were perfectly natural, but can't or won't discuss any of the steps that led to this. That woman, too—delicate ground there." Van der Valk was sick of hearing what delicate ground Stasie was. "Naturally, I ordered a psychiatric examination at once; devilishly tiresome it all is when one has to do everything in English. We're all up to here in sworn interpreters and shades of meaning; the Advocate General insists that this Irish lawyer be given every facility—you can just imagine how troublesome it makes things." It went on for some time: the magistrate was sorry for himself.

"I quite see," said Van der Valk. "I recall that I had much the same experience in Ireland. But you've a confession, surely—and her signed statement."

"Oh, come, come"—irritably—"to listen to you one would think it was open and shut. None of that has any evidential value. She was his mistress, granted. She broke it off and the boy went to Holland in a state of turmoil. Some kind of crisis was precipitated by Martínez, who presumably got to know about all this, and on this point the boy is totally withdrawn; after the event, it all follows a classic pattern. The boy's escape is not from the crime, of course, but from pain-

253

ful associations which were its cause. He runs away, wanders about Europe, is ashamed to meet or face the father—significant that a father, any father, is seen as a menace—rushes onto this boat, a half-hearted effort to attack you; that's all easy, usual ostrich performance of a powerful perturbation. After you brought him back, of course, period of complete withdrawal, apathy, inability to respond; whatever one asks, it's 'Don't know.' If one wasn't so familiar with these states, of course, one would take a dim view, but it's 'Don't want to know.' But there's no attenuation of responsibility—everyone's agreed on that—simply a violent rejection, which Dr. Scheepstra characterizes interestingly as quite involuntary, a corrosive element violently rejected by the stomach. Now, you've talked to this woman—can't you throw any light?"

"I honestly believe she doesn't know and that she's telling the truth."

"She's obviously very unbalanced—the attack upon you, the subsequent effort to seduce you."

"She was extremely devoted to her father in a warped way, and his death threw her into a perfect panic."

"Yes, quite; she sees herself as responsible for the boy's action, and that's clear enough. You're convinced there's nothing further to be got out of her? Well, as a matter of fact, the Procureur Général agrees with me that it would only confuse matters further: two perturbed persons in place of one. But it's this Irish lawyer. . . . I couldn't go into court anyway with such a lamebrained tale—the crucial point is missing. Why did the boy kill this man? Was he betrayed, threatened, frustrated—these psychiatrists keep humming and havering."

And what has that to do with me? said Van der Valk, but to himself.

"There's something we've missed," said the Officer of Justice. "Something evidential. You're the only person who's had the necessary contact with everyone involved. I want you to go over all your notes, search your memory. There's nothing in the dossier but bits and pieces. It doesn't add up." Van der Valk was forced into silence.

"Scheepstra agrees," said the magistrate in a friendly, persuasive way. "He is convinced that there's a piece missing, which he wants to make his synthesis cohere. He says he hasn't enough information. There's no criticism of you whatever: in fact, you've done very well. But whatever may be lacking, only you can supply it."

"I'll go over my notes," grumbled Van der Valk, "but it's very unlikely I'll make any more of them than when it was all fresh. I obeyed the rule."

To be sure he did. He was at home, gloomily sipping orange juice from Israel: there had been altogether too much whisky and his liver was bad. Grated carrots (Arlette was a great believer in grated carrots; one of the hazards of having a French wife). To be sure, the rule that notes must be written up within twenty-four hours, the rule about fear or favor, about imprudence-carelessness-or-neglect, about conduct expected of a diligent and conscientious officer, about tampering with witnesses, about being tampered with by: hmm, the syntax was getting muddled, as his generally did.

A senior officer in the Amsterdam hierarchy had once called him in to explain that he had posted him an adverse report that would have bearing on his promotion.

"You are given to minor indiscretions and you believe these to be unimportant. In your present position, no doubt they are, but I have a fear, and I believe it justified, that in a position of greater responsibility you might commit an indiscretion light-heartedly, believing it to be unimportant, and that without wishing it or imagining it, a judicial instruction may as a consequence come tumbling about your ears and justice as a result be perverted."

It had never happened. It hadn't this time. His report stated that after considering ill-guarded remarks and unbalanced behavior in the course of a private interview, he had been led to believe that Mrs. Flanagan would attempt a form of corruption, since she was seeking loopholes enabling her to avoid etcetera. That with this in mind he had sought the advice of Inspector Flynn and in accordance with standard procedure they had set up a mousetrap, blah blah.

Well, there was nothing about that which was technically untrue. He had known with certainty that Stasie was the key to the affair; he had had to find means to make her talk; they had been unorthodox, but so was she.

His conscience wasn't very clear. He had got into a compromising position. He had been diligent, all right, a bit too much so. And not very prudent. Tumbling Stasie in his hotel bedroom had not been foreseen, and was that due to a bit of a wish not to foresee it?

Well, yes, Flynn had just laughed. He had said, "You're in the shit now"—but that had been a figure, hmm, of speech. Had there been tampering-with-witnesses, Flynn would never have agreed to play his part in ensnaring eager Jim Collins and his candid camera. Flynn had thought the episode funny. It was, anyway, evidence of the lengths to which Stasie was prepared to go. Quite.

He still had a bad conscience. He wasn't proud of himself. Out it would have to come. The fact that it did not have to come out officially—where it was irrelevant anyway—made no difference. Yes, it did. That was just why it did have to come out privately. He had played Arlette a dirty trick, but he had also played one on Stasie. He owed it to both of them.

"Arlette."

"Mmm?"

"I've something to say."

"Do."

"A confession."

"How badly that begins," frivolously.

"Yes, well, it doesn't improve as it goes on."

"I'm listening," seriously.

"You know about the three sisters—they sound just like a Chekhov play. Come to think of it, they wanted to go to Moscow, too. Or something that they wanted extremely badly. Respectability, perhaps. Pa had immense charm, and in a way a lot of class. But he was a shady—or perhaps just unstable—figure. However," hurriedly, "with them it takes the form of various lovers, who got passed around in kind of an eccentric manner. The boy Denis was perhaps more than that—she was genuinely in love with him. I don't know why. Perhaps that way she recaptured a sort of innocence. The old man might have done the same thing—he married a very young innocent girl, all loyalty and fidelity."

"You're rambling."

"Yes, I am. She has, of course, a very strong taste for men."

Arlette's face twitched. She had already guessed. But she kept her mouth shut.

"She thought up several bizarre notions for getting rid of me, which I didn't tell you; it would only have worried you. She even pushed me under a car—no, no, I'm here, aren't I, all in one piece? I broke my collarbone. She also tried a seduction act after I had rather stupidly let her get inside my room. I wasn't as disinterested as I thought I'd be. Of course, I didn't take advantage of any innocent victims, but I wasn't altogether the innocent victim myself, either. It's not very creditable, and—ja, I can't feel I should hide it. It didn't go into any official report, of course, but there it made no difference, whereas personally—well, I can't pretend it was just an irrelevant incident."

Arlette generally looked younger than her age, which was forty-five. She had good skin, and well-modeled bones. Now all the little lines were showing deep and sharp, like cuts.

"How often did this happen?"

"There wasn't any often. On this one occasion, for about five minutes, I simply lost my head completely."

"That, no doubt, is what they all say. Has this ever happened before?"

"No."

"That woman in Innsbruck—the one who shot you?"

"No."

"You do expect to be believed?"

"That's up to you."

"And you know that the journey of a thousand miles

begins with a single step? It also ends with a single step." She hissed it out and despite self-control he felt fright. Arlette could on occasion be extremely violent. If I end up, he thought with a flash of what might not be whimsy, getting knifed on Stasie's account . . . well, I'll shake Martínez by the hand, that's all, and tell him I, too, found out the hard way.

"I have no excuses."

"But you did tell me."

"No doubt I shouldn't have. I make mistakes frequently."

"No, you were right. But let me tell you something. You're often away, and when away you often have got into difficult and dangerous situations. That's your job, and so is getting out of them. One of my jobs is seeing that I never get into them. I've never been anywhere with a man."

"I know."

"And you do not, I imagine, think seriously that I might be les, either, while we're at it?" Her voice was going off key, with a nasty edgy screech like a jolted phonograph needle. Her face was getting shakier, the little cuts whiter. "I'm being abominable," she said, and burst into tears. He forced himself to stay still. The difference between these women, he thought—there are, to be sure, a good many more—is that Stasie cries fallen down, with her face in the floor. Arlette stays upright.

He waited for ten minutes, rubbing his nose and shifting from one buttock to the other, as though on a hard bench in a police station. Arlette blew her nose and went and got herself a drink, slamming the fridge door, and then opening it again and shutting it quietly.

"Never?" she said, standing in the doorway. "Never?"

"I promise."

She believed it, but she could not resist a last, coughed-up, spat-out jet of bitterness. "No wonder you were so ardent on your return from this exciting town. I innocently put that down to eating too much steak. I suppose I should be speaking of a transference of affection."

The words, as they were meant to, stung.

Like a whip, he thought a day later, rubbing his face as though there really were a mark across it.

Luckily—yes, luckily—the office was suddenly very busy. A couple of days' furious—or, at least, exceedingly busy-bee—work was needed. His department, the criminal bureau of a largish country district including a lively (and nowadays petulant) university town, was understaffed (chronic complaint of all police bureaus), and though he went on a good deal about the efficiency of his arrangements, and there was even some truth in the boast, he still had not got to the end of the administrative bumf that had accumulated during his absence among the fleshpots of Dublin; horrible great piles of paper needing his signature, about half of which actually had to be read. Indeed, about a quarter had to be read with comprehension. Being invariably either in the opaquest of officialese, or in scientific jargon, these had to be read twice, as a rule.

In addition, there arrived in rapid succession an abortion, an indecent assault, some phony Swiss banknotes, and a robbery with unpleasantly wanton violence committed by juveniles. There was no leisure for meditation.

Still, his staff noticed that he fell into trances, drank large amounts of tea, and rubbed his nose a good deal, besides being ungenerously short and tetchy for someone who's just had a holiday. (Everyone was convinced it had been a holiday, and he was aggrieved when the Chief Commissaire for the Province of North Holland, his remote but invariably tedious superior, rang up in a mood for eating captive goats and went on for hours about Van der Valk never being there when needed, and he would take this opportunity of reminding him—all at great length, and he couldn't even say "Oh, go and . . ." down the dead telephone at the end, because the switchboard might still have the plug in, and what about Discipline.)

A holiday! Back in '45, in the army, he recalled, the English used to call it a "skive." His language was full of English words, these days, since Mr. Flynn's conversation lessons.

It was true he went into trances, and in them there was a recurring theme: Arlette's wounded and wounding phrase about transference of affection. What did it mean? Of course, it meant that he had slept with Stasie and then leapt hungrily into bed with Arlette; that this was disgusting and unforgivable and a beastly betrayal, and a mean and dirty insult. But it meant something else, too, and he did not quite know what. It was "on the tip of his tongue."

Poor Stasie! To bed her, while sneaking about to catch her out in her pathetic, secret, neurotic life—it had been unforgivable.

What was she?—who was she, this pretty and attractive female, this intelligent and cultivated woman? For a start, she took after her da. And straight off one fell into the clutch of hundreds of learned gentlemen, all brandishing behavioral sciences the titles of which sounded as though just invented by satirical weeklies: Van der Valk had the greatest skepticism toward all of them. Because one knew little about Mr. Martínez, deceased, and that little was already too much. Intelligent, witty, charming, a fantasist. Temperamentally incapable of staying on rails. Alarming capacity for justifying dubious performances by bizarre personal codes of conduct. Wealth of possibilities: far too much already—what had Stasie's childhood and upbringing really been like?

Was she vicious? He didn't know and was sure none of the learned gentlemen did, either, however many behavioral hand grenades got rolled around and tossed out to explode in a hail of jargon. One could say that she was fertile ground; that was easy, as easy as pointing to the thirst and need for affection and stability, the pathetic reaching for a "normal marriage," the equally pathetic belief that each new love would bring happiness—and, wound about everything she did, the cloudy sandstorm of deception and self-deception, the passion for intrigue and endless clever little schemes —and oh! that amazing plausibility. What chance had Denis against this formidable female, when he himself had been caught, however momentarily, in the snare? And the result of that second's vanity and greed and happy foolish lechery? A horrible blow in Arlette's vitals.

Luckily for her—and him—that she had such resources: she had tried for a day to "punish" him, failed, cried, and flung herself at him, shouting, "Love me, go on, obliterate that devouring cow" ("cette vache engloutissante"—it sounded better still

262

and more terrifying in French). What chance had Denis had?

Lynch and his wife had been deeply, bitterly wounded as the first result: crime spreading, as it always did, like a cancer, destroying love, trust, honesty down endless ramifications for a long, long way. They thought they had "failed." He had tried to tell them that it was not so, that there was nothing "failed" in Denis, that it would all pass. . . . He had talked a lot, and what good would that do. . . . He had done harm, but he had tried to make up.

He had written a closely argued report stating his conviction that Denis was an accidental killer, that it had been, as so often, "the victim's fault." But the prosecutor was determined to make up his own mind about that. He had let Van der Valk see that he wanted no theories—they were three a penny any day. A fact or two, an essential complementary fact. There were a few around somewhere.

Why did he feel so pestered by that nasty little phrase about a transference of affection?

When he hit on it—or guessed, at least, that he might have—it was exactly like searching all over the house for his spectacles and finding them perched on his forehead.

"Get me Mrs. Martínez on the telephone, will you? If there's no answer, try the city hall to see if she changed her address." He signed two or three papers without seeing what was written on them.

"Not moved? . . . Oh, you have her? Put her on. . . . Commissaire van der Valk, Mevrouw, good morning. As you know, there've been considerable developments since we last spoke. . . . Yes . . . yes, that's normal that you should be called on to amplify, if need be, your statement: the magistrate has a dossier now and doesn't want dust to gather on it. That's just what I called you about; I wanted a word with you. . . No, no, quite separate from the Officer of Justice; the police have nothing further to do with the instruction that is now going forward. . . . No, I've no further power to intervene. Like you, I'm just one in a cloud of witnesses. Just that before handing in my file I'd like to round out a detail or two. I wondered whether you'd allow me to call. . . . No, you're working; I understand—this evening then? . . . Quite so, but I won't take up much of your time. . . . Till then and thank you, Mevrouw."

She didn't sound in the least enthusiastic about seeing him, but that was nothing new—nobody ever was!

"Could we have supper a little early? I have to go to Amsterdam."

"We could, but what a bore. Business?"

"Unofficially business—the Martínez woman. With benefit of hindsight, I find there are a few things I still have to ask her. The file's been hanging about and I want to tidy it up before sending it in."

"You don't have to make so many excuses. Why not this afternoon?"

"No, the woman's working—reasonable; she has her living to earn."

"Then there's no choice, and supper can be early. Just don't take her to bed, that's all." His mouth open until he grasped that this was humor.

"Don't say such things," reprovingly, very much the government servant of upright life and severe morals.

"No, and don't think them, either, is what you

264

mean. I was teasing you—if that is allowed. O.K., it's understood."

He did rather wish that the administration would discover some other official transport. As prudent, cheap, and reliable as a Volkswagen beetle; just something else, that's all. He parked in the Rivieren-Laan and plunged into the rabbit warren. The card in the name slot was the same: simply had "F.-X." crossed out and "Mrs." written in. He rang the bell.

Anna looked unchanged; her hair style was altered, but it was the same pleasant-looking youthful woman —quite pretty in her dairymaid style, neat small body trim in a close-fitting wool frock—who opened the door, recognized him, frowned a little, smiled a very little, said good evening quite politely, and motioned him in with not too bad a grace.

A few changes had been made inside the little flat. He didn't quite know what: subtly, it had become "working woman alone" instead of "married couple." No sign anywhere of any man's presence. She offered him coffee; he refused and got a glass of vermouth. He disliked vermouth, too, after supper but didn't want to appear stiff.

"I'm glad to see you're readapting with no trouble."

She shrugged; what useful answer was there? "One can generally do things when one has no choice."

Exactly; like murders, but one didn't say such things. She offered a cigarette, very formal and courteous, sat down, upright on a straight chair, legs crossed professionally as though she had a shorthand pad on her lap. Straight serious face. He leaned back, gazed vaguely about, said "I suppose you're right," vaguely.

"You've not altered much," he said with a kind of good-natured curiosity.

"What could I afford to alter? I have met with much kindness. Several old business acquaintances of—of my husband's—made a point of offering me work—serious work, not just charity. I earn my living. Fortunately I have no children to worry about." Poor old Martínez, thought Van der Valk. All that long, active, often brilliant life. So many women. He's left a trace all right, but not the one he wanted.

Anna, plainly ill at ease, propped her elbow on her knee, put her chin on her palm, and looked severe, not wanting any more beating about the bush. "What was it you wanted, Commissaire?"

"Oh, I had been wondering whether in your situation you wouldn't have preferred to go back to Ireland."

She seemed much surprised; frowned, thought about it, looking narrowly. Ireland? What was he getting at?

"This is my town," she said. "I was born here; I've lived nearly all my life here."

"You have family here?"

"That is to say—I seem to remember telling you that my family disapproved of my marriage—there was a certain coldness."

"Which your husband's death has not altered?"

She made a grimace, giving her a schoolgirl look. "Rather the contrary, if anything."

"You mean an attitude of 'I told you so'?"

She seemed relieved at his catching on. "Yes, I saw them rarely—perhaps once a year. My husband—wished to avoid quarrels—and not to cause me pain."

"You didn't want your family feelings to interfere with your marriage."

266

She flushed, all over her high, rather bumpy fore-head.

"I just wondered whether his death impelled you to heal the breach, so to speak."

"No. I don't understand why you should think I might want to go back to Ireland."

"But it's simple, surely. I recall your saying you regarded your husband's daughters almost like sisters. Which I agree is simple and natural. So that under the painful circumstances it would seem a natural thing to do. Quite an attractive solution."

She flushed again—she was an easy flusher—and fidgeted slightly. "That is so, possibly. Was, I should put it. Things—alter."

"Oh, quite. You're a young woman. Doubtless you'll marry again."

"That remains to be seen," prim. "You're very interested in my personal life."

"Yes," blandly.

"It seems exaggerated. Surely your inquiry is finished."

"Not altogether."

"But you said yourself—the magistrate—Denis," painfully, "poor Denis—I mean—he's confessed, hasn't he?"

"You've been wondering—like all of us—poor Denis, what could have got into him to behave like that. You'd be interested to know."

"I—er—I don't know. It's a very painful subject. I don't like to talk about it."

"And of course you never met Denis, did you?"

Her eyes were her best feature. A clear cornflower blue, unusually large in her small face. Perhaps a little too round. Another flaming great blush.

"No." Squeezed out.

"But I'm afraid we have to talk about it—if only to do justice to him."

"I was summoned by the Officer of Justice" with an effort. "He didn't tell me much—he said that Denis —had been in love with Stasie. Do we have to go on about this? It's hateful."

"There are a few inconsistencies."

"But it can't—it isn't any longer your business. You said so. I don't like your—routing about—in my feelings like this. You haven't any right to question me."

"Mevrouw Martínez, as long as my file is not closed, I'm afraid I do have the right to question whom I please."

"I'm sorry; I beg your pardon. It's—you must see that this is a wound that isn't healed. I was very much attached to my husband."

"Of course. You know that I spent a week or so in Ireland? I had the pleasure of meeting your sisters."

"Yes—I mean, I didn't know exactly; I supposed as much."

"Interesting woman, Stasie. Very attractive."

"Er—yes."

"Understandable that Denis should fall in love with her."

"Er—yes." Scarlet all over. Hating it.

"Sex at the bottom of our misfortunes, as usual. Its place in modern society is possibly exaggerated, though, would you say?"

She had assumed a look of worldly wisdom. Enlightened people were not bothered at talking about sex. On the contrary, they discussed it with alarming fluency.

"To understand something about Denis," he said

268

in an odious, jolly voice, "we have to draw a picture, mmm?" I am being bastardly, he thought, but professionally so. There is a difference. "Denis refuses to," he went on. "Another proof—if one were needed. Denis in love with Stasie, mmm. One of these affairs in which a lot of excitement is generated by concealment. Secret assignations, breathless meetings at queer times in peculiar places, fear of discovery—spice of danger, hmm? All unbeknown to Denis, everyone knows all about this famous love affair. Her sisters know, the excellent Mr. Collins knows, and, while he's good at pretending the contrary, I'm convinced Mr. Flanagan knows: he can hardly not know, and he's a better judge of his wife than anyone gives him credit for."

"Why are you telling me all this?"

"Why, you know your sisters, and I've too much respect for your judgment not to give weight to your opinion. Correct me if I seem unfair to them."

She said nothing, remained sitting upright, and still, quite collected.

"A woman like Stasie—she gets satisfaction from this kind of situation," he said. "Answers various deeply rooted needs—that's no especial business of mine, wouldn't you agree?"

"I wouldn't really know. I suppose so."

"But a boy," warming to it. "A young romantic boy. He has of course pleasure, hmm, physical pleasure, excitement a good deal. And perhaps, too, some splendid illusions. He caresses notions of giving her help and healing, understanding and devotion, sun and rain in her desert garden. He glows with sensations that are very far from wicked or vicious. I suppose," said Van der Valk sadly, "that such notions sound intensely ludicrous to anyone my age or yours—but I had ideas like that, too, once. Didn't we all burn to change an evil world?"

She was following him, all right, with an attention so close that her face and neck were rigid with strain.

"And then there was a crisis," in accents of classical tragedy. "Isn't there always? Stasie broke it off. The world is a villainous place and Othello's occupation's gone. And, like many before him, our Denis goes for a big trip to the South Seas. His parents are delighted. Instead of wasting his time in Dublin, what could be better than travel—broadens the mind. They have many friends well placed to keep a benevolent eye on cherished son, smooth his path, mmm? Lucky Denis. He can go to Paris or Rome—but he goes to none of these places. He goes to Holland. I wondered why. I suppose that, like other young men, he didn't want any of these oversmoothed and supervised paths provided. Wanted more of an adventure—somewhere he could be independent, real, courageous. So, clinging to happy memories of what he thought of as his first adult adventure, he came here to look you all up. You met him then—what did you think?"

"I—" She went scarlet. Suddenly downstage, and suddenly a spotlight, and suddenly she had to open her mouth and sing. "I—" And not unexpectedly she dried dead.

"You told me a lot of lies, didn't you?" said Van der Valk in the most tranquil voice imaginable.

"I—" She didn't have anything to say at all.

"You were afraid. Very well. We'll leave that— bear in mind," still mildly, "that the examining magistrate will want to know. Just tell me about Denis."

"I spoke to him— Well—yes, I did tell a lie about

that. I mean, I was worried about the scandal, I mean, about Stasie. . . . He spent an evening here," hurriedly. "He had projects and notions about finding a job here, and he wanted to get—my husband's advice."

"Quite odd. No? Don't you think so? He's had a break with Stasie—not a row, but a grand renunciation—very emotional, knowing her, with weeping and tremendous words about not ruining each other's lives. Then he comes here, where he is constantly reminded of her, where memories and reflections crowd in at every corner. Can you explain that?"

Anna's forearm was crossed tightly over her chest, her hand on the upper arm, squeezing the flesh nervously. "How should I explain it," irritably. "You seem to make a big thing of all these psychological ins and outs—I don't know. Anyhow, it might be all supposition—you say this and that was so, but it might not be so in the least, however convincing it sounds."

"It doesn't sound at all convincing to me," silkily. "These little casebook histories seldom do. Oversimplified. People are full of inconsistencies and contradictions."

"Yes," gladly seizing on this. "It's a big mistake to sit theorizing in this way."

"That is just why I came to see you," very bland now. "I had a theory, and I hoped that you would give me your opinion on its value."

"Well, none of this, really . . . means much to me, I'm afraid."

"Perhaps this will mean more. I make a suggestion that Denis renounced the grand love, but he kept intact his portrait of women he could devote further grand loves to. The first one was fun, and he intended there should be more. The model was intact, too.

Stasie in a little rocky alcove in a long white nightie"
—dryly—"like frightful statues of the Madonna. I
suggest he came to Holland carrying his little alcove
with him, looking for a new statue to put in it. A Stasie substitute. To whom he could transfer his affec-
tions, his warm heart, and all his illusions. And I further suggest that right here he found one. You."

Anna had not blushed for some time. Now—it was
one of Arlette's phrases that made him laugh, though
he was not now laughing—"her blood made one
jump." She went perfectly white.

"There you are," to the Officer of Justice, who was
listening, for once, instead of talking. "He fell straight
heels over in love with her. Superficial, or facile? No,
he was just on the second trip round. Stasie all over
again. Another Martínez, same age, same situation—
less encumbered. Old husband, no children, lonely all
day with nothing to play with."

"She struck me," said the judge, "as very loyal,
unusually devoted. She struck you that way, too. Did
he seduce her? Or what?"

"No idea. Theorizing, as she told me snubbingly.
None of my business anyway," pointedly.

"What happened then?"

"How the devil should I know?" crossly. "She had
hysterics. Any of a hundred things might have happened, and ninety-nine probably did. Did he seduce
her? He's quite an expert by now and she's a push-
over. What did she do? Tell the old man? Or did Martínez—quite an expert, too—see through it? Had he
seen through Stasie, or did Denis tell him? He must
have decided to straighten the boy out, and said or did
something that had a fearful effect. He was quite a

272

one for resounding pious platitudes and could be excruciatingly smug, but what did he do? Some threat that to Denis was intolerable, hitting him somewhere he couldn't bear touched. That picture gallery—what went on there? What was said?"

"Please stop asking these rhetorical questions," said the judge crossly. "You sound exactly like an advocate with a poor case."

"That's exactly what I am."

"Well, please spare me the flapping sleeves," shortly. "I'm a jurist, not a jury."

"Oh, Jaysus," said Van der Valk.

"What's that?" startled.

"It's what the Irish say when they meet a situation that is inextricably balled up."

"I propose," primly, "to disinextricate. I say, that's quite a splendid neologism."

"The French talk all the time about disintoxication. I could do with some of both."

"We'll confront this precious pair," said the magistrate, cheering up at the thought.

Senator and Mrs. Lynch paid a visit to Holland. The instruction showed every sign of being long and painful. Each of the magistrate's questions, each of Denis's fumbling, foggy answers had to be laboriously translated by the sworn interpreter, besides being written down in Dutch by the greffier. This was bad enough without being interrupted all the time by Mr. Dillon, who started every phrase by "With great respect, Monsieur le Juge," had acquired a Dutch accomplice as punctilious as himself, and was all set for an immense amount of sleeve flapping, by proxy or otherwise, in front of the assizes court.

Van der Valk met Lynch in the corridor outside the judge's office, after a weary and fruitless interview with Denis.

"Appallingly numb," said Lynch with a slow patient sadness. "He doesn't communicate at all."

"Ah," said Van der Valk with sympathy. For the last fortnight, he had not thought about the affair at all, had indeed been busy with other things, and was in the Palace of Justice on a totally different errand. He was also in a hurry, but the least he could do was stop and be polite. "I'm afraid he's a bit disillusioned with the world." He knew that things had not gone easily. Anna had told her tale and stuck to it. She had certainly not been seduced by Denis. Nor had she seduced him. No, she hadn't put ideas in his head. She had felt nothing but a sort of maternal kindness. She might have been misunderstood but, no, she had not behaved flirtatiously. It had simply never occurred to her that Denis could have killed her husband. Well, yes, perhaps she had concealed the truth. No, she hadn't told lies; well, possibly lies by omission, but she had not wanted to bring the family into disrepute. She had been sorry for Denis. Yes, it was true that he had poured out to her a long tale about her sister Anastasia. She hadn't believed it at first. She had been much shocked. Yes, perhaps she had mentioned something of the matter to her husband. She had felt sure that he would know how to handle it. She had felt so overwhelmed by the tragic consequences that she had determined to suppress the whole thing.

"Cold-blooded bitch," muttered Van der Valk. "What did Denis say?"

"Nothing, Dillon tells me. Just sat, with a miserable sort of little smile. Refused to challenge her at all. I'm

convinced myself that even if she didn't seduce him—
or allow him to be familiar with her, which comes to
the same thing—she flirted with him and encouraged
him, and that it was a sense of guilt that sealed her
lips."

"She took me in at the time, I'm afraid."

"Yes," said Lynch bitterly. "Butter simply doesn't
melt in her mouth."

"You showed me much kindness, besides fairness,
in Ireland," said Van der Valk suddenly. "I hope
you'll allow me to invite you to dinner—and Madame,
of course."

Lynch looked at him with a humble simplicity he
found touching. "We'll be glad to," he said.

Arlette was nervous about this, and on her best behavior.

"I'm not used to entertaining the grand bourgeois.
I'm afraid they'll find my kitchen a very peasant affair.
Well, tant pis pour eux."

She produced smoked eel, Holland's glory, with an
endive salad. With this, Riesling, which she got from
the grower in Dambach-la-Ville, a tiny town in Alsace,
not far from the "little house" they had bought to retire to when he got his pension. After this she had
daube, because she came from Provence: a piece of
beef braised in an earthenware pot, its lid sealed on
with flour-and-water paste.

"But what gives this marvelous flavor?" asked Mrs.
Lynch.

"A small piece of orange peel," blushing slightly,
"and a very tiny bit of marjolaine. I'll show you, if
you want." With this came pink plonk from Cassis,

bought in Albert Heijn's Supermarket, probably, though she wasn't going to admit it.

As vegetable, fennel, done with a slice of marrow.

As dessert, a grand stroke, another "Holland's Glory": frangipane wrapped in flaky pastry, made by the baker, and Taittinger champagne—madly expensive, she confessed in private later.

She got a great deal of praise, all genuine, and blushed some more, with pleasure this time. She looks very pretty, thought Van der Valk proudly, and smells perfectly delicious, of cleanness and Madame Grès, and a scrap sweaty from the kitchen, which adds piquancy. Mrs. Lynch, nice woman, said, "You're going to let me help with the washing-up," and the two women disappeared into the kitchen, from which came a smell of coffee, earnest female conversation, and, very unexpectedly, shrieks of laughter.

"What are we?" asked Lynch suddenly. "Who are we?" Van der Valk, ashamed at offering rather a plebeian cigar to his illustrious guest, struck a match.

"It's a sensation common to everyone arrested for a misdeed of whatever sort. Whether one has committed a really ingenious fraud worth a million dollars, or simply pinched a bottle of milk, the result is the same. Loss of identity, a feeling of no longer belonging. An impersonal, indifferent society has seized one. It is bloodthirsty, because it is frightened, and must appease strange gods like the Balance of Payments. The high priests are quite kind and civilized—it is rare now for them to be cruel or even very vindictive—but they tie you down, just the same, to the stone and wait for the sun to rise."

"Having been one of those high priests," said Lynch

in his slow way, "having belonged to the caste, having been respected and even honored. . . . To retire from public life is easy enough; to retire from the image one has fashioned, to take off the mask—it's harder; one had come to believe in it oneself."

"To retire from anything at all would be a great mistake, I believe. You feel, after being in that awful Palace of Justice, as though it were you on trial. Put another way: when you think about Denis, you feel that you should be on trial, that you deserve it quite as much as he does. A pretty sound instinct. Nobody knows who should be on trial here. Anna—Stasie—Martínez himself. The whole pack collectively; Collins and all the lovely ladies of Belgrave Square and even Eddy Flanagan, who precipitated the whole thing, in a way, by closing his eyes and pretending it wasn't happening. Even me—my conscience isn't clear in this matter. We're all standing by the dike with our thumb in the hole." Lynch looked at him curiously, and decided to say nothing.

"That picture you have in your office," Van der Valk went on, "the man playing cards. You and I have the advantage of being experienced card players. We know when to go softly, and when to shake the big stick. We know how to lull and how to cajole. We know how to frighten people with the big bristling eyebrows and the stony little eye—to make them lose their confidence. While Denis—at that age, one is so utterly vulnerable. No craft, no cold blood, no reserves to draw on at all. Courage has to make up for everything."

Mrs. Lynch, who had come back with Arlette and the coffee, had been standing quietly listening.

"Is there any answer, Mr. van der Valk, and can you give it to us? Why did Denis have to commit this act, this gratuitous piece of violence? What forced him —what was irresistible? We have asked ourselves the question repeatedly, and we haven't found any answer. And we had thought we had some knowledge of the world."

Van der Valk thought. Arlette gave him his coffee cup. Everyone sat immobile. He felt a fool. "I can give you a sort of answer. It won't satisfy you. It doesn't satisfy me. The judge will think he knows. The lawyers and the doctors will have answers. Theirs are better, probably."

"I'd rather have yours. Whatever it is . . ."

"I think it's a sort of challenge thrown down to the boys which they can't resist. A danger—a mortal danger—which must be defied. I suppose you remember reading about the motorbike gang in California—the Hell's Angels. They covered themselves and their clothes in filth; they painted themselves with obscene slogans, to show that they rejected society, that they were putting themselves outside it."

"But—"

"I told you it wouldn't satisfy you."

"Go on."

"You say that there's no comparison with Denis. No, but there's something in common—all these boys— they've only courage; it's the only way they have of proving themselves men. If I chose this example, it is because they had simplified and stylized their lives into a clear formal pattern. They had these big powerful bikes, the one thing they seemed to value, to care for. Everything else treated with contempt and derision—

278

men, women, money, shops, institutions of any sort, but the bike carefully cleaned, polished, tuned, beautifully cared for. His sort of a symbol of purity, liberty, honor. And then somehow it seems that it's not enough. I don't know. . . . You take the big bike, very fast, exceptionally powerful, you feel it in your arms, gripped between your thighs—you master it. And then somehow the challenge is not enough. There is speed, there is danger, but it's not enough. They aren't satisfied. They have to push it faster and faster, on curves, on slippery roads, in bad visiblity, at night . . . anything."

"Rosemayer," said Arlette suddenly, remembering.

"Yes, Rosemayer." Lynch and his wife looked at each other, but asked for no explanation. Mrs. Lynch at least knew that Arlette understood, which was enough. "I have two boys," Arlette had said suddenly, in the kitchen.

"More than that, even," went on Van der Valk laboriously. "They have to destroy the bike—the one thing . . . and themselves with it. If you go off a big bike at a hundred miles an hour, there's not much left of you. If you go on pushing on a curve, there comes a moment when the centrifugal force takes over, when you feel the back sliding away and know you can no longer stop it." He was looking at the wall straight in front of him, trying to feel, to understand.

"They seem to seek that moment, to desire it passionately, that moment when the bike takes over and they know they're helpless and that they may have only two or three seconds left to live. They've a name for it, which they all understand because they've all been there. They call it going over the high side."

"And Denis? . . ."

"I don't know, I tell you. That's how it seems to me, that's all."

"Over the high side," repeated Lynch slowly. "I think I see. I think even that I've been there myself."

"I think we all have," said Van der Valk gently.

ABOUT THE AUTHOR

NICOLAS FREELING was born in London and raised in France and England. After his military service in World War II, he traveled extensively throughout Europe, working as a professional cook in a number of hotels and restaurants. His first book, *Love in Amsterdam*, was published in 1961. Since then, he has written seventeen novels and two non-fiction works. His most recent books have been *Gadget,* a novel of suspense, and the third Henri Castang novel, *Sabine.* Mr. Freeling was awarded a golden dagger by the Crime Writers in 1963, the Grand Prix de Roman Policier in 1965, and the Edgar Allen Poe Award of the Mystery Writers Association in 1966.

Mr. Freeling lives in France with his wife and their five children.